PRAISE FO

The Last Time We Met

ALSO BY CAROL MASON

After You Left
The Secrets of Married Women
Send Me a Lover

The
Last Time
We Met

Carol
MASON

LAKE UNION
PUBLISHING

Text copyright © 2010, 2018 by Carol Mason
All rights reserved.

Published by Lake Union Publishing, Seattle.

First published as *The Love Market* by McArthur & Co in Canada in 2010. This edition contains editorial revisions.

www.apub.com

Amazon, the Amazon logo, and Lake Union Publishing are trademarks of Amazon.com, Inc., or its affiliates.

ISBN-13: 9781503902558
ISBN-10: 1503902552

Cover design by Debbie Clement

Printed in the United States of America

For my mother, Mary Mason. Never enough thanks.

PROLOGUE

September 2014

Someone once told me that there's no such thing as a coincidence, only synchronicity. That likeminded people often travel down similar paths that can converge unexpectedly. That's why you'll bump into the mother of your daughter's school friend in the wine shop at six o'clock on a Friday, or your old art-history professor while touring the Louvre. But sometimes chance encounters don't seem to result from any kindred purpose. And you'll see someone from your past in a place that is so unlikely for either of you to ever be in that you can't quite explain it. You can't even read into it, because very often life – just like who we end up loving – is a random thing.

In my case, I just get off a bus at the wrong stop.

I haven't really been paying attention to where we are, given that we've seemed to spend ninety per cent of the journey in the snail's trail of London traffic on this Saturday afternoon. What is far more fascinating than anything outside the window is my left earlobe reflected in the glass – and the fiery little diamond twinkling away with each slight movement of my head. I happen to glance at Mike sitting in the seat facing me. He is grinning in affectionate despair.

'It's too lavish!' I said to him in the jewellery store yesterday, as I reluctantly handed the little diamond studs back to the salesman.

'No, it's not. I want you to have them.' Mike cocked me a glance that said he was quite enjoying being the big man footing the bill for an expensive anniversary present, just this once. 'Try them on again,' he said.

'We can't! They're two grand.'

'We're taking them.' He pulled out his credit card.

Mike had known I'd wanted little diamond studs for a while. I'd managed to drop them into the conversation just enough times to have the hint tiptoe across his consciousness so that buying them would seem like his idea – a romantic gesture – rather than just me engineering my own gift.

'But we could finish our bathroom with that money. Or put it towards a new car. Or Aimee's education fund . . .' I thought, *Please, God, don't let me talk him out of it.*

'You're right,' he said. 'Let's put them back.' He pretended to pocket his credit card again, and to try not to see how my face must have fallen. Then he smiled. 'Two thousand pounds, Celine. What's that work out to over ten years of marriage? You don't think you're worth that to me?'

I rubbed my chin. 'Hm . . . Maybe I should try a bigger pair.'

Mike snapped his card down on the counter. 'Done deal.' I tripped out of there like I was Ginger Rogers. I slept in them; and, this morning, grinned all the time I was brushing my teeth. Mirrors, windows, backs of spoons have all become irresistible.

'Come on,' he says now. 'We're getting off.' He pulls me up from the seat, spoiling my love-in with my own earlobes.

'But I thought we were staying on until Knightsbridge?' We're going to Harrods, because I can't go home to the north-east of England without buying my sister something that comes in a green-and-gold carrier bag. Even if it's just a box of tea – which is probably all we can afford now.

'You can stay on if you want, but I'll hurl if we don't get off this bus,' he says, dragging me through the throng of people.

Mike and his legendary travel sickness. Some people suffer from piles, eye twitches, or gluten allergies; with Mike it's an overdeveloped gag reflex whenever he's on anything that gathers speed and turns corners. He jumps off before the doors close, pulling me with him, and for a moment I feel like I'm flying. But not in a good way.

We're only down here because Mike was given tickets to see Van Morrison through his job as a radio producer for a late-night talk show on Newcastle's Blaze FM. The palm-greasing from the station's advertisers usually just runs to tickets for a football match, which always makes my upper lip curl because I happen to be the only person in northern England who doesn't give a damn about football. So this was quite exciting. Plus Aimee is staying with my sister; Mike and I rarely get away just the two of us anymore.

The bus spews diesel into the air, and Mike does a wet burp. I stroke the back of his head. His hair is going grey quite rapidly for someone not quite forty. The style has been the same since the day I met him: collar-length and side-burned – a 1950s rockabilly pompadour. I remember thinking, when I first laid eyes on him, on a flight from London to Newcastle, that he looked a little like Henry Winkler from *Happy Days*. While this wasn't a selling feature in itself, there was something appealing about the way he didn't conform to the 'David Beckham faux-hawk' standard that every other bloke did in 2002.

'Are you all right?' I ask him.

Another wet burp. 'Come on, let's walk.' He takes hold of my hand, his cold and clammy fingers lacing between my warm ones. Given that he's not feeling well, I will lift my ban on handholding this one time. The problem is that, at five feet nine inches tall, I'm an inch and a half bigger than him in my bare feet. Now, there are some men who love the idea of doing a Dudley Moore, and I have a feeling Mike is one of them, but it's not reciprocated. I will often joke with him that sometimes, by the time you put me in shoes, I feel like I'm taking my child for a walk.

'Hang on; I think we're going the wrong way,' he says now, when we suddenly arrive at Sloane Square. 'Harrods is back there.'

We're just turning to go back the way we came, and I'm registering an uncommonly carefree feeling: no work, no Aimee to get off to school or pick up, no endless round of gym classes, meals to make, shopping, cleaning . . . when I see him.

He is coming out of a building about fifty feet ahead of us. I know this man; I know him so well that it makes my world become a surreal sort of still.

The stature of him is unmistakable. The height: a not-so-common six feet four. And the physique: muscular enough to save him from looking lanky, yet not so bulky that you'd think he must have to work at it. But it's the way he holds himself that makes him stand out in a crowd: that difficult-to-strike balance of confidence and graceful masculinity. Patrick would never think to stoop to anyone's level. Not literally or any other way. And just looking at him you'd know that, and you'd be torn between admiring him and assuming he'd be an arrogant bastard.

My mouth has gone dry. My heart is a strange clash of surprise and sadness.

I am dragged back twelve years to when I was twenty-one, in the middle of an around-Asia trip, not realising that when I got to Vietnam I was going to meet someone who would change things for me so completely. We first met properly in Sa Pa, the misty mountain village where the famous Love Market takes place – young lovers go there to find one another and old ones return to remember. Patrick was in the Love

Market looking for a story. I remember how he stood across the square and held my eyes, and never once looked away. And in that moment, I knew I was going to have a grand, groundbreaking, heart-crushing romance. He was it. Nobody had to make the first move. It was somehow already made.

But it can't be him. I believe he lives in Canada. How could I possibly find myself in London for the weekend and see Patrick, who doesn't even live in this country?

But, even though I don't have time to study him and I can't see his eyes because he's wearing sunglasses, I am certain it's him. I would know him anywhere.

I don't think about what I'm going to do next. My hand slips away from Mike's. There's a blare of horns, a squeal of brakes, a group of Japanese tourists running after a bus, their feet smacking the ground, then everything is soundless.

'What's wrong?' I hear Mike's voice, distantly, from beyond the other side of my shock. Memories rush over me, as though it had all been yesterday. As though nothing had happened since. There never was a since. Never a Mike or an Aimee. Never a life.

The man is stepping off the kerb, raising an arm to flag down a taxi, and in a flash this moment will be gone. Time seems to slow right down, giving me ample chance to do something. But do what? I can't speak or move. I'm a strange mix of wildly excited and ill.

Mike takes hold of my arm. 'What on earth's wrong with you?' Patrick is bending now, talking through a taxi driver's window. I even recognise the shape of his head. 'Celine?' Mike says again. I hear the concern in his voice; his fingers grip me tightly.

Is Mike trembling, or is it me? What I do now is going to be one of those pivotal moments that change everything. I know this, and all my instincts say, *Don't do it!*

All but one.

Patrick – if it's Patrick – is climbing into the back of the taxi, and I am in such a heightened state of panic that I start trotting towards it, hearing Mike call after me, bemusement and slight annoyance in his voice. But I've taken those few steps; the damage is already done. As the taxi starts pulling away, I find myself, inconceivably, starting to run after it.

Then two buses hurtle past, and I can't see the taxi anymore but still my legs have a will of their own. When I'm able to see around the buses, there is now more than one taxi, and I don't know which one he's in. But on I go. I'm a high-speed train about to wreck itself. All the while, my common sense is telling me this can't be Patrick, so what on earth am I doing chasing a stranger?

Then I have a stitch in my side, and a painful airlock in my chest. It crosses my mind that I might be having a heart attack.

The buses and taxis are converging at a set of traffic lights, and I have to stop because my body is giving me no other choice.

I flop forward, my breath coming in gulps, thoughts piling on top of each other: I've just seen Patrick. Or was it him? The face wasn't quite . . . Maybe this man wasn't as tall.

But it *was* him. I know it was.

I remember how I lost him the last time. I can still visualise him standing there, in the dim morning light of his cabin, with his bag packed. And me thinking, *You'll walk out of this door and I'll never see you again.* And as he left, my reproachful tone: 'Don't look back at me once you walk out of this door.' I listened to his feet, to the sound of him leaving, somehow hoping he would turn around and come back, that his love for me would prevail. But it didn't. He never once looked back. With his every step, I was thinking, *Go after him; he's only at the tree; he's only at the road* . . . Then, *He'll only be on the bus; he'll still be at the airport.* Then, *He's somewhere in Hong Kong; he's still in Asia* . . . Like the way I would write my address, when I was a child – placing where I lived, positioning my small and insignificant self in the broader context of everything else: Celine Walker, 22 Duke Street, Newcastle, England, United Kingdom, Europe, World, Universe.

The memory fades and I suddenly remember where I am. When I look down the street, Mike is standing exactly where I left him, as though he has cautioned himself against coming any closer. London returns to real time but I continue to stand there, helpless and inoperative. I should be thinking only of how I can explain myself to Mike, but I am imagining the interior of a black cab with Patrick in it, gazing out of the window, unaware that our lives have just synchronised again.

Why didn't I just shout his name?

I sit down on somebody's doorstep. And I want to stop the tears, for Mike's sake, but they come anyway. To think we'd been having such a lovely weekend. The earring shopping; our really nice dinner out. The way we'd linked arms as we walked back to the hotel along the fairy-light-strung Thames Embankment. We chatted all night. Not the routine stuff of his work, my work, the state of the house, Aimee, but frivolous things, almost flirtatious. Or so it felt; maybe it was the wine. Then, in bed, his tender kisses down my throat, his hands gripping my bottom under my nightdress. The way he knows my body better than anyone else, yet fails to ever really excite me. And sometimes I'm able to pretend different, and sometimes I can't.

The coldness of the concrete penetrates my jeans. All the good things about my life that I don't want to lose by losing Mike line up in my mind, urging me to remember that Mike is the one I'm with and the one I love. Not Patrick, who has spent more time in my fantasies than he ever did in my life. But all I am is numb, defeated before I even try.

Next, I'm staring at Mike's slightly scuffed brown Clarks as my tears turn cold on my cheeks. When my eyes travel up his body and finally reach his pale face, I can see him waiting for an explanation. Dismay and disappointment gather around him, like a man just realising that there's something about his wife he doesn't know. Or maybe he does. Maybe there are things he suspects, and wishes he didn't. The weights and measures of a marriage: we know things but we choose not to think about them. We choose to bury our heads in the sand.

Mike says only one thing. 'That was him, wasn't it?'

ONE

Here's what I remember.

The café in Hanoi. I always say that's where we met, because, to be precise about it, it's where I first saw him. If there hadn't been a second time, this one would no doubt have been washed of all significance in the way that generally happens when people merely catch your eye and give you a moment's pause in the grand programme of life.

The city was in the grip of a typhoon. I had run down a skinny alleyway through ankle-deep water, my jean jacket clinging to me like a stiff sail, into the first dry haven – an open-air café that fortunately had half a dozen tables indoors. He was sitting at the one nearest the opening, which had the best vantage on to the storm – the seat I'd have taken if it hadn't been occupied. A bowed head of beautifully thick, close-cut blond hair. Tanned neck. Broad shoulders in a chambray shirt. From this view of him from behind, he could have been a young Robert Redford. There was something very at peace about the way he was sitting there; Patrick is a person who is more than happy with his own company. As I passed him and glanced at him side-on, I saw he was tinkering with a camera, one of those fancy ones that come with all kinds of lenses and complicated component parts. His sleeves were rolled back, pushed halfway up his arms. There was a watch on his right wrist with a brown leather strap, and for a moment I found myself paying undue attention to the raised veins along his tanned forearms, the fine golden hairs. He didn't seem to be aware of me. Whatever he was doing with his camera, he was lost in his own world. I thought how striking he looked against the background cinema of torrential rain, which seemed like it might just be white noise to him, aiding and abetting his patient purpose.

I left a table between us, going for the next one along. There were plenty to choose from, us being the only two people in there. As my chair squawked along the floor I was conscious of him looking up. It was the barest notice, a beat – one, two – where I felt his eyes on me and I registered the thrill like a tiny Cupid's arrow right through me. I wouldn't have dared describe it to anybody because it seemed like such a non-event, yet once I'd sat down I was utterly hijacked by his presence, hyper-aware of everything about him, even the gentle rise and fall of his chest. My twenty-one-year-old romantic psyche was entirely disarranged by him, and I hadn't yet managed a decent look at his face.

I ordered an egg-yolk coffee from the waiter. I remember noting the sudden sprightly quality in my voice, and how his fingers stopped their fiddling when I spoke, as though he was listening for something quite particular and needed to be perfectly still in order to hear it. On my travels, especially in places off the beaten track, where you ran into very few tourists, I had noticed myself doing a sort of covert information-gathering about other Westerners as I sparingly encountered them – were they Australians? Canadian? Someone with whom there could be if not common ground then a little symbiotic conversation about our shared adventures?

My coffee came and my hand was slightly unsteady when I went to pick it up. I was capable of recognising the absurdity of this, a part of me inwardly shaking my head at myself. While I tried to make the drinking of it last forever, I also mastered the fine art of staring in his general direction, but slightly past him, at the rain, while frantically willing him to look over and start a conversation. In a way, our lack of acknowledging one another was becoming a form of dialogue in itself, I thought. Even objects around him – two small tables, a narrow shelf with some black-and-white photos on it, the ragged, exposed brick and bumpy plaster of a wall – helped me frame a picture of him that, little did I know, I would carry around with me for many years to come like brutal, exquisite torture.

His beer was almost done. Any minute now he was going to drain his glass and leave. So I took a risk and said, 'That looks like quite the labour of love,' nodding to his camera.

He stopped what he was doing and looked at me. There was something laid-back yet alert in that look – alert to me. I was held there by the enquiry of his intense, dark eyes, oddly unable to draw breath. I never quite forgot it. 'Yes. I suppose,' he said, after a moment or two. 'I just bought a new flash for it and there's something wrong with it already. Driving me nuts.'

The accent was American. He was older than me – possibly by ten years. I had quite literally never spoken to a person who had a more astonishingly handsome face.

'That's a shame,' I said. I was aware of being riddled with a nervous delight that was about to rip out of me, and I hoped like hell I wasn't wearing it all over me. 'It looks sort of . . . I don't know . . . rugged.' I tried to look at the thing but could only stare at his hands.

He cocked his head as though my word choice gave him pause. I liked his strong, slightly-on-the-large-side nose. Those intense eyes that weren't without kindness. 'Rugged,' he repeated. 'Yes. I suppose it is.' Then his attention returned to his camera. It was as though I was no longer there.

I almost turned stiff with embarrassment. Fine. I got it. He didn't want to talk. I hadn't reached the grand old age of twenty-one without recognising the brush-off when I got it. I wasn't the type of girl to go running back for more. I quite pointedly turned my attention back to my coffee right as he glanced at me again. I felt that look for perhaps three beats of my heart until he turned away again. Next he was packing his camera into his holder. I was aware of my profound dread of him getting up; of wanting to keep him there, to press pause on time. A few seconds later he hurriedly drained his beer glass and then I heard the scrape of his chair along the floor.

'Have a nice day,' he said, when I almost wasn't going to look up but decided to at the last second. There was a look in his eyes that held us there, like a brief pulling of elastic.

Still to this day I've never really known what to say to this easy-come, banal expression that doesn't really demand a response. An equally banal 'Thanks; you too'? So I said nothing.

I'd booked the tour to Halong Bay through the hostel but the weather was playing havoc with everybody's plans. Rather than sit it out – I was getting a bit sick of Hanoi – I decided to jump on the tour bus for Sa Pa. After three months touring around Asia my heart had gone out of travel. I longed for the simple comforts of home, in particular my own bed.

The rain hadn't let up by the time we arrived in Sa Pa. With inadequate footwear for the weather I took a tumble on a hike that put me in bed feeling sorry for myself for a whole day. By the next, the rain had thankfully eased; a low mist hung over the village, grey on a blanket of green. I was wandering the buzzing market around suppertime and had stopped to watch one of the Black Hmong women making fabric dye from an assortment of plant leaves. Despite the dazzling array of colours, scents, and textures to keep my senses occupied, there was a point where I had the strongest feeling I was being watched.

When I turned, he was standing not fifty feet across the square, the only blond head in the crowd. Standing so very still, yet alert, which told me he'd been looking at me for a while before I'd felt it. He was wearing an adventurer's khaki jacket, with big, patchy pockets, his camera holder slung over a shoulder. As we held gazes, recognition beat indelibly between us, and a small fire started up in my heart.

I knew he was going to come over, so I turned away, giddy, quite sure my face was burning. I busied myself by fingering through brightly coloured, embossed fabric, calls of *You Buy! Buy from me!* coming from the Hmong women, as though the very act of my touching their wares had indicated my interest. But I was hearing and seeing it all from a distance, everything around me muted by rabid anticipation. Yet when he arrived at my side I neither felt, nor showed, surprise. And I wonder now if my subdued acknowledgement of his presence was when it all became preordained somehow.

'If you're going to buy, you have to haggle with them,' he said. 'Thirty per cent less is a good start but any more than fifty is insulting. And, of course, if you've no intention of taking the item, best not to start the ball rolling in the first place.' He talked to the tableful of fabrics, only lastly turning and meeting my eyes.

I hadn't quite forgotten the brush-off in the café. 'Don't worry. I got all that from the guidebook,' I said, and started to slowly walk away from him.

'Glad I was helpful,' he said, following me, a note of amusement in his voice, and I suppressed a small smile. There was always something in me that was determined to play hard to get. It had perhaps accounted for why I'd had so few boyfriends.

'Any other suggestions?' I stopped and finally looked up into his milk-chocolate eyes. He was, impossibly, more handsome close-up, with perfect, lightly tanned skin and healthy pink cheeks.

He studied me in a way that felt significant. 'I'll save them for another time,' he said.

We smiled and something between us relaxed enough for me to breathe.

'Do you know what this place is?' he asked after a moment or two, right as I was conscious of the impossibility of breaking away from his gaze. I sensed he was finding the 'make conversation' part awkward; there was an air of desperation about it.

I had heard something in the hostel about a Love Market though I hadn't known what that was. I told him this.

'Yes,' he said. 'It's been a ritual for many years. A sort of mating rite. Tradition had it that a very long time ago a girl and a boy met here and fell in love. But they were from different tribes so the union wasn't blessed. The families did everything they could to keep them apart. But the couple were determined not to be broken. So every year at the same time they agreed to meet in the market to make it known that their love for each other hadn't faded. And it started a thing . . . It somehow became the place where young people came to meet their future partners and older people came back to remember how they had met the ones they'd married.'

'Seriously?' I asked, euphoric he was telling me all this, though the content was least responsible for my excitement.

His eyes went over my face in an arc. 'Well, when you think about it, if you're a guy and you spend your entire week working hard up in the mountains, you've got limited opportunity to meet a girl. And similarly if you're a girl and all the dudes are working up mountains . . .' He watched my face give way to a smile. 'So every Saturday evening the boys come here looking to fall in love and the village girls come to sell their local produce and meet a husband.'

Before I could get a comment out he said, 'You don't believe me. Come.'

And then he surprised me by taking hold of my hand.

I will never forget that feeling of my hand in his, a virtual stranger's, the natural, dauntless, almost instinctual way he went to clasp it, and that sense I had of giving myself over to him. I was on air. He led me around the bustling square, eyes taking in everything he saw – so many of his observations sparking a story he'd then tell me. 'See this boy playing the pen pipe?' He raised the hand that still clutched mine and pointed out a teenager who was playing a strange-looking reed-like instrument to a gaggle of girls in colourful costumes and headdresses. 'If one of these girls likes the look of him, you'll hear how she'll pick up the tune and sing the words of the song back to him to indicate her interest . . .'

We stood and watched for a little while. 'No one's biting,' I said.

He looked vaguely amused. 'I guess I jinxed it.' He finally let go of my hand and shot a picture.

I smiled to myself. 'You're a professional photographer then?' Observing him was like a delirium, a strange disruption of the chemicals in my brain.

'A journalist,' he said, glancing at me again. 'Though part of my job is to take pictures. Six tourists died in a landslide a couple of days ago. I was here reporting on it.'

'They sent you all the way from America?' My cheeks were hot and my heart was skipping.

He stopped clicking pictures and turned to fully face me. 'No,' he laughed a little. 'I'm Canadian. But I'm based in Hong Kong for the time being, working for the Associated Press.'

'Ah . . . I was in Hong Kong two weeks ago. I had a bit of a drama because the hostel I was staying in lost my passport.'

He frowned. 'But it turned up?'

'Yes, after a lot of worry and half a day in the embassy filing a report.' I indicated around us. 'So you being here . . . it's work?'

He studied me closely again but as though his mind was going back and forth on something. 'Kind of. A sideline. It's interesting, mainly, isn't it? A festival of food, song, dance and custom, all centred around the most universal of human desires . . .' His gaze stripped through mine for a second or two, making me blaze from the pointedness of it.

'So you're going to write about love in the Love Market?' It wasn't the cleverest thing to say.

'Who knows? Maybe if I've something worthwhile to say.'

He went on studying me so unyieldingly, a bit like someone contemplating a dive. Then he seemed to visibly snap out of it. 'Do you want to go get a drink?' he asked.

TWO

March 2017

The post rustles through the box and falls softly on the carpet. I leave my morning coffee and the newspaper and walk down our short passageway to the front hall.

There's the usual stuff: bills, flyers, the odd shares certificate for Mike that still comes to this address. But it's the letter-sized white envelope with the solicitor's return address on the front that stops the casual flicking of my hand.

I walk back into our kitchen, conscious that the rain, which has been spitting on and off all morning, is now lashing on the window like a rushed and eerie whisper through a dream. That relentless rain that is so common in early March, sweeping across the wild and exposed Northumberland moors where we live, in a small rural hamlet, some twenty miles west of Newcastle upon Tyne. The kitchen has suddenly gone dark. I switch on the light and find myself just standing there looking out of the window, through my reflection, as though gazing at a ghost. The letter dangles from my limp hand, its contents on a slow parasail in my mind.

Beyond our crumbling stone wall, the wispy mauves and taupe and moss green of the rolling moorland are blanketed by a grey, slow-swirling mist that is probably in for the day. Our plum tree has dropped its blossoms all over the grass. They lie there like confetti long after a wedding. I pull out a chair from under the kitchen table and sit before rereading the letter.

The words are all there, saying what words on a decree absolute are supposed to say, but suddenly I can't quite believe them. I stare at them for so long that they merge and fuzz, and tears burn in my eyes. As four or five drop on to the page, I want – irrationally – for them to have the effect of a magic eraser. But when I look again, it's all still there, telling me the same thing.

We had split up once before; Mike had unfortunately overheard a conversation I was having with my sister, and it had stung. He made a transparently unconvincing production of moving out, with a tie hanging out of his suitcase, putting himself up on the couch of a mate from work for five nights. By the Friday he was home, because a) his back was killing him; b) he realised he wasn't the one who was unhappy – I was – so, if anybody should leave, it should be me; and c) we'd planned to go camping in Scotland that weekend and Aimee had been looking forward to it for ages. But this time when he left, he'd already rented a house. He didn't want us making up our minds and changing them again because we were too afraid of life without the anchor of each other, too afraid of the 'over' in case it was worse than staying together. But somehow, through all the business of him going, I'd still imagined him coming back.

My phone rings, shocking me for a second, and my first thought is that maybe it's him, because he'll have no doubt received the same post. The kitchen table that doubles as my work desk is covered in papers, magazines, client files, questionnaires, surveys, research findings, my empty cereal bowl, old coffee cups, a wrapper from a Mars bar. I find my phone just before it stops ringing. From my call display I see it's a client. I let it go to voicemail.

The rain rushes at the window again and slides down the glass like tears. I'm cold even though the fire's on in the living room and it heats the entire main floor of our small, detached, two-storey stone cottage. My gaze goes to the photo of Mike and me on the shelf above the kitchen table. It was taken a while ago at a wedding: my first client's. Mike's hair, ever the same Fonzie style. His straight, almost too-perfect teeth, and kind, shyly sexy smile. I am taller than him even minus the hat. But it's still a good picture of us.

One thing I've noticed is that no matter where I stand, those eyes always seem to be watching me. They've got this uncanny ability to change when the mood demands it. Sometimes they're smiling, if Aimee and I are locking horns. But other times, like now, they seem to be full of pent-up sadness. We are here, at the end of an era. I have known this is coming and yet I am finding myself so struck by how I'll never wake up beside him again, he won't ever walk in and kiss me and ask me how my day was, I'll never attend another one of his tedious office Christmas parties, try to match another pair of his socks, be afraid to follow him into the toilet, argue over visiting his mother, grumble about the predictability of our lives or why I don't think we're as happy as other couples seem to be. *Never* is such a hard word to swallow. Somewhere inside me it feels like a colossal tragedy that our marriage has come to this. All those assumptions we had that, because we were together, we would stay together; as though the two were somehow interknitted. There was a part of me that fought against them and yet I also trusted them. I know all these are strange thoughts to be having now.

I drag my eyes away from his. I can't stand him looking at me like this, though of course I realise I'm making way too much of a photograph. In fact, today would probably be a good day to take the thing down.

I remember years ago a friend getting divorced and telling me that we get so few actual 'jumping off' opportunities in life. Divorce was hers – her second chance to take a running leap at happiness, either by herself or with someone else but certainly and finally not with him. It had sounded so exhilarating. I'd felt almost envious. Then I'd felt awful for imagining myself in her shoes. Now, I'm in them. I am free to jump. It should be a better feeling than this.

I come downstairs a little fuzzy-headed from my short nap and go over to the couch where my daughter is sitting, and drop a kiss on her silky brown hair with its one tiny plastic clip keeping back the fringe that she's trying to grow out. 'Hi, sweets.'

'Hi, Mum,' she says, flatly, and waggles her fingers in a wave. She has pulled out an earbud and I can hear Ed Sheeran singing 'Shape of You'. 'Granddad's here,' she says.

Lately, after school, my seventy-five-year-old father has been teaching my twelve-year-old daughter to draw – art being the only subject she seems to do okay in these days. Aimee has reached that age where even she no longer believes what her report cards used to say to encourage her when her marks were lagging behind those of her friends: 'Aimee has not yet reached her full potential.' She previously took some pleasure in the fact that she had something ahead of her to look forward to that her friends had already achieved. I'd thought, *What a fine way to look at life!* But since Mike moved out there are very few traces of this quirky, positive Aimee. It doesn't help that, back in the autumn, she fell off her bike. She was dodging a deer that had stalked out from behind trees along a country road. She broke her right arm and her leg in two places and had to miss six weeks of school and could no longer compete in the under-16s regional gymnastics championship that she'd trained so hard for.

I'm not much in the mood for chatter but go into the kitchen and find my father sitting at my messy work table in his perfectly pressed trousers, navy blazer with the shiny brass buttons, and cufflinked shirt. I run a boutique matchmaking service for professionals across the north of England. When I was racking my brains to come up with a name, it suddenly just occurred to me that I should call it The Love Market. I was unsure about it at first; could I ever see, hear, or think those words without being pulled back to everything I've tried so very hard to forget? Then again, the other way of looking at it was that perhaps a new context would be a healthy thing and might even help me in my mission.

'Sandra Mansell, thirty-six, from Jesmond. Do you think she'd be interested in modelling for me? She has very good bones.' My father is holding an 8" x 10" photo of my buxom spa-owner client.

'What are you doing? That's private. Give it back!' I try to wrestle it off him but he hangs on like a drowning man with a life raft.

'If you leave me alone with a trove of treasure, I'm going to open the lid!'

'I'm sure Sandra wouldn't want a man of your tender years getting his jollies from her picture.' I manage to get it off him and put it back in the envelope.

'You never know,' he chuckles. 'She might.' Then he salutes the envelope and says, 'So long, Sandra. You're a real man magnet. It was wild while it lasted.'

I try not to let him see me smile – just pleased, in a way, that I can manage one today. Being the daughter of a diminutive dirty old man has been the cross I've borne nearly all of my life. When I was Aimee's age, my father left my mother and me for a young woman. Not because he no longer loved us, but because he loved *his Marie* more. He tried to explain to me that if my mother hadn't loved him so much, he might have loved this Marie less. And even though he loved me more than he loved any of them, he still had to leave us for her.

I was already confused. All I knew was the bottom line: I had lost my dad. And, because my mother was so stung by life, in a way I had lost her too. Even more confusing was that my mother never looked like she loved my dad too much – not by the way he would do something that would harden her against him for weeks. And even when she'd forgiven him it was still there: the hesitant return to trust; the anticipation of another transgression later.

So this was what love was, I used to think. The slow un-beguiling.

The truth is, how our parents love shapes our own expectations for better or for worse. That's why, for Aimee's sake, I never wanted to be where I've found myself – officially – today. Are we now a family that hands down divorce like the heirloom silver? Will Aimee, in the years to come, make a better job than I have done of everything? Sometimes I find myself wanting to blame my father. If he had been more accepting of his reality perhaps I too wouldn't have been such a romantic who was destined to sabotage the good thing I had. 'Did you say you're staying for dinner?' I ask him.

'Not tonight. I have plans.' He sends me a coy glance.

'Where did you meet this one, then?' I look at his fantastic hair: the thick, undulating, white curls. The perfect pencil-line moustache a shade too black. My dad is dapper, and handsome – 'for a little fellow', as he calls himself.

'At the Grope a Grandma night at the old town hall.' When he sees me smile he says, 'No. At an exhibition at the Laing, actually.'

'She's an artist?'

'Would meeting her at a gallery imply she'd have to be?' My father speaks posh for a council-estate boy, always sounding his 'ing's. Winning a scholarship to the oldest and most esteemed art school in England was one of those flukes of fate that somehow validated his belief that he was too good for where he came from, and therefore made his fall greater when life went pear-shaped and he had to come back.

'How old is she?' I ask him. My father used to love showing off his girlfriends – each one younger and more beautiful than the last – but now we never lay eyes on them. 'You sure she exists?' I'd asked of his latest one.

'She exists,' he'd said. 'She just hasn't yet had her coming-out at the debutante's ball.'

'Which means she's about seventy-five, right?' I'd teased.

He'd grimaced. 'Don't be ridiculous. I've never gone out with some-one my age, and I'm not about to start now.'

'How is it relevant how old *Anthea* is?' he says now.

'Oh God! Anthea!' I chuckle. I'm picturing a thirty-year-old wanna-be co-host of a celebrity ballroom-dancing show, and he knows I am. When he was young, my father took himself way too seriously; now he uses our mutual capacity for finding him slightly funny as something that brings us closer.

Despite the fact that he is theoretically past it, he has lost none of his old ability to beguile women. It's an art form how he lauds the often-invisible minutiae of their beauty, as his hand finds its way to the curve of their lower back, so they are never in any doubt about the masculinity that wrestles in his trousers. But it's the way he talks about his passion for my mother and his era as a painter in Paris that makes people recognise that men like my father don't come around every day. And not only do these men deserve to have you humouring their stories about their life, you do so willingly, for the chance that something they say will change the way you look at your own.

'Anyway, how is The Love Market these days?' he asks, with scoff-ing emphasis on my company's name. Progressive as he is, a romantic like my father finds it morally indefensible that anyone would actually pay someone to find them a partner. I look over and see him peering at a report from the University of St Andrews on 'Face Values Applied to Love Game' – the latest research on what people believe your face says about your attitudes to sexual commitments. My bedtime reading.

'It's doing well. Thanks for asking.'

'And how are *you*?' He exaggeratedly lets the paper float out of his hands, making sure I see, to emphasise his scathing disregard for it.

I stop clanking things on the bench. What is it about an innocent enquiry about your wellbeing that makes you realise you're actually not doing well at all? 'I'm all right, Dad.' I don't want to tell him that my divorce is finally through – not right now, anyway.

'That doesn't sound very convincing.'

I shrug. Even though we've been largely absent from one another's lives, my father still has a way of knowing things without my having to tell him.

'Remember what Gwyneth Paltrow said. The best way to mend a broken heart is time and girlfriends. And in my experience it has always worked,' he says.

I smile at his joke. 'Why's your heart broken this time?'

'I wasn't talking about me.' His eyes slide to my decree absolute sitting on the table.

'Have you been reading my letters?'

'Now, would I?' He looks aghast. 'But if you leave things lying around then you have to accept that eventually they become public property.' Then he adds, 'But this is a sad day.' Because my father always liked Mike.

We meet eyes, and in that moment, all the things I want to say line up for me to speak them, only I can't speak them, and I wonder why, after all this time, it should be so hard. He stands, because he knows we're not going to have a big heart-to-heart about things that are done that we can no longer change. And, inwardly, we will use the fact that Aimee is right here as the excuse to keep this emotional bridge between us that we just can't cross. He slips his raincoat on over his blazer then goes and kisses 'his favourite granddaughter'. Aimee will usually remind him, disdainfully, that she's his only granddaughter. Although lately

Aimee seems to act as though she considers everything and everyone to be beneath her, not just her granddad and his tired jokes.

'I better be off, diddle-doff,' he says. '*Anthea* will be waiting for me.' He shoots me a prankish smile.

I go over to him and give him a quick cheek-kiss, wishing I could cuddle him, but how do you suddenly start being tactile when you never really have? What you do is you hug your daughter all the more, when she'll let you, to give her what you never had. 'Don't do anything you shouldn't do,' I tell him, affectionately, just glad that he's alive and he's got this much spirit left in him, and hoping I'm half as frisky in my old age as he is in his.

'Oh, I'll try,' he says, with a wink.

THREE

'I was reading an article the other day,' I tell my stepsister, Jacqui, while we're out running, attempting to get fit for summer, though personally I always tend to leave it a few months too late. 'It was about how memories of your first love can ruin your future relationships. It said that if you had a passionate first relationship and allow that to become your benchmark, it becomes inevitable that future partnerships will seem a big disappointment. It said ideally we would all wake up and have skipped our first relationship and be in our second one.' I am panting hard. My legs don't seem to want to work and my heart has gone out in sympathy.

'I'd happily have skipped mine,' she says. 'Remember Darren who wore the T-shirt that said *I Love Laxatives*?'

I grin. 'Did he really love laxatives?'

She chuckles, and then says, 'So I take it you've been thinking about Patrick again.'

The mention of his name after all this time is like a groggy regaining of consciousness to a life almost so forgotten that it might not even have been mine. 'I wasn't, no. But of course now I'm going to. Thanks.'

'Welcome!' she sings.

'Back to the article, though . . . I do think that first love sets the standard for all who are to come.'

'But would you have wanted to have skipped knowing Patrick and have just found yourself with Mike?'

I can't really have this conversation while running. I don't really know why I'm even bringing it up. I don't feel like getting the lecture on how I should be out there dating again. Apparently, according to my sister, the one date I actually did force myself to go on, a few months back, didn't count as a proper effort.

'Divorce is like a death, Celine,' she carries on, oblivious to my discomfort. 'But it means a marriage is over, not a life. You have to grieve the marriage but you have to move on too. There's no point in moping.'

'Who said I'm moping, Jacq?' My pace slows and she follows suit. 'Anyway, it's only been a week. They say it takes two years to get over a divorce.'

'That's when they've walked out on you when you're three months' pregnant. Or they've been putting their willy on the internet. When you're the one that wasn't happy, life begins the minute he's down the garden path. In theory, I suppose. Though in your case not in practice.'

'Well, even if I wanted to run out and get someone else – which clearly I don't, because I haven't as yet – I feel a bit like discounted goods now.'

She scowls. 'That's a peculiar thing to say!'

'It's true. It's not exactly a selling feature, is it: telling someone you were so fixated on your first love that it ruined your marriage. I mean, they'll hardly be lining up for me!'

'The worst kind of truth is the whole truth!' she says, pulling out her water bottle from her waist pack. 'No one ever need know all the gory details.'

It's stopped raining so I take off my nylon jacket and wrap it around my hips as our pace slows to a walk, enjoying the early spring air on my bare arms. 'Do you think that's why I've never exactly cracked up over the divorce? Because I was so convinced it was what I wanted?' The worst I've done when he first left was spill the milk when I was putting it on my cereal – poured almost half a litre into my lap – because I was distracted by a moment of extreme missing him. 'I mean, I've never totally lost the plot, have I? Never walked around Hexham market in my dressing gown, stockpiled Prozac in the garage, backed my car into a small person who I mistook for a street lamp . . . What's wrong with me?'

Jacqui's striking almond eyes latch on to mine. Even though we're not real sisters – Jacqui is the daughter of my mother's second husband – our thoughts and fears definitely seem to spring from the same well. We've even been told we look alike. Similar height – I'm an inch taller – and we have similar body types: slim enough, but prone to packing on ten pounds after two weeks of pigging out. At thirty-six, I'm already going grey and colour my long hair a dark chestnut brown, whereas Jacqui, two years my junior, has naturally mousey hair, highlights it blonde and wears it in a bob. When my mum married Len, his kids – Jacqui and Chris – had lost their mother to cancer. Somehow there we were, a miscellany of identities put together under one roof: a five-piece family in a doll's house. I just thought that Len was a pervert, Chris a lamebrain, and Jacqui was always there, trying to be my friend. Maybe I'd not have resented her if she hadn't seemed to have my mother's approval in a way that I never did, even if it was just my mother sucking up to Len – who was there, earned good money and wasn't my father. That is, until he started going out in Chris's shirts and coming home covered in love-bites, then ran off with a nurse and became exactly like my father. Then Jacqui, Chris and I had a bit more in common. We all had absentee dads, and in a way we were all motherless: theirs had died, and mine was there in body but little else. Chris now lives near Hull with his high-maintenance girlfriend, and once in a while he'll phone and we'll end up talking for an hour, and then he'll disappear for two years. And Jacqui is the human equivalent of my ligaments, always holding me in place to prevent dislocation.

'You don't have to have a public breakdown to prove to the world that you carry pain,' she says.

I shake my head, surprising myself by feeling the tears build. 'Knowing our marriage is officially over has just really made me reflect. It's just odd thinking of Mike – this man I've known for most of my adult life – being out there living a life without me and maybe with someone else. Or me, with somebody who doesn't know any of my history, who isn't Aimee's father. Who never actually stood there and shared that joy and amazement when she was born. How do you suddenly not have someone in your life anymore when for so many years they literally were your life?'

We stop walking. Jacqui looks at me with that expression in her eyes of someone who will always want to protect me from my worst self. 'This isn't because you want him back, is it?'

Her question shocks me. 'I can't be that messed up, can I?'

'It's got definite Taylor-Burton elements to it. But where's the law that says you can't get back together again if you've made a mistake?'

I lean over and pant, realising that as I've not been running in about two months I seem to have become seriously unfit. 'Yes, but we were never Liz Taylor and Richard Burton, were we?' Jacqui will always confer romance on everything, and I've become so cynical that I don't know whether she's right to want to or mad to try to. 'They had something indestructible that destroyed them. We were empty vessels who wanted the other to fill them.'

'How do you know he's not divorced and out there thinking about you?' she asks.

I stand up straight again. 'I don't suppose we're talking about Patrick again by any chance, are we?' My sister is like a dog with a bone over this topic. After I told her the story of him all those years ago, Jacqui was the only one who seemed to fall under the spell of him the way I had. She was the only one who didn't judge him, or me, when I told her why we couldn't really be together. I could say things about him and she knew. Plus she was the only one who ever tried to drill me with good advice about how to forget him. Which couldn't have been brilliant because it clearly never worked.

We walk now. Jacqui strides it out, employing both legs and arms, always convinced she has to shed a few more pounds than she really does. 'I don't know anything about him, or what he's doing. It's been fifteen years. It's a lifetime to people our age.'

'But the point is, you still wonder.'

'Thanks,' I tell her. 'For being in my head. But actually, I don't. Not anymore.' With the death of my marriage, something else has died: my spirit, my unfettered belief in matters of the heart, the electric colours of my world; I am a flatter, wan version of myself.

'Have you googled him lately?'

'I don't do that kind of thing.'

'Why not? You did it before.'

She forgets nothing. 'Once. Ages ago.'

'But didn't you look him up after you thought you saw him in London?'

I tut. 'Okay, twice then. And I decided it wasn't him. We've been through this a million times.'

'All because he was wearing sunglasses and you needed to see his eyes to be convinced.'

'That . . . and I rang the hotel I'd seen him come out of and they told me there was no guest by that name.' Sometimes we will find ourselves talking about Patrick as though he wasn't old news.

'You did?' She gawps at me. 'You never told me that part!'

'Didn't I?' I avoid her eyes.

I remember how I'd sneaked away from Mike to use the payphone, how my heart had hammered as I'd dialled that number. How I'd been worried Mike would know what I was doing just by my face. I'd been outside myself, watching myself do it, heartily disapproving but powerless to stop myself. If it was Patrick – if he was in London at the same time as me – I had to know. And if he was staying at that hotel, then I'd have to cope with whatever act of insanity I would commit when I found out. The fact that I was even contemplating a reckless act of insanity of course spoke volumes to me about my marriage, which depressed me for days. And that was a side effect I'd tried to hide, but Mike already knew.

'Everybody wonders about somebody, Jacqui. It's called the politics of disenchantment. But most reunions with old flames don't work out.' Believe me, I'd researched that too, pretending I was really only doing it because it was my job to have insight into these things. 'Not unless it was a war separation or something on that scale.' Or – like the story Patrick had told me that day – if you were just from the tribe that everybody loved to hate. 'The moral is, you have to live the life you're living. Not some parallel life that you wish you could live.'

She pretends to play the violin. 'Nice words. I've got some too. Life is short. Botox is just round the corner. You have to grab your happy by the horns. Maybe seeing him that time – or even just *thinking* you saw him – meant you were on some parallel cosmic track. Maybe it meant you weren't supposed to forget him.'

'Have you ever thought that maybe you should try taking your own advice?'

Not a part of me believes that Jacqui wants to marry the man she's engaged to. And yet she's hurtling down a course without using her brakes and I can't seem to stop her. Though I have a feeling it's all going to come to a head soon.

'Can we not talk about Rich right now? This is way more exciting,' she says, looking sad for a moment.

'Well, I'm sure he's forgotten me,' I tell her. 'I mean, it's not as though he's ever come looking for me in all these years, is it?'

'Who knows? Maybe he really wanted to. Or maybe he did and he couldn't find you. If only you'd been a modern gal who keeps her own name in case old boyfriends try to look her up.'

I laugh.

'Seriously,' she says. 'You're thirty-six and gorgeous. You're a good person, a great mother – even if Aimee doesn't think so at the moment – and whatever you felt deep down, you were a good wife. So it's guaranteed that you're going to find another man, which would be a great thing if only there wasn't still this unfinished business in you. And even if he lives in another country, even if you've not spoken to him in fifteen years . . . who's to say that there's absolutely no way it can ever happen? What have you got to lose by looking him up? Really? When you think about it, Celine – not one single thing. Sometimes you have to just take a leap of faith into the unknown. And – God – if you're not going to do it then I'm doing it for you!'

I give her a sweaty hug. 'You talk a load of pipe dreams, but I love you nevertheless.'

A leap of faith into the unknown? Jacqui's words tick over in my head much later when I pour myself a glass of wine and sit on the couch. Didn't the old me used to be such a daring girl? I dove headlong into life, and the thrill of it was fantastic. Then marriage made everything feel a little too certain and established for my comfort level.

Much as I hate any conversation that centres on the fact that I haven't made any proper effort to start dating again, I suppose, if I were my own client, I would think it a little odd that in the two years since Mike and I split up I've made no effort to get back out there again. Jacqui is right: there is this unfinished business in me.

I stare at my computer sitting just feet away on my work table. Then I get up, go over there, log on to Google and type in Patrick's name.

FOUR

I remember the bump-bump of the jeep he'd rented as we climbed to 2,000 metres above sea level, striated paddy fields falling away behind us and new ones emerging; my heart performing similar tiny undulations. He'd said he had to go out the next day, 'into the field', as he called it, to shoot some photos, and that I could come . . .

'Have you seen a lot of the world?' I asked him. The landscape was striped with sunshine, dots of colour from the clothes of Hmong women harvesting rice, some of them pausing to watch us and wave. The day was playing out as though in a dream. Patrick was very much in work mode. He hadn't again reached for my hand. I was an accessory, I thought, just tagging along with him. Though by the way he would occasionally look at me, I was clearly a bit of a distracting one.

'No,' he said. 'But I intend to.' He shot me a meaningful glance over his shoulder. 'You?'

'The summer before uni I travelled Europe. We weren't a family who holidayed much, so France, Italy, Greece . . . it was all a big deal to me. And I absolutely loved the freedom of doing and seeing it all on my own! Then when I graduated I got the idea to come here – get the travel bug out of my system.'

'Why do you have to get it out of your system?'

I couldn't tell if he was teasing me. 'Well . . . I mean, see and do as much as I can before, you know . . . before I have to settle down, I suppose.'

He gave me a look as though I'd just said the most outlandish thing. 'Settle down?'

I found myself smiling and squirming. 'It's an expression.' I realised it wasn't really something I'd normally say, so where had it come from? I hated it when aunts and uncles said it to me! The presumption that I would have to follow the book of life exactly as they and everyone around them had. That I might have a window of carefree living before-hand, but that was going to be it and I had little choice in the matter. 'Don't they say that in Canada?' I stared back at him, challenging.

He beamed a smile. 'No.'

I still couldn't tell if he was mocking me.

'What does it mean?' he asked.

I huffed a small laugh at the silliness of it and found myself hav-ing to consciously break away from his eyes. 'Well, if you're dying to know . . . It means get a job, save money to buy a flat, get married, propagate the species . . .' He was looking at me as though he was highly entertained by me, and quite enthralled, which surprised me. 'It's a stupid expression,' I said.

Much later, when we pulled over to collect some food and a beer, and sat on the ground, having a sort of spontaneous picnic, he chinked his bottleneck to mine, held my eyes, and said, 'Here's to never getting it out of the system.'

We smiled.

I remember him saying, 'I'm married.'

We had been bumping along again in pleasant silence. The admis-sion came out of the blue. There seemed to be an urgency about it, even though he spoke it casually, like it had been born from his thoughts more than from any actions or words.

'Anya's back in Hong Kong,' he said.

'Oh?' I tried not to show I was in any way ruffled but the word just kept ringing in my head. Had I expected him to be? I hadn't thought about his existence beyond the corporeal one right in front of me. It was distorting everything in the most beautiful way I'd ever known possible. If you'd asked me there and then, I could have stayed stuck in that point in time forever. I'd somehow been taken out of reality by him, and there was nothing even vaguely appealing about going back. But, I suppose, the conversation about settling down probably had suggested to me that he was still single. 'How long have you been married?' I asked, casually.

'Fifteen months, though we've been together since university days, off and on. Been out here a year . . .' His gaze slid across to me. I tried not to hold it but couldn't resist. We were so close spatially, and yet I suddenly felt several thousand miles of distance. This felt like an end and we'd barely had a beginning. It was catastrophic.

'I want you to know because it would feel deceptive keeping it from you, and I'm not like that.' He looked at me so earnestly that it didn't occur to me to not believe him. 'That day in the café in Hanoi . . . I left because I felt myself being drawn in a way that was only going to complicate things.'

This surprised me. Really? I'd had no idea!

'We're not together. We're under the same roof mainly for practical reasons but it's not working and hasn't for the last six months. Anya didn't adapt to being over here. She's got some issues. It's . . . I don't really want to get into it . . .'

I could see in his eyes the difficulty he was having with this so I didn't want to press him. Instead I banked it, tried to process it, to see my way around its significance and why he was making this point of telling me. 'Does *she* know it's not working out?' I asked, as though if I was only going to ask one pertinent question it had better be the right one – one I could make something with. I remember holding my breath. It felt like my entire life hung in the balance while I waited for his answer.

'Of course,' he said. 'But nobody else does . . . certainly not the reason why . . .' He stopped the vehicle, shifted in his seat so he could better see me. We were the only two people as far as the eye could see in every possible direction. It felt symbolic. 'We agreed that when I get back either I'm moving out or she's going back to Canada. We know – I've made it plain – that we can't go on . . . And she knows too.' He looked down for a moment or two. I waited, hanging on every word of this to see how much he was going to give me. He looked up again. 'It's difficult because I want the best for her. She's a good person. But we made a mistake in getting married. I think I always knew it, so in many ways I can only blame myself. But it's gotten really bad in ways I could never have anticipated.'

There was so much revealed in the very little he'd told me. Later, when we sat squeezed on to the small seat of a patio bar, chatting about the concept of brevity – in words, in love, and in life – while he pulled strands of my hair through his fingers, as though they were fine, fascinating yarn, I told him this.

He was telling me, *I shouldn't be here with you. And the reason I shouldn't be is that I want to be.*

FIVE

There are endless articles on him. Every time I do this I feel the same rush, that sense of tasting the forbidden again. Many of them I've seen before; because of course I've googled him way more than I've ever admitted to Jacqui, which always felt like a form of infidelity in itself. Would I have liked Mike looking up the same ex-girlfriend? Would I have been able to convince myself that his curiosity was purely idle or, at worst, nothing more than nostalgia? That it was enough it was me he'd married? Then again, is infidelity the most destructive thing that can happen to a marriage, or is giving up?

I digest everything on Patrick like it's new to me. Wikipedia references. Career profiles. Something about him winning an Emmy for his coverage of Hong Kong being returned to China. A fascinating interview with him in *Frontline* magazine. But it's the image results that spellbind me. So many of them are familiar, from when I combed over them to answer that one question: was it him I'd seen in London?

There's a new one, though. He's wearing a khaki combat jacket, and is posing against a parched mountainous backdrop of some foreign war zone. It looks like it's probably recent. It's his most 'close-up' shot on here. The face is older. Shockingly so: the cheeks fuller and softer with age, a flush of a suntan across the bridge of his prominent nose. His once-fair hair is greying, and in his eyes there is a sadness and seriousness that never used to be there. Wikipedia tells me his birthday—which I already knew. Patrick is forty-three now. Journalisted.com catalogues every article he's written on wars. And yet I can't find anything very telling about his personal life. Nor is he on Facebook, or I might have drummed up the nerve to add him as a friend.

Just purely to see if there is anything, I type in the words 'Patrick Shale contact information' and hold my breath. But all that comes up is the name of a literary and talent agent who, it seems, represents him. I try again with 'Patrick Shale email', not expecting the result to be any different.

But hang on . . .

There is a Patrick Shale who lectures in the journalism school of a place called Ryerson University, in Toronto. When I click on the link, there it is – an email address.

My heart scuttles. Even without there being a photograph it has got to be him.

SIX

'Kim!' I say, finally deciding that not answering my phone isn't good for business – even when it's the client I love to hate. Mike's photo is staring at me from the shelf. For Aimee's sake I left it and placed one of her and me at a church fete next to it.

'Celine, thank God! Do you have a minute?' she says. 'Something completely awful has just happened to me!'

I should be jumping up saying, *Oh my God! Something really awful has happened to Kim!* But I know her personality type. I saw it when we met in her Newcastle Quayside office three months ago. Kim runs one of the largest public relations agencies in the country. The girly way she tried to bond with me over my leopard-print boots was more than over the top. Then when she cut me off and barked at her secretary to come in and clean her desk, citing *Allergies!* to me as the reason for the dusting crisis, I recognised histrionic personality disorder a mile off.

'What happened?' I say now. I'm not too concerned. This is the person who refused to go on a date with a man because his last name was Schmink. A renowned heart surgeon would have been The One, if only he'd had shoulders and wasn't 'just a pair of arms pinned to his throat'. And then there was handsome, easy-going Frank. Didn't he just order dessert for himself when she told him she didn't want any?

Then again, perhaps I shouldn't take her so lightly. You never know, this might be the one time I've matched a client with Jeffrey Dahmer II, or someone who keeps albums of teenage girls in his night-table drawer.

'I'm just so shocked and disgusted. It was horrible!'

Kim has been on three dates with David Hall, a widowed property developer. I had hoped that this was a sign that everything was going quite well.

'Tell me,' I say. 'Try to calm down . . .'

I am guessing it's an issue of a deviant sexual preference, or an odd-looking private part. One thing I have discovered in this business: women will always clinically dissect their sexual encounters. Whereas my male clients never talk about their dates disrobed, and I've never yet heard a man say that the sex wasn't good enough.

She launches into how the salmon was overcooked at dinner, and then about a film. 'We couldn't agree on which one to see, so we ended up going to see one that neither of us wanted to see – just to make it fair – which, of course, was a complete and utter disaster, because if there's one thing I can't stand it's anything to do with aliens . . .' Now I get fifteen minutes on the plot of the film that neither of them cared to see.

As she chatters on about aliens I stare out at the garden. It looks so barren in the rain. The empty planter boxes. The vegetable patch that has been a bit neglected over a couple of summers, since Mike's been moved out. 'Kim,' I interrupt her. 'I thought you were telling me about David.'

'I'm getting there!' she growls. 'I'm just trying to set the scene. But as you're obviously in some sort of hurry . . . if you must know, we went back to his very nice Newcastle loft. One thing was leading to another. I had tugged down his jeans . . . Oh.' She makes a strange vomiting noise. 'It was awful!'

The Apollo rocket will come back from the moon before she finally spits it out.

'It was just . . . it was just there. His raw, exposed . . . willy . . . The man doesn't wear underpants!'

'Oh!' Well, she had me this time! I really was preparing for something that would end up on the next episode of *Embarrassing Bodies*. 'Well, have you thought that maybe he was just behind on his washing?'

'They weren't in the laundry. And I checked his drawers. His entire flat is an underpant-free zone.'

'So, hang on a second. You were in his bedroom? Does this mean you slept with him?'

'Does it sound like I was attracted enough to sleep with him after that?' Her tone has *imbecile* written all over it. 'I had a quick mooch when he got up from the couch to go to the toilet. To *clean* himself – I mean, who knows what they have to do.'

I try to force away the rather distasteful picture of David doing unsavoury things in the bathroom, and of Kim ferreting in his dirty laundry. While I'm always intrigued by what makes people tick, and the blend of part-science, part-instinct that goes with matching two human beings – a bit like pairing wine with food – I never bargained for how this job would take over my life. I am called upon at any hour to be a psychologist, babysitter, best friend, life coach, stylist, punching bag, hatchet man, walking dictionary of everything . . . I'm always contemplating ways to charge them a retainer for the hours I generally spend just listening to them talk, which they seem to think comes free with the service, but I've never quite worked out how to do that. I've got to get on to it. I could be rich.

'He's a freeballer,' I tell her. 'They're not as rare a breed as you might think. Freeballers feel cleaner and healthier without underwear. Often it's because they've had air-flow problems in the past. Freeballers aren't a known sociopathic group, so we're really quite safe with him. And – I know you'll disagree, but – you actually can't make a judgement about anyone by their underwear status. And wearing underwear does not guarantee that you are a cleaner person.'

Norman, Mike's old black-and-tan tabby cat, comes into the kitchen to eat his food and rubs up against my bare leg. I reach down and stroke his bony body.

'I'm just not sure it constitutes a serious problem, that's all,' I tell Kim. 'I mean, not if everything else is good about him. Remember the Seven Deadly Sins? David Hall doesn't commit a single one of them. He's not chronically late, or rude to waiters. He's got no scary divorce stories, or satanic kids; he doesn't have anger issues, isn't unduly attached to his parents, and he didn't suggest splitting the bill on your first date. I'd say we shouldn't write him off just yet.'

'I don't know . . .'

'Try to remember what's out there. You know that David is one of the few men who can handle a successful, independent woman, and he isn't looking for someone thirty years younger.' A subtle reminder to her that, at forty-five, Kim is not likely to attract a man her age. Most men in their late forties and fifties want to try out their inner Ronnie Wood when it comes to romance, and that doesn't bode well for women like Kim, who don't need an older man for his money and prefer the standard age difference of two point two years. It pains me to think she might be giving up on him this fast.

'Can't you just give him another chance?' I plead.

'Shall we give it another try?' I can hear Mike saying, after every time we'd fought and talked about whether we should break up. I'd feel like I had a renewed sense of purpose somehow, and yet, at the same time, I'd know it was wrong.

'I don't know,' Kim says. 'Honestly, I'm not sure I can be attracted to him after this.'

'Look,' I tell her, brightly. 'Why don't you tactfully present him with a pair of underpants, and tell him you'd find him really sexy if he put them on?'

'Or, I have a better idea,' she says. 'You could have a talk with him. Tell him Kim says the underpants are going to be the deal breaker.'

I picture Kim as the Mafia Don, and me her 'made guy'.

'After all, I do pay you,' she adds.

With types like Kim, retaliation to irksome comments is no-win. You have to appeal to the higher power that controls them: their ego. Sweet talk them round to your way. 'I'm well aware you pay me, Kim. And you know I'll do anything to help. But you're a very persuasive person; I think you can pick your moment and tell him how much you'd love to see him in a sexy pair of briefs.'

'Do you think that would work?'

'His goal will be to please you,' I tell her. 'I think you're in with a very good chance.'

When we hang up, it strikes me what a change I've undergone. How conceited I used to be about being a married woman with a child. I was lucky enough to have been lured into this false sense of security that you have when you are attached legally, and in other ways, to another human being. Where you can say and do virtually anything to them and they will tolerate you and try to understand you, and put it down to you just being you – for some greater goal that even they don't clearly understand. It somehow put me above the petty criticisms that the single confer upon their dates. I had deeper, more justifiably petty things to find fault with. Back then, that seemed to signal that my life was in good shape.

It was clearly a very warped way of measuring success.

SEVEN

'What's wrong?' I ask Aimee, as we sit in an empty Italian restaurant called The Godfather, down a Newcastle city-centre side street, at lunchtime. Three bored Italian waiters stand around aimlessly watching our every move, while the Gypsy Kings sing 'Bamboleo'.

I kept her off school today. Not that I make a habit of encouraging my daughter to play hooky. But sometimes they call it retail therapy for a reason. And I know from experience that satisfying Aimee's addiction to shoes once in a while has healing powers that all the mothering in the world can't compete with. 'It's about your dad and me, isn't it?' I ask the top of her head as she stares for a disproportionately long time at the four lunch specials on the menu. She could be me, twenty-four years ago. Although my mother never took me out for my favourite food and asked me how I was doing.

She shakes her head. She has been unusually quiet since I told her that her dad and I were officially divorced now. I look at her shiny mane of hair, the porcelain skin like my mother's, her lowered gaze and the natural Garbo-esque sweep of her thick eyelashes. My daughter, who turns herself out like a rebellious street urchin, is lately in the habit of wearing a short-sleeved T-shirt over the top of a long-sleeved one, a pleated denim mini-skirt, and colourful chequered tights – sometimes with holes poked in them. 'If you want to talk about it, we can.' The waiter swoops, brandishing a notepad. We both order the lasagne.

And then she says the words that cut me open. 'Why don't you love him anymore?'

I close my eyes, and it's a moment or two before I can look at her again. 'I do love him, Aimee. Of course . . .'

'Then why aren't you together? Why aren't we still a family?'

Tension gathers in my brows. 'We are still a family. We both still love you. And we both still care about each other. We just can't go through life as a couple anymore.'

'Why not, though? If you both care for each other?'

'It's not an easy answer,' I tell her. 'The love between a husband and a wife is different. It's not quite as unconditional as the love your dad and I have for you.' In the way she looks at me now, I can tell that explanations are just fancy word games to her. She's asserting that one selfish right we both know she has: to have us be a family. And I know that because I've been there.

'Aimee, please don't think I have any bad feelings towards your dad. This is hard for me. These last couple of years, I've just been trying to learn how to live without him and it's still a very strange place to be. I may have to figure it out as we go along. Other than loving you very much, that might be the best I can offer you right now. It might be all I have.'

Nothing. I can't read her. I sometimes want to beg her to cry, scream, anything. Not this. This flatness. She used to be such an expressive child. Then Mike left, she fell, and a part of her has stayed fallen.

I remember Patrick saying all those years ago, 'We tried. We really tried to make our marriage work. But sometimes you realise it shouldn't require all that effort.' And I realise that's exactly how I feel too.

The Gypsy Kings are singing 'Volare' now, and the waiter sets down garlic bread that we didn't ask for, angling for a flirtatious glance. Aimee stares at the top of the table. I can almost see her young little mind grappling its way around adult truths.

But am I lying to both of us? Since my daughter has become the very thing I hated being – a fixture moved back and forth between two parents and no longer part of a mathematical set determined precisely by what's in it – did we try hard enough?

'We didn't really split up,' Mike said shortly after we separated the first time. 'We were just taking a little break from each other.' He rubbed the tear off my cheek with his thumb. 'I'll never part with you,' he said, as though I was his favourite record from his prized seventies collection. I can still feel the way his thumb stretched the skin under my eyes.

I never had to ask myself if Mike only came back for Aimee. I knew that in Mike's mind he'd never really left.

'I hate this dumb song,' Aimee says. The waiters are leaning up against the nearby wall, watching us, in competition for our attention. Aimee looks right over and catches them gawking. 'Who are they? Dumb, Dumber and Dumbest?'

I have a small chuckle at her childish cruelty. 'We could go shopping after this for something for you to wear to Rachel's party.'

She lifts a sheet of bubbling mozzarella with her fork, her T-shirt sleeve reaching to her knuckles. 'I'll get third-degree mouth burns if I eat this,' she says, peering at the steam coming off it. Then she adds, 'Why? It's not like I'm going.'

I set my fork down. 'Since when?'

'Since she didn't invite me.' She meets my eyes. 'But I'm not upset or anything.'

'Why didn't she invite you? Did you ask her?'

She sends me a plaintive look. 'How would it be better if I knew?'

I try to find an answer for that, but, as often happens, my daughter outsmarts me.

'You're not distancing yourself from her because she won the championship and you resent her for it, are you?' This would be out of character for her; and besides, it feels like old news now.

She drops her jaw and it hangs there. Then she says, 'No! I am totally over that. It was ages ago.'

I am glad we agree on that. But something in her expression . . . I am not convinced. 'Good,' I say. 'Because, as I told you when you had your fall: yes, it was bad, but imagine how much worse it could have been if you'd hit your head. You will win other competitions. There are so many opportunities ahead of you.' I know that my 'You can still lose the battle and win the war' line isn't all that much consolation, but it's the best I've got right now.

I look at her fingers seized around her fork. They are long and gangly and pale and perfectly tapered, with their pearly painted nails. I have adored them from the moment I first laid eyes on them. Sometimes I think I've watched Aimee grow through her hands. I'm like a fortune teller, except I don't read palms and I just see the present. If only I could see what was even a short distance ahead for all of us. That might be a gift worth having.

'Her mum said that marriages only break up because one person has met someone else.'

It's me doing the jaw-dropping now. 'Aimee! You shouldn't listen to things like that! Yes, people sometimes do fall in love with others. But in our case neither one of us was looking to meet someone else. That's not what this is about.'

We eat the rest of our food in silence, though I am beyond furious at that remark. When we're done, I glance over and accidentally catch the waiter's eye, which seems to make his day.

'You've got yourself a boyfriend,' Aimee says.

'And hands off; he's all mine.'

I catch a hint of a smile. 'Listen, we're going to pay up and shop till we drop. And we'll plan our own party. How about that?' I pull out my money to pay the bill. The waiter is on me in a split second.

'Who'll be left to invite?' she says, pulling a smile. 'They'll all be at Rachel's.'

'Don't worry.' I wink at her. 'We'll think of somebody. Even if we have to pay people to come, just for show.'

She tuts. But it's a happier tut. And right now, that feels like a major achievement. 'Can we get out of this dumb restaurant?' she asks.

'Gladly,' I tell her.

EIGHT

'What are we going to do?' he whispered into my temple.

It wasn't a question that really demanded an answer. I could tell he was thinking out loud. Every hour we were spending together was bringing reality to press on us – but it was a confused reality; a surreal one, still.

We were in bed in his dimly lit cabin, where we had been the entire day, as though by staying within those four walls all outside threats to what we had couldn't reach us; only this narrow world of ours was real. He had just snapped a picture of me, a close-up of me looking at him with bare honesty and desire, a slight teariness in my eyes because, even though he didn't know it, I was pitching ahead to the possibility of him being gone and my never seeing him again. It was one of a great many he took of me over the course of a couple of days. I was starting to just give myself up to the clicking of his camera, to accept what he told me: that this was how he framed things he knew were too precious to forget. It was raining hard and we were convinced we could hear it landing on every leaf of every tree. I had only slept with one other person, when I was eighteen – an episode born more from a desperate need to lose my virginity than from passion springing from every pore of my being. This – sex with Patrick – was rearranging everything I knew about myself. Patrick's kiss, the way he touched me and seemed to know me, the way we just fit – it wasn't awkward, we just seemed to flow from two similar places into the same perfect one – felt like the making and remaking of me.

'We could start with you not going back to Hong Kong tomorrow,' I said, semi-seriously, propped up on one arm, endlessly staring into his eyes as he stared into mine. My eyes were the only camera I needed. At this point I loved everything about him. There were no doubts in my mind. It was magnificent and massive to be this sure. The degree to which I'd attached to him was something I'd never known or even really imagined knowing. When I was with him I had the most complete and utter sense of belonging. But now I had this horror of him going back there to his apartment and somehow making up with his wife. I remember that overriding sense of self-preservation – of preserving *us* – and my own fragile selfdom. I had always been a kind-hearted girl who tended to place other people's feelings on the same plane for consideration as my own. Yet I could only think of one thing at all costs: not losing him.

'I have to go back,' he said. 'For work. I was supposed to be back yesterday.'

I puzzled this. 'But when we met in the Love Market . . . ?'

'I was only supposed to be there that day and fly home yesterday morning.' He smiled, playfully devious. 'I managed to change my ticket but I have to go back tomorrow or I'll probably end up fired.'

'You changed your ticket because of me?' I couldn't bear to believe it because I felt like I would burst even more than I was already bursting if he said yes.

'Because of you.' He stared at me with a sort of loving intensity that I will always remember. 'Mad, eh? I meet you for five minutes in a village and I'm rearranging my life so I can be with you. Because something about you . . . I just couldn't stop myself. I would have had an easier time cutting off my own legs . . .'

I smiled. 'Well, I'm glad you didn't try to cut your legs off but to be fair it wasn't exactly five minutes. We sat in that bar until they almost threw us out.'

'Oh, I'd made my decision long before that,' he said. His eyes were so full of truth, a fervour written all over his face, and in that moment I believed in him with everything I had in me. 'You had me in that café in Hanoi. I couldn't concentrate for wanting to just sit there and look at you. And it was even more than that. Something I can't explain. Maybe I'll never be able to.'

'You barely glanced in my direction!' I mimicked his slightly arrogant, flippant *Have a nice day!*

He laughed. 'I know. That was bad. Like I told you before, it was purely because the situation was complicated. I . . . I just thought, *Man! Don't go there . . .*'

'Was complicated?' I half-teased, and bloomed with so much hope. 'So what is it now?'

He answered by making love to me again. I honestly believe, looking back, that at that point in time it wasn't complicated at all, for either of us. It wasn't until much later that he answered the question that I'd just assumed already had been answered.

'If I didn't feel any degree of guilt about her, and responsibility for her, I'd not much care how I acted,' he said, almost apropos of nothing. 'And you really must believe that there is a huge part of me that just wants to throw caution to the wind and literally not care – to think only of myself . . .' The way he was looking at me I could tell he wasn't fully communicating what was flying around in his head. All I could do was read between the lines, and yet the lines still felt so full of promise. The way I saw it was he was just rationalising what he'd already intended to do. I felt safe in that.

He'd already told me they met in journalism school. They both worked in smaller cities for a while then found themselves in Toronto together. They lived together for a couple of years then Patrick had applied for a job with the Associated Press in Hong Kong. She'd just landed a placement at the *Toronto Star*. They had to make a decision. His opportunity was the bigger career move. They both knew that he couldn't *not* take it. So they decided to get married and come out to Asia together.

'It could have been fantastic,' he'd said, looking a combination of wistful and jaded. 'There are many two-journalist couples with the bureau. There was every opportunity for her to have a great career in China, freelancing. You have to understand, when you're both out here trying to figure out a whole new culture, a new language, you're as likely to get a good story in the grocery store as you are sitting at your desk in the bureau. In fact, more likely. And it wasn't just me telling her that. Some of our friends are doing exactly what we could have been doing. But something in her changed. She became very negative. Didn't seem motivated anymore. It was almost like she resented the fact that I had a regular gig and she thought she was the only one struggling . . . The truth is, I was so busy finding my way. I was learning on my feet how to file daily news reports for the most influential news-gathering operation in the world, and she was just sitting around being angry and resentful and sorry for herself.'

'So why the guilt?' I asked him now, because I could see how much this was still weighing on his mind.

'Anya has a drinking problem,' he said, after a moment or two. 'And when she drinks she's a violent-tempered drunk.'

I scrutinised his face. I didn't massively want to talk about her and yet I needed to know. 'You mean it just . . . developed? Because of the move to Asia?'

'No. She was a big partier in university. Could get pretty verbally abusive after a few. She knew it and tried to keep it in check. But it got bad after we moved here. Just spells of explosive rage. Completely unprovoked. She's hooked up with a buddy – the wife of an ex-pat chef. They sit at the bar in the Shangri-La half the day drinking.'

This new information floated around. 'Okay, but I still don't understand this issue of you feeling guilt, though.'

He flopped over on to his back and stared at the ceiling. 'It's because I dragged her away from her world, from a good job . . . I led her into this. I should have spotted the signs earlier but maybe I just ignored them . . . I wasn't one hundred per cent sure I really even wanted us to be married and yet we somehow found ourselves deciding to do it before we came out here – to sort of make us more of a team . . . Then when I got here I was feeling so responsible for her and yet angry and frustrated that she was making me feel so responsible for her.' He looked at me frankly, shook his head in lingering exasperation. 'I thought she might be depressed at first. I tried to get her some help but she wouldn't hear of it. I suggested we fly her sister out, because they're very close. She wouldn't have that, either. I couldn't motivate her in a single positive way. It killed our relationship. But I couldn't just abandon her. I felt I had to at least try to make our marriage work, to make something worthwhile for her.'

'Worthwhile?' I stared at his fine nose, at the weight that was suddenly there in his eyes again – one that had arrived with just the mention of her. 'But you don't stay married to someone as an incentive for them to be happy.'

'No. And this is what I'm faced with now. The fact that I can't stay in the marriage anymore. But I'm trying to extricate myself in a way that I can live with. I'm trying to do the right thing by her . . .'

I was scrambling to make sense of it. He didn't sound like he was undecided. I believed it was over. He didn't love her, but he obviously cared about her, and I wouldn't have wanted to find myself falling for anyone who felt differently. And yet I still wasn't sure why it had to be complicated. At the heart of me I felt a little threatened by the fact that he somehow wasn't managing to say, *Don't worry about a thing; you and I are going to be together no matter what.* But I didn't want to press it. I was fully convinced that by tomorrow we'd have sorted it all out.

'We'll think of something,' he said, as though finally answering his earlier question, and my prayers, at the same time.

NINE

Aimee and I get on with the ebb and flow of our daily existence, and just as I'm racking my brains to come up with some new ways of growing my client base, I am handed a referral from one of my favourite female clients, Trish Buckham. Trish is a lawyer with a sparky, infectious personality – though you might not imagine that's what she does for a living, going by her micro-minis, funky hairstyle and foul mouth. I've known her a couple of months and have sent her on a few coffee-meets, because she prefers the quick-exit strategy, rather than the way I normally like it to happen – in a restaurant, where you're forced to get to know your match for the time it takes to consume a civilised meal. She never sounds over the moon when I ring her about a possible date. So sometimes I wonder if her heart really is in meeting someone, or if she's doing it just to convince herself – or others – that she's trying.

It's usual for clients to refer friends to me; but it's almost always people I've already successfully matched, referring someone of the same sex. So this is a bit different. I always meet potential new clients before taking them on. I will go for lunch with the women, as well as talk to them a lot on the phone. I always ask the men to meet me in a restaurant for dinner, in a fake-date situation, so I can see them the way a female date would see them, and iron out their kinks before I put them on The Love Market.

Manchester is a bit out of my net, but Trish all but begged me to help her friend.

I didn't set out to do this for a living. I'd been a recruitment consultant to start with. But the twenty-mile drive into the Newcastle office wasn't really working out once I had Aimee. Mike worked nights at the radio station and looked after Aimee during the day. He rarely got to sleep and I rarely saw my daughter and was always burned out.

I had loved my job initially. I was good at the business-development side of attracting new clients, the relationship-building. But best of all I loved searching the market for suitable candidates, the interviewing and the psychology of evaluating their personality tests – seeing how they might react in certain situations and using the findings to determine if they were the right fit with a certain corporate culture. I loved the whole exploration of who a person really was, compared to how they saw themselves – and saving them from ending up in jobs they weren't suited to. Then two things happened around the same time. I had recently headhunted an accountant called Sharon Gillespie for a new position that was being developed in credit control for an international retailer based in Gateshead. It was the only case I'd been involved in where the fit was wrong. But I'd got to know Sharon quite well while she'd tried and failed to settle into her new role, and I also knew that she was single and wanting to meet someone. I had an inkling she might get on nicely with another client of mine who also worked in the financial sector and was having a career crisis of his own. They were similarly educated, similarly attractive and both quietly spoken. I introduced them, and love bloomed. Two years later they were married – Mike and I attended their wedding – and Sharon ended up returning to the job I had headhunted her away from.

Around that time, I read an article on how internet dating had become too algorithm-led and was not always even close to being successful. The article had humorously cited a woman from Wales who had supplied a popular dating site with a fairly standard wish list for a partner and had ridiculously been matched with a plumber from Missouri and a man who claimed to be a Saudi prince. Serious or not, it got me thinking about a business idea. After a lot more research into the market for personal introductions, I reasoned that I could apply my existing skills of people-fitting while offering a high-end, very personal matchmaking service, the likes of which wasn't really being done in the north-east of England. Mike and I had already decided I should leave my job and stay home until Aimee was school age. So I decided to run some ads in the right magazines, to treat it more like a hobby at first and see what happened. I came up with my branding, bought a Mac computer and designed my own website – all while Aimee took naps or played beside me. After the first six months I had eleven clients and growing. After the first three years I was successfully matching more than fifty per cent. Now, I have a manageable and growing portfolio and a success rate of seventy per cent. Is it a bad life? Well, sometimes it's frustrating. Occasionally it puts me on such a high that it renews my faith in the concept of there being 'the right one' for all of us. That's more than you can say for most jobs.

My train to Manchester is at twenty past ten. I drop Aimee off at school at ten to nine, and plan to run a few errands around town before heading to the station. Just as I'm pulling out of the school drop-off area, I see Rachel's mum's shiny white Range Rover pulling in behind me. I put the car in park, wait until she has waved off Rachel, and then get out of my car just as she is about to leave.

'Sorry,' I tell her, when she emerges from the vehicle. 'I didn't mean to flag you off the road like a policeman, Sandi!' We exchange a bit of friendly chatter and I try not to imagine her cosying up in bed with her husband and them talking about me and Mike and assuming one of us must have had an affair. I tell her that Aimee is sad she hasn't been invited to Rachel's party.

As she listens, nothing moves except for her blonde hair blowing around her face in the stiff breeze. Then her expression hardens. 'I'm sorry, Celine; I wasn't really aware . . . They don't really tell you things anymore, do they? They think they're so independent now.' She blushes, avoids my eyes, and holds on to her hair to stop it blowing – something I think she wants me to see is irritating her so I'm aware it's going to be a short conversation. 'You know, it's not really up to me to tell her who to be friends with.' She tries a smile, her Rolex gleaming from under her jacket's sleeve. 'They go through phases, don't they?'

I feel my spine elongating and try not to come off as though I'm steeling myself to doff her on top of the head with my cheap handbag. 'You know, Sandi, Aimee's been very down since her fall and everything. Not being able to compete for the gymnastics trophy after the months of hard work she put in—'

'It wasn't Rachel's fault she had an accident! Aimee didn't have to make her feel so bad for winning!'

I was going to say that it absolutely devastated her. But this outburst stuns me for a moment or two. So instead I say, 'I'm sorry, I didn't know that. I thought Aimee rang and congratulated Rachel?'

'She did. But Rachel could tell she didn't really mean it.'

Rage pounds in me. 'Well . . . Sandi, if she wasn't squealing with excitement for Rachel it's because she was just so gutted!' Can't she see? Has she absolutely no idea? She has a child herself!

Sandi gives me a withering look. 'Well, you have to teach her that it's no way to behave.'

I open my mouth to say, *Well, maybe you could try asking Rachel to imagine how she would feel if her parents had split up, then she falls off her bloody bike and is laid up with broken limbs. Then she can't compete in the one competition that she practically lived for.*

The words are bursting out of me, but instead I look at her Hermès scarf, neatly fastened around her neck, and remember that in life you can't expect everyone to behave and think and feel as you. So I say, 'You're right. And you know, if you and Rachel think it's fair to invite every girl in the class except Aimee, well . . . if you can live with that, then I suppose I'll have to.'

Our hard stares last two beats of my rattling heart before Sandi Bradshaw says a snooty 'Good heavens!' and starts walking back to her car. Then she gets into her supercharged petrol-guzzler and drives off.

James Halton Daly is everything that Trish said he is. I can tell this the moment I catch sight of his handsomeness at the table. When he looks up from the menu and sees me striding towards him, he stands to greet me, beams an honest, warm smile and gives me a quick and shameless once-over.

The Instant First Impression. Hair: blond and shaggy, like a Wheaten Terrier's. Handsome, in a 'Sebastian Flyte meets Hugh Grant' way. I already know he went to one of the top public schools in England, then Oxford (where he met Trish), and that now, at thirty-eight, he's a partner at a top Manchester law firm. A charming, like-able toff. *A* for style. The tweed blazer with the turned-up collar. The pink striped dress shirt, open at the neck, and the dark jeans with the turned-up cuffs.

'We could forget that I'm about to hire you to find me a girlfriend, and *you* could be my girlfriend,' he says.

I laugh and feel myself blush. 'I'm taken.'

'Are you?' He lays a hand on his heart. 'Well, I imagine it must be one of the leading credentials of being a matchmaker, right?'

You'd think.

'How do you become a matchmaker, anyway?' he asks, before I've even sat down. 'I mean, I thought you'd have to live in New York and look like Cher.'

I tell him I wish I looked like Cher. Then I tell him how I got started, and what it is about the business that gives me a buzz. He seems fascinated. We chat easily. He is shamelessly checking me out, but I'm flattered. I like his boldness. I like the thick silver ring he wears on his left index finger and the way he corrects the waiter by reminding him he should be taking the lady's order first.

I finally get him on to the topic of women.

'Well, the last ten I went out with—'

'Ten?'

'Well, obviously not all together. Over a period of . . .' He pulls a thinking face. '. . . a year and a half maybe – went from bad to catastrophic. There was, in no specific order: the smoker, the inferiority complex, the one who was more interested in my friends, she who thinks all lawyers get murderers off, Jen who was obsessed with tango dancing . . . Then there was Miss Religious, Miss Missing Front Tooth, the one who was only fourteen years older than her daughter, and Franny Fat Fingers . . .' He recoils, squeamishly. 'Oh, and the one who compulsively checked her mobile for messages.'

'Whoosh! That's quite a list of fatal flaws. Especially the compulsive checker of messages.' I tease him, sipping on the Kir Royale he insisted I order, feeling a little more free and easy than I normally do in a Fake Date scenario.

'Perhaps I've just had bad luck, but I've found quite a few single women in their thirties have issues – confidence issues, desperation issues . . . I could go on.'

'But you're in your thirties. Maybe that means you've got a few too. Have you ever thought of that?'

He beams a big, cheeky smile. 'Admittedly this would be the first time,' he says.

'Fat fingers aside, though, what is it that you're looking for in a partner?'

He seems to think about this, lolling back in his chair, totally at ease, and I recognise how much I'm enjoying this. Perhaps it would be easy to start dating again – if all the men looked like him!

'Well, an independent, free-minded brunette who doesn't take life or herself too seriously. Who likes to travel, be spontaneous, is perhaps unsure if she wants kids. She'd be a fabulous mother if she had them, but she'd feel just as complete in an exciting, child-free marriage.'

'You've clearly given it no thought, then!'

'You asked! I'm trying to be helpful!'

I titter. 'So don't you want kids?'

He looks at me candidly. 'I don't know. Possibly. Perhaps it's because I've not yet met anyone I could see as the mother of my children.' He gazes at the ceiling. 'Oh, and I don't want any "golden retrievers".'

The waiter has just set down my appetiser – poached egg and bacon on frisée lettuce – and I dip some French bread into it. 'What's a golden retriever?' I have a horrible feeling he's not talking about pets.

'Blonde. Beautiful but generic-looking. Always needs brushing and combing. Eager to please but suffers from separation anxiety. Destructive when she gets bored.' He chinks his spoon off the edge of his escargots dish.

'You're being serious, right?' I gawk at him, poised to go off him.

'Of course. Shouldn't I be?'

I shake my head, a little lost for words. 'No, no . . . It's good to know. Very illuminating.'

'Plus, I don't want a lawyer.'

'Why not?' I know I should probably hate him by now, but for some odd reason I'm finding him rather entertaining.

He leans across the table to whisper. 'Generally, I don't find them very interesting.'

I study him. 'What about Trish?'

'Trish?' he frowns. 'Well, Trish is definitely not your typical lawyer. But she's a mate. I'm hardly going to have a romantic relationship with a mate, am I?'

'Aren't you? Why not?'

'I don't know.' He narrows his eyes, as though he's never considered the question before. 'By the way, did she tell you that she and I are in competition? We have a bet on to see which one of us is going to find our soulmate first.'

'Are you? No, actually, she never mentioned that.'

He nods, studying me now. 'So what were you asking? Oh, yes, if I was going to have a romantic relationship with, say, Trish, for the sake of argument . . .' He splutters a laugh. 'Then I wouldn't be here, would I? Hiring you.' He leans across at me. 'No. Frankly, I don't want a lawyer for practical reasons more than anything. The balance of work and home life. I just don't think lawyers get the concept of balance very well.'

'So you don't want any woman who has a demanding career?' They never do. Even though most intelligent men don't want intellectual dingbats either, or women with no interests or ambition.

'Not true. I'd love a woman who had an absolutely fascinating headache of a career. I just want it to be different to the headaches I have in mine. And I want her to work to live, not the other way round. You can't have two people doing that in any one household. And if we ever did want kids . . .'

'You'd want her to stay home to take care of them.'

'Politically incorrect. But true.' He pops the last of his six escargots into his mouth, then he adds, 'But only if she wanted to. I'd prefer if they didn't get brought up like I did, by a parade of nannies.' He watches me put my napkin on my side plate. 'I'm in the bin now, aren't I? Did Trish warn you you'd go off me this fast?'

'Not at all,' I grin. 'If I put you in the bin, then I don't know what that would mean I'd have to do with some of my other clients. Cremate them, maybe, and then bin their ashes?'

He laughs. 'That bad, eh?'

'Actually, no. I'm just joking. I have lovely clients.' I realise it's completely out of character for me to be talking like this. What's happening here?

'So what's with this personality-profile thing you had me fill in?' he asks over his steak frites and my Roquefort-stuffed free-range chicken breast. We have talked about his university days, his travels, his social life, and his last proper relationship, which lasted six years. 'Can you really match a person with another person based on their answers to those particular forty questions?'

'You mean, as opposed to any other forty questions?' I'm surprised to find myself feeling so lit up by this man. He's gorgeous, classy and, with that roguish, confident way he has, I have a feeling he'd be very good in bed. I clear my throat and reign in my thoughts . . . 'Actually, you'd be quite surprised. If a woman answers that a mate's physical attractiveness is extremely important, then I'm not going to set her up with a six-stone jockey with a third eye, am I?'

'Do you have a three-eyed jockey on your books?'

'I used to have a two-eyed one.'

'Did you match him?'

'Eventually, yes.'

'Hang on . . .' He wags a finger, then reaches down and digs in his briefcase. 'Question, what was it? Thirty-two?' He pulls out the questionnaire I emailed him. 'Ah yes. Love it! *Is your bedroom messy?* He turns serious-faced. 'I mean, if I say yes it is – which, yes, it always is, actually – does that mean you'll match me with an equally messy person so we'll live in complete chaos forever? Or are you going to pick a neat freak? That way she'll get so frustrated with my mess that our marriage will become a constant nag-fest!'

I'm about to answer, when he says, 'Or this one: *Do you enjoy a good joke?* I mean, I'm just curious, is there anyone who will say, "No, personally I bloody loathe a good joke. Despicable things!"? And what about,

How often do you get angry? Once a year? Once a month? Once a week? A few times a day? Are we talking angry as in ready to singlehandedly open fire on a care home of snoozing senior citizens? Or your more garden-variety anger, like, "That wanker just cut me off in the passing lane"?'

'Are you done mocking my questionnaire?' I shake my head in disbelief.

'Yes,' he says. 'I mean, I could go on if you like.'

'No. No need to overstate it! Actually, I never used to have any sort of psychometric evaluation—'

'You call this a psychometric evaluation?' His eyes are a mischievous twinkle. 'Oops, sorry, go on.'

I push a rosemary-basted potato around my plate. 'What I mean is, I used to just go on instinct. You know – do they look right together? Do I sense a similar outlook, views, values, humour? But so many of my clients expected to fill in a personality profile, because other dating services have one. Personally, I think they're people who are looking to pass themselves off as somebody they're not. You don't have to fill it out if you don't want to.'

'Now if I say I want to, you're going to think it's because I'm dying to lie about myself.'

'It's okay, I've got you sussed already as it is.'

We smile at one another. His eyes are flirting all the way to bed. And if this wasn't a professional relationship, he'd already have me there.

'Did Trish fill it out?' he asks.

I think back. 'No. As a matter of fact, she didn't.'

He drops it on to the floor by his briefcase, sits back, looks at me, and beams. 'Fancy sharing a dessert?'

I conclude, after our date, that, of the four main masculine personality types (thinker, doer, ideas man, dreamer), James is the classic thinker: the type that forty-one per cent of women are drawn to. Thinkers will immediately command attention when they walk into a room. Thinkers are logical and challenging; they're the managing directors of every

63

big business you've heard of. Communicative, emotional women are attracted to them because they represent stability and security.

All that, and he's sexy as hell. I'm going to enjoy finding the lucky lady who will think this guy's fantastic.

Or perhaps I should just scrap that and start dating him myself!

A high has to be followed by a low. On the train home, Kim of missing-underpants fame rings me.

'It's no good, Celine. I went out with him again last night. I picked the right moment and I just came out with it and asked him how he can think it's hygienic to have his bottom free to the breeze.'

'What? Kim, that's not exactly how we planned to broach the subject.' I attempt to whisper, cowering in my seat and trying not to look at my travel companion opposite – a businessman who is glaring at me around his copy of the *Financial Times*. I accidentally got booked into a quiet carriage and should not be using my mobile.

'Well, he said it's completely unreasonable of me to tell him how to dress!'

'He has a point, doesn't he? I thought we were trying the subtle approach? You were going to tell him how much it would turn you on to see him in a sexy pair of briefs.'

The man across from me has lost all interest in his paper.

'I know. But I'm an out-with-it person! I can't bear pussyfooting around. It's such a time-waste.'

'Well, what would you like me to do, Kim?' I ask her. 'If the knickers are the deal breaker, which I'm sensing they are?'

'Find me someone else,' she says.

I pointedly switch off my phone and smile at my now rather stupefied-looking travelling companion. No wedding ring. Should I give him my card?

TEN

'Who's that dude you've been googling?' Aimee looks up from her history book in the middle of my quizzing her on Peter the Great for her test tomorrow.

'Which du—, I mean person, are we talking about?'

'Patrick Shale.'

For a moment I can't fathom Patrick's name coming out of my daughter's mouth. 'How do you know that name?' I ask her.

'Your internet history.'

My jaw almost drops. 'Since when do you check my history?'

She refuses to meet my eyes. 'Since you check mine.'

I have no time to react because she says, 'So who is he? Is he your new boyfriend?'

'Boyfriend? No! He's just someone I used to know a long time ago. A Canadian I met when I travelled Asia.'

I see the rare interest – and tinge of scepticism – in her eyes. 'When did you ever go to Asia?'

'When I was twenty-one. Right after uni. I went travelling for three months.'

'You never told me this!' She looks so excited suddenly.

'I suppose it never came up.'

'So you had a boyfriend centuries ago, and now you're back in touch with him again?'

I laugh a little. 'Well, it was hardly centuries. And he wasn't really my boyfriend. And I'm not in touch with him. I might have googled him when I had nothing to do, but that's all.'

She frowns. 'Why was he not really your boyfriend?'

I have never imagined myself having any sort of conversation about Patrick with my daughter. I have sometimes regretted that I've told Jacqui so much – as though by sharing any of it I have defiled it in some way. My instinct is to clam up, to erect a wall around it and protect it. Yet I remember being Aimee's age and thinking that adults moved in such a covert world. My mother never gave me an 'in'. I was like a dog sitting waiting for table scraps of knowledge about her interior life. But they never came. I spent my twenties tiptoeing around her, the legacy of my never having felt like I mattered. Then she died from breast cancer in her late forties. A sad life cut unfairly short. I was never to know if we could have eventually become friends.

I lie down on my side and stroke Norman, who is curled in a sleeping ball.

'Because he was never really mine,' I say. 'He was a Canadian foreign journalist working as Asia Correspondent for the Associated Press, in Hong Kong. He was my first true love.' Saying it is the equivalent to letting out a heavy sigh; there is so much lead weight in it. I honestly don't know whether I feel better or worse. She pretends to go on reading, which amuses me. 'Patrick was intense, spontaneous, hungry for life and devastatingly attractive. He was the most exciting man I'd ever met and, despite us knowing each other for a ridiculously short time, I fell head over heels in love with him.'

She puts her book down now, turns on to her side, with her back to me, and pulls up the duvet, leaving an ear peeking out.

'There's a village in the mountains of Vietnam, called Sa Pa . . .' I tell her a bit of the story.

'The Love Market! That's the name of your company!'

'Yes.' I smile. 'I thought it was so appropriate. The real one was more of a marriage market. We go to our local market to buy food; these people went to sing and dance and find a husband or wife.'

'That's very twisted.'

'Actually, it wasn't. It was charming. The boy made up a love song and sang it into the darkness, or played it on an instrument. And somewhere in the crowd, a girl sang her own words back to him. Soon they'd be singing in perfect harmony—'

'I'm going to barf. What did they sing about?'

'I don't know. It's not like they sang in English just for me!' Her ear moves up. Is that a smile? 'Families would bring their daughters to the Love Market every Saturday night. They were probably the same age as you. And the young boys would come looking for a wife.'

'What? At my age?'

'Yep. If you lived there, Aimee, you'd probably be married with ten oxen, a couple of dozen buffalo and seven kids by now.' I see her ear move up again. 'Anyway, the two lovers would then disappear into the forest for three days. And when they next emerged—'

'They'd had sex?'

I've never quite got around to finding out exactly what Aimee knows about sex but I have a feeling it's more than I knew at her age. 'Well, maybe. But over there, Aimee, once you'd had sex with a boy that was it for you; you got him for life. The girl would go off to live with the boy's family. Her parents would lose a daughter, and another family would gain another pair of hands to work the land.'

'Drastic! I am *so* glad I don't live there.'

'It was better than I'm painting it . . . Perhaps you had to be there.'

'No thanks. I am so never going there!'

I smile when she shudders. 'It wasn't just young lovers, though. Many of the people were there because they were married to someone but their hearts belonged to another. I remember Patrick telling me that people came to the market to find what they had lost, or what they'd never had.'

She turns slightly again, and looks at me, a little intrigued. 'Tell me more about Patrick.'

For some reason I smile. I'm enjoying talking about him now that I've got going. 'Well, he was staying in one of the tribal settlements, in a rather primitive cabin in the middle of the woods, the typical place you'd imagine a foreign newsman roughing it in. And I was staying in a fairly westernised little one-star hostel.'

And, from the moment I set eyes on him in that café, in my mind it was a swift, wordless passage from 'hello' into bed. It's incredible to me how despite all these years I can still relive that connection, that fire. It was almost like I knew that I would never feel that with anybody else. And that was possibly the saddest part.

'Did you have a lot in common?'

The maturity of the question takes me aback. 'Actually . . . I've never thought of that before but I'm not sure. Patrick was hugely driven. I'm not. He wanted to be a nomad, travelling the world. I'd had my fill after three months . . . I'd say we both appreciated the same things – beauty, peace, calm – the simple things life has to offer. We could certainly talk easily, if that counts. I remember us saying we both thought it was like we'd met before, as though some of the ground between us – the awkward stuff – had already been covered. It was odd . . .'

'Go on. It's just about getting interesting. Did you have sex with him on the first date?'

'Aimee! You're twelve. I'm not talking about my sex life with you.'

'But did you?'

'No. You never ever have sex on a first date, with anybody. And you have to be at least eighteen before you have it at all.'

'So after how many dates is it okay to have sex with someone?'

I think for a while. 'This is a bit off the topic, but . . . ten.'

Her jaw drops and for a moment she can't speak. 'Go on then, get back to what you were saying about Patrick.'

'Well, there's not much more, really. We only had four days. We never got to know what more it could have been because of circumstances. All we really knew was it felt way, way more than what it probably should have done in such little time.'

'Only four days! But what circumstances? Why wasn't it longer?'

It's weird, being plunged back into the memory. 'Well, I had a ticket home to England and he had to go back to Hong Kong for his job. He had to go back to his life.'

I don't tell her that he was married. That the morning he left he said, 'I think I had to meet you for a reason, Celine.' And he didn't add any more. And because he didn't, a part of me was left wondering, *So all I did was serve a purpose? To help you get some clarity on the rest of your life?* And that was when everything got very confusing. I started to feel the tiniest bit used, and the hurt started to push its way in.

'When I came back to England I remember thinking I'd never get over him. That this was what having your heart broken was about. I told a friend this and she said, *Wait four months!* And it was true, in a way. I had to look for a job. I wanted to rent a place because being back home with your gran was hard . . . And then, of course, I met your dad.'

And Mike was FedEx to forgetting. Like me, Mike wasn't particularly ambitious. Work wasn't his world. He had no real desire to travel beyond a beach in Portugal. He didn't have a deep-thinking side, nor a particularly sensual side. He wasn't complicated. Unlike Patrick, Mike knew what he wanted – he wanted me – and he was quite single-minded about getting me. And I respected that. I loved that. But as much as I loved him for his guilelessness, his steadiness, his gentleness, it wasn't a rip-me-open sort of love. Though I'd already decided I didn't want that ever again.

'Tell me how you met him again? Dad.'

'Well, the first time, it was on the London-to-Newcastle flight on my way home from Asia. We were seated next to one another.' I tell her that we really hit it off, but in reality I spent the entire hour telling him about my failed love affair and my broken heart. And I remember when I got off thinking, *Blast! I never asked a single thing about him! He probably thinks I'm so all about myself, and he seemed so nice.* 'Then I saw him again a few months later, when your aunt Jacqui won tickets to a concert sponsored by Blaze FM . . .' I smile. I recognised his unique way of dressing, the Fonzie hair and his kind face. And we chatted and he said, *If you've forgotten about who you said you'd never forget about, then I'd like to ask you out on a date. But if you haven't, I won't.*

I hadn't of course. But I realised that I had moped for long enough and Mike felt like a great stride in the right direction.

'Do you wish you'd been married to Patrick rather than to Dad?' Her voice sounds sleepy now, and I love her so much in this artless little second where her attention is slipping.

'No. But you never forget your first love. That's just the way life is. Before we meet him, our hearts are like a blank slate. With him, we're able to discover those romantic feelings for the very first time, and express that new and wonderful part of ourselves, and we never, ever forget what that feels like. So when you meet yours one day, recognise him for what he is: someone who will probably always linger in the quiet corners of your mind over the course of your life.'

'Did you always want to set people up after that?'

'No. But if two likeminded people meet and fall in love and I've helped that in some way, then that's no bad thing, is it?'

She seems to think about this. 'Maybe I could go into The Love Market business with you when I grow up. I hardly think I'm going to have to know all about Peter the Great to know about matching some men with some women.'

'Maybe,' I tell her. She yawns and reaches to stroke Norman. I trace a finger over the part of her ear that's curled like a dry leaf.

'Maybe you can tell me more about it tomorrow.' She moves her head just slightly to look at me. 'Oh, and, erm, Rachel invited me to the party.'

'Did she?' I'm surprised. 'And you're going?'

'Of course. Why wouldn't I?'

I love how quickly my daughter forgives and forgets.

When I walk out of her room, I go straight into mine feeling oddly wired. This is why I hate talking about it! A restlessness is beating in me now. My head is pulsing with *What If?*

I haven't done this in a very long time. Perhaps because it serves no other purpose than to cause me aching misery. So I don't know why I find myself going over to my jewellery box, but from beneath the tangle of beads and baubles I pull out the folded piece of paper he sent me two years later, and read.

ELEVEN

From the top of Ham Rong Mountain, a grey mist settles over the village of Sa Pa, North Vietnam, like an exhalation of breath into the cold. The red-roofed settlements of hill-tribe life sparkle below like garnets dropped from a hand in the sky. Little stirs across the never-ending paddy fields from this great height, which makes life and all kinds of possibilities feel wide open.

I don't know why I came here, or why I now feel a part of me will always be unable to leave. I have never believed in the concept of true love, or that there is one person in this world who is meant for us, and we either find them or we find something inferior. I have never wanted to believe in it, perhaps because I am not a lover of limitations. For the Red Dao tribe, easily identified by the red headdresses worn by the women, marriage is a commodity that can be bought for the price of a song. The Saturday-night ritual of the Sa Pa Love Market isn't quite what it used to be before it fascinated tour operators and travellers worldwide – bringing me there and bringing her there. The Red Dao are private people. Few will accept your American dollars in exchange for your right to take their photograph. On Saturday nights, Red Dao hill-tribe youths of both sexes gather in a weekly courting ritual. The males strut around doing a sort of tribal version of Harry Connick, Jr in the hope of attracting a pretty young female. The songs are rarely romantic. Mostly it's a bragging rite chronicling the boy's physical prowess, or his strong work ethic. But it's well known that the men don't work as hard as the women and can usually be found sleeping off opium in the shade of a lethargic water buffalo. However, in the Red Dao culture, everyone is meant to find a mate. So on that one Saturday night at the Love Market, when they walk off into the sunset with a faith in each other that's built on nothing more than a melody sung in harmony, you can't help but wish that finding a partner was as simple as that in your own village square.

It definitely wasn't as simple as that for me. I met her there. By chance. I won't give her a name. By not giving her a name I am pretending that she's been easy to forget. I didn't have to sing to her. Fortunately Western mating practices prevailed and I didn't have to work that hard. But I was so unprepared for it. If a marriage is wrong, you can end it. But only a noble coward puts a dying marriage before his happiness with someone else.

Being a journalist, you'd think the most natural thing for me to do would be to find her. But, just like in the Hmong and Red Dao cultures, not every meeting in the Love Market has a fairy-tale ending. Sometimes love is a tune we sing to ourselves that no one else can follow.

Two years after I returned to England, this came in the post to my mother's address, which I had given him in desperation and haste – not even sure he wanted to take it. I saw it sitting on the hall table as I was hauling my wedding dress in from the shop. I recognised the writing immediately.

Exactly seven days later I was walking down the aisle with my father. Mike stood at the altar watching me, and for the briefest of moments when I smiled I knew that smile was beautiful and it glowed from some magical place far in me. Because as I was looking at the man I was about to marry, I was imagining it was Patrick standing there.

He didn't even write a letter with it. All he said was: *A piece I wrote on spec for* National Geographic, *which they rejected. The editor said there was too much of me in it.*

Years later, Mike found it when we were clearing out drawers to make way for some new bedroom furniture. We ended up having a huge argument, probably because I got so defensive about why I'd kept it. I remember tearing it up in front of him, and throwing it in the bin, out of anger, not capitulation – to prove something more to myself, really, than to him. Then I went to bed devastated that I'd destroyed something that had meant so much to me. I felt like I was relinquishing a part of myself to Mike that he had no right to own; and what's more, he hadn't even really asked me to.

A while later he came into the room. I saw he was holding something. It was Patrick's crumpled letter. He'd dug it out of the bin and taped it back up.

'I don't want you to think you can't keep something because I'm going to feel threatened by it,' he said. 'Because I'm not.'

Taking it from him seemed like an acknowledgment of Mike's insufficiency and my conflict. He looked at me for a while as though establishing a truce. Then he got into bed and put his back to me, and I sensed the whole thing was over. It was clearly just one of many glitches in me, which he was used to now. Our marriage wasn't going to end over a letter.

But in a strange way, it did.

TWELVE

'Special delivery.' Mike is standing at my door with Aimee, even though he only picked her up a short time ago.

It's his Saturday to have her sleep over. Since he left, I can only imagine that our relationship has been as civilised as breakups get. Mike is fair. I am fair. And we both have Aimee's best interests at heart. Because of his night-owl hours at the radio station, and Aimee being in school all day, he doesn't get to see her as much as he'd like. We made a deal that, in addition to every second weekend, he can see her as much as is convenient for everyone during the week. He just gives us a little bit of warning so we don't trample each other's plans.

'I don't understand,' I say. I am half-dressed to go out with Jacqui for a drink.

Aimee slinks past me into the house, leaving Mike and me facing one another on our doorstep. I often think it must be so odd to have to knock at the door of your old home, and not be able to just walk in.

'She's fine. She just said she felt homesick.' He looks down at my oyster silk top and my new black jeans. 'Sorry to sabotage your night on the town.'

'It wasn't really a night on the town,' I say. 'Only the pub with Jacqui.' I wasn't really into it anyway; I was just fighting my inner tendency to be a hermit on weekends.

Instead of turning to go, he leans casually against the doorframe and we hold eyes. It's like one of us is visiting the other in prison, and even if we both put our palms against the glass it still wouldn't feel like we were touching. A boundary has gone up because we've moved from the intimate thing of being married to the hostile thing of being divorced. Or we're supposed to be hostile, but neither of us can even manage to get that right.

'So, how's things?' I ask, for want of something better.

'Things?'

He continues to look at me as though he's drinking every bit of me in, instead of just seeing a face he knows as well as his own. And in an attempt to look everywhere but into his sad eyes, I see him more objectively than usual: as Mike this human being who I happen to know quite well, though he's once or twice removed from me, as if we're an impossible form of related strangers. He's wearing a jacket I've not seen before. A dark-brown leather three-quarter-length thing that, because he's short, comes almost to his knees instead of to his bum, where it probably should. Mike has always had a distinctive style. There's something 1970s about his oversized jackets, skinny jeans, winkle-picker shoes and the prematurely grey Fonz hair. Rather than not being a follower of fashion, Mike is his own fashion. He's comfortable with himself. And I always respected that about him.

'I'll have her next Saturday if she's happy to come.'

'We'll see,' I say. 'She did rubbish on her history test.' I try to change the subject. 'I even helped her study for it.'

'Maybe that was the problem.'

I smile. 'I was thinking maybe we need to get her a private tutor. Just for the main subjects.'

'I think maybe we should back off pressuring her. She's only twelve. Don't you think she's had enough to deal with these past few months?' He sounds annoyed at me.

I nod, feeling a bit miffed at the implication that I'm some sort of hard taskmaster, though he makes a decent point. 'You're probably right,' I say.

I still sometimes miss our conversations. Even our arguments had a certain comfort value. Not that we had many; Mike tends to be more passive-aggressive than full-on confrontational.

'You got your hair cut. How was your business trip?' he asks.

My hand goes to the strands around my face. My 'divorce cut', as Jacqui calls it. The first time I've radically changed it in years. 'It was only down to Manchester. I left Aimee in good hands. She loves having Jacqui stay over.'

'I know. Why do you sound like you're apologising?'

'I'm not. I'm only saying . . .' What am I saying?

'Anyway, I know she was fine. I took her out for pizza. With Jacqui.'

'You did?'

He must see my surprise.

'Didn't she tell you?'

'No, actually.' Why does it bother me that he went out with my sister? A divorce shouldn't mean families have to take sides, yet selfishly I don't really want to share my sister with my ex-husband. 'You're allowed to take people out. It's a free country. You don't have to give me reports.' I realise I'm being childish and unreasonable.

He looks down at my feet, diverting a potential argument perhaps. 'You've only got three toes done,' he says, of my nail polish.

'And they're smudged and have bits of carpet sticking to them.' I say, feeling glum. He continues to stare at them, as though my feet are an emotional stop sign he's trying to get past but can't. I think of my unprovoked outbursts about why I wasn't happy – they didn't happen often and certainly less as I got into my thirties. There was always this feeling that marriage had become some kind of stopping place, some destination we'd reached only to find that I'd hoped for more when I got there. The strange thing is, what did I ever think it was that he stopped me from being or doing, that I want to run out and be and do now?

When he finally looks up, he stares somewhat unseeingly into my eyes and it's as if he's just quickly reread his *Coles Notes* on the section that deals with how you learn not to care. 'Anyway, while I have you here . . . Before you shut the door on me . . .'

'I wasn't going to shut the door on you.'

'Yes you were.'

'I wasn't. Why would I do that?' It hurts me he'd think this.

'Because, finally, you can.'

I don't answer this. He moves closer, his eyes going fleetingly to my mouth. 'I've given a lot of thought to this business of being alone, and I have a proposition for you.'

'I don't like the idea of any of your propositions.'

'You won't. No. But I'm going to make you an offer you can't refuse.'

'You're going to put a horse's head in my bed? I suppose I deserve it.'

'Actually, that was going to be my last resort.'

We smile at my lame attempt at a joke.

'What I mean is, given that we are now officially divorced, and given that I for one am ready to take some giant step to move my life forward, I thought you might be able to help me out.'

'Doing?'

'I want to employ you. To help me meet somebody else.'

He scrutinises my presumably stunned-looking face. 'It makes sense. You know me better than anyone. You'd know who would be good for me, probably better than I would. And I'm obviously going to pay you. I'm not asking for favours.'

Mike always looks at me in shades of many conflicting emotions. But I always sensed that, while I might have doubted him, he never doubted me. Another thing – Mike never looks at you as though he's seen it all before. And I've never been made to feel that he'd fancy me more if I put lipstick on for him, or had bigger boobs. I know this is rare, from many of my SADs (Sane Attractive Divorcees, who are grounded, healthy, normal, and just want a second chance at happiness), as opposed to the SAFs (Spinster Attractive Females, who have never been married and are getting more inflexible the older they become). Mike may not be a six-foot, wheeling-dealing hulk of testosterone, but he knows how to appreciate a woman. Which makes me picture him appreciating someone else.

'No way.'

'Hear me out.'

'No. I'm not doing it.' I fold my arms.

His eyes linger on my throat. 'I'm an opportunity for you to make another two thousand pounds. I'm a good candidate. I want the full service, though. The Fake Date. The whole works. Just like I was any client. Just because you were married to me doesn't mean you can hold it against me. No assumed prior knowledge.'

'You don't meet the MIS.'

'What's the MIS?'

'You know what it is.' Minimum Income Standard of £60,000 for the men; I don't have one for women.

He wags a finger in front of my face. 'No prior knowledge, remember?'

When my face doesn't change he says, 'So this is the one time when you can bend the rules a bit. And I'm not asking you to set me up with Angelina Jolie. One of your dodgiest sevens will be fine.'

Mike knows that I have an attractiveness scale for both sexes. It might seem unfair, but it's easier to match women who are of average height, slim to curvy, and have symmetrical features and good skin. And women – even the hot ones – will still date a much less attractive man if he's got money. I hate saying it. I'd hoped we'd all evolved over time. But in this regard we haven't.

'I don't need a pin-up,' he adds. 'After all, I'm more into personalities than I am looks. I mean, I was married to a gorgeous woman and see what happened there.'

We hold eyes in the aftershock of the remark. This is Mike doing his passive-aggressive thing and I'm not up to it tonight. 'I'm not doing it, Mike.'

'Will you at least think about it?'

'No. And I can't believe you're even suggesting it. What normal person would do this?'

'But we know you're not normal. And who cares what others think? Most people don't have an ex in the business, do they? And you're so good at what you do; why wouldn't I want to try to benefit from that? I could meet someone else still. Maybe even have another family – not that any other child would ever replace my first. But a wife certainly could.'

'You know what? I've changed my mind. I am going to shut the door on you.'

He puts his foot out to stop me in case I'm serious. 'Is it too much to want to see me happy? Do you hate me that much?'

'I don't hate you!' A pain blazes in me. 'I'm just . . .'

Puzzled. Why would he insist on the Fake Date? The purpose of that is for me to get to know the candidate as if I were a prospective date. I hardly need to do that with Mike. 'I hope this isn't some strategy to get me back.'

I regret saying it the instant it's out. All the good humour slides off his face. Then his gaze travels quickly up and down me. 'You know what, Celine? Even in my darkest moments – because I still get them, far more than I would wish – I would never want to go back to being married to you.'

We stare at one another while my humiliation robs me of a comeback. I go to close the door now.

'Just tell me you'll think about it.'

I look off to the side of his head, through a spring of tears. 'Move your foot or I'll slam this and break all your toes,' I bluff.

Tense moments tick, and I get a quick flashback to one of our last fights. Mike usually has a personality like a calm sea but he can occasionally lose his rag – something that comes off more funny than threatening. That time he pelted a shoe across the room. I don't think it was ever designed to hit me and it missed me by a country mile. What it hit, though, was the Lladró figurine of a little boy that Mike's mother had given him. He'd loved that ornament. I personally thought it was awful and a strange gift to give your adult son. It seemed poignant that he'd broken it. As though what we were fighting over had succeeded on some darker level in breaking him rather than just an ornament.

He studies me closely, and then he moves his foot. Finally, I am able to close the door. I lean up against it, holding my breath. As I hear the scrunch of gravel under his feet as he walks away, I realise one true thing. No one will love me like Mike loved me. I know it without anyone having to wag their index finger in front of my face and tell me. I have lost what was probably the most abiding love I ever had.

THIRTEEN

Aimee sits by the window swinging a leg over the chair arm, in her jeans and the powder-blue satin top I just bought her. 'Why didn't you want to stay with your dad?' I ask.

'I . . . I don't know. I don't want to talk about it right now.' She stares at me vacuously for a moment. 'What does an orgasm feel like?' When she sees my face she says, 'If you don't want to tell me, I'll ask Granddad. Or Rachel's mum.'

'Don't be silly,' I say. I know she has no intention of asking anyone but me.

'Well tell me then . . .'

'Like a sneeze,' I say, trying to be offhand about it. 'Ah-choo! Only not with your nose.'

She twirls a long piece of newly blonde hair around a finger. Jacqui just took her to the salon as a treat. She got soft golden highlights put in but they're only temporary and won't damage her hair. 'Would it be completely inappropriate of me if I asked you why you want to know this?'

'I kissed Rachel's boyfriend.'

I frown. 'I didn't know she had one. Where?'

'On the mouth, of course.'

'I mean, where in the house?' *If they were in a bedroom I am going to kill him and Rachel's irresponsible mum.*

'Outside. No one saw.'

'You don't kiss a friend's boyfriend, Aimee. It's a big no-no in life. Are you still jealous because she won the competition?'

'He wanted to do other things.'

He's dead. I'm never letting her out of my sight again.

I try not to rise to her bait, in case that's what this is. 'And you? What did you want?' I ask. She stops playing with her hair, stops wagging her leg. With the slight change of hair colour she looks older – stunning, and for the first time I try to see my daughter through the eyes of a boy. She's sexy, which is a very odd thought to be having about your own child.

'I don't know,' she says. Then, after a moment, 'Mr Bradshaw caught us kissing.'

I frown. 'I thought you said no one saw.'

She performs a coy little upwards flick of her chin. 'Well, he saw.'

'And?' I study her, wondering where this is going to go.

'He wanted to kiss me too.'

There is a sudden glint of mischief in her eyes that quickly disappears just as I catch it. This is how I know this is all fabricated.

'That's not funny. You don't make up lies about people, Aimee. Somebody might take you seriously and that's a very dangerous game to be playing.'

We hold gazes while the opportunity for a snarky comeback dies. I tell her it's time we both went to bed. As I'm about to leave the room she says, 'So I take it you're not going out boyfriend shopping tonight then?'

I freeze, aware of a beat of annoyance. 'Go to bed, Aimee,' I say, in a tone that tells her I'm not messing around.

'I'm sorry,' she says later, when I peek in her room. 'About the boyfriend shopping.' She pulls a rueful smile and removes her earbuds. 'That was a dumb thing to say.'

'It's okay,' I tell her. I go in and sit on the edge of her bed. 'Are you all right?'

She puts her book down and looks at me, like she's grasping for the right way to say something, like someone trying to work her way around a speech impediment. 'I know I've done it plenty of times before but tonight it just suddenly felt weird me staying there when you're here . . . Then having him bring me home and leave me at the door.' She casts her eyes down and looks, for a moment, as though she might cry.

'I'm so sorry . . . I know. You wish he was coming home with you.' Even after all this time . . . Children aren't as resilient as some people like to tell you.

One hand uncurls from her book and her thin fingers meander down the cat's belly. 'I don't know. Not if you don't.'

This show of unity touches me.

'It was just weird.'

I go to stroke Norman as well, and our fingers meet, briefly. 'I know,' I tell her. 'You're allowed to feel as you feel. Once in a while we all get our moments.' I wonder how it will all play out once Mike properly starts dating. To my knowledge he hasn't done much of that so far – certainly not that he's told me. I remember how I had to share my dad with his new girlfriends, often getting dropped at the last minute for a better offer. Could I see Mike suddenly rearranging us around his dates? Neither of us has had to share him before.

'Oh, and Mr Bradshaw never tried to kiss me. I made that up.'

'I know that too,' I whisper. 'Don't worry about it.'

I can't sleep when I go to bed because I can't stop feeling a little sad and guilty that my daughter still gets her low moments, that she's mature enough to feel the finality of divorce compared to merely the process of divorcing. So to try to distract myself I pick up my book on physiognomy: the assessment of a person's character or personality from their face. While I thought a big nose was a sign of a big something else, it's apparently an indicator of health and vitality. Big ears? More comfortable taking risks. A thin top lip? Watch out, this person may be serially unfaithful. And a woman's eyebrows plucked into a tiny line, like my client Kim's, is a sign of suppressed rage. I put the book down after ten minutes and try to focus on sleep.

But now Ian Dury's 'Hit Me With Your Rhythm Stick', which was on the radio earlier, is playing on a never-ending loop in my head, so I reach for my laptop on my night table and decide I might as well check my email.

I've got quite a few. The first four are from Kim. Speak of the devil. Her first email is titled 'Urgent'.

> Time is ticking. I haven't heard from you in a while.
> Do you have anybody else for me?

The second is titled 'Urgent!!!'

> On second thoughts, I'm not sure I can go through with any of this again. Will phone you early in the morning to talk – unless you're up now? I can't sleep.

The third is titled '*IMPERATIVE* you read this!!!'

> I'm having serious second thoughts, Celine. I just don't think you and I are working out. I'm not even sure you even WANT to match me anymore.

The fourth: '*Have you DIED?*'

> Sorry, I can't do this anymore. I've just had enough.
> Please prepare me a refund.

Oh dear.

No one's asked for a refund before! Number one, I don't like to admit failure. Plus I've put time and thought into matching Kim, and every time she brushes over clients, writing them all off after one date, I lose a bit of credibility with them. But also, I don't really believe the solution to her unhappy singlehood is to dump me. So by giving her a refund I am failing both myself and her. But if I reply now, knowing her, she'll be at the other end of the email, and then I'm never going to get to sleep. I'll wait until morning, until she's cooled off.

The next one I see is from Fran Kennedy. Fran married Allan, the man I'd matched her with; only, very sadly, Allan now has lung cancer and she often pours out her heart in an email. I open every one she sends me fearing the worst, but, true to form, in this one Fran's spirits are high even though he's not doing well. I read it several times and then type a long reply. By the time I am done, I am sleepy. I'm just about to put my laptop aside when another email pops in.

Good heavens! When I see the name, I almost bolt out of bed.

FOURTEEN

Patrick has sent me a message.

Have I just had a painless heart attack?

I blink a few times. No, it's still there.

Whoosh! I throw the sheets off my legs, suddenly boiling hot. Okay. This cannot be. Surely I must have fallen asleep and this is a dream – triggered, obviously, by the fact that Jacqui and I have been talking about him recently.

I notice there's nothing in the subject line. Strange. Whistling out air, I open the message.

But wait . . .

He hasn't written anything.

I scroll up and down a few times, close my browser and re-open it. Still a blank where the message should be. As a drastic measure I even shut down my computer, wait a tense two minutes, then reboot. Technology, as we know, can do the strangest of things.

But there's still no message.

Hang on . . . Let me get my head around this. Patrick has sent me a blank email? Why on earth would he do that? In fact, why on earth would he be emailing me at all? My mind immediately jumps to Jacqui. Is this a practical joke my sister is playing on me? My cheeks are blazing hot thinking of her doing this. I'm somewhere between curious and furious.

One more scroll down to the bottom just to make sure I'm not missing something. What I see makes me squeal out loud.

There, in a way that can't be misconstrued, is a small line of text that reads:

<On 04/04, Celine Lewis at CelineLewis@hotmail. com wrote>

Hang on . . . *I* wrote?

I look to see what I've supposedly written but there is nothing.

So I supposedly sent an email to Patrick saying nothing, and he sent one back also saying nothing? When I look up, Aimee is standing in my doorway, staring at me as though she's seeing an alien. 'I heard a noise,' she says. Her eyes shoot to my laptop.

'Sorry . . . I got up for the loo and stubbed my toe.'

'Can you stub it more quietly next time?'

'Yes. Go back to bed. It's late. Can I take you back to your room?'

'Why? Has it moved?'

She's just turning to go when I say, 'Aimee, you didn't look up Patrick on the internet and send him an email, did you?'

'Hm?' She rubs her eyes, vigorously, with the knuckles of her index fingers, like she used to do when she was little. 'No,' she says, after a moment. 'Why would I do that?'

'I don't know. Maybe because you knew I'd been googling him. Maybe you found his email, intended to type something, got distracted, and the message accidentally got sent anyway?' I try to give her an *out*.

She looks at me like I'm raving. 'Mum? Are you sure you don't think that's a really strange question? Why would I want to email your old boyfriend?'

'I don't know, Aimee.' She's blushing. I can usually tell when Aimee is lying but why would she blush if she's not guilty? It's late, so I just say, 'You're right. Forget I asked.'

I watch her traipse back to her room, not plod-plodding her feet like a herd of pet elephants – something she has taken to doing lately. Right now she's too tired for attitude. Her nightshirt is stuck in her knickers, a milky-white bottom cheek peeking out. 'Aimee,' I say, getting up and following her before she disappears behind a closed door. 'Aunt Jacqui didn't google him, did she? She hasn't said anything . . . ?' Way too much of a coincidence that the message was sent when I was in Manchester, when Jacqui was staying here with Aimee! I think of her egging me on to email him and her saying something like, *If you don't, I will* . . .

'No,' she says, as though the subject is getting tiresome. 'Now can I go back to bed?'

When I close my room door, I climb back on to the bed and stare at his name for about ten minutes, and the blank space where he could have written something but didn't. My heart is pounding with daring and anticipation.

Patrick. Back. After all these years.

For some mad reason I click on 'Reply'. Whoosh! Now what? I breathe out long and hard through my mouth while I ponder what on earth I could possibly say. I have to account for why he received an email from me in the first place, but any way I think of putting it just sounds contrived or desperate – and downright strange after fifteen years.

Then I think, well, *Just be honest.* So I type:

Dear Patrick,

I have a very odd family who think it's funny to meddle in my personal life. The truth is, I don't know how either my sister or my daughter (not sure who is the culprit yet, but I will find out) found your email address, or why they went looking for it in the first place. I am sure you were surprised to receive a blank message with my name on it – as was I to receive yours. So as we are here . . . what can I say after all this time except I hope you are doing well and that the years have been good to you. Sorry for the strangeness of this!

Best wishes from Celine

After a moment or two of *Can I? Should I?* I think, *Heavens, just do it!* So I press 'Send'.

FIFTEEN

Five minutes later, he replies.

Dear Celine,

I am not sorry to have received your email – quite the opposite. But yes, it did come as a surprise. And the main reason I emailed you back without writing anything was, to be truthful, that I was puzzled and I didn't know what to say. But other than that lame excuse, it was a pretty dumb thing to do.

I followed the link to your website in your email footer. I was so surprised when I saw the words The Love Market. You can't imagine how that took me back. Although you probably won't believe this, I actually thought of you a couple of weeks ago. I was sorting through some boxes in my apartment and I came across the old Dictaphone I used in Sa Pa. Remember? When I stood by the window in my cabin and you sat there watching me?

He means, when I sat on the end of the bed naked except for his thin white T-shirt, and watched him slowly pacing in front of the window as he was trying to work. 'You're distracting me,' he'd said, mid-sentence.

I'd smiled.

He'd looked at me in that lingering way that said he was trying to bank every detail of me because these were our last hours together and we could barely speak of them. And then, without moving his gaze even a millimetre, he'd thrown his Dictaphone on to the table and taken purposeful steps across the floor.

> I hope these last fifteen years of your life have been good ones. I always imagined you would have married a great guy, and ended up settling and having a fine life. And from what you've just said, you have a daughter, so perhaps I am not far wrong . . .
>
> Patrick

I read it twice, marvelling at how the moment with the Dictaphone managed to be so marked out among his memories. I am swept by such a powerful nostalgia that when I hear my mobile ring I reach to the night table, not bothering to look at the call display but assuming it's Jacqui. I am so ready to give her a good telling off!

'Hi,' I hear a voice say.

I am suddenly thunderstruck and can only manage, after what feels like a very long silence, to say a faint, 'Oh my gosh.'

He laughs a little, nervously. 'Sorry, I was just on your website again and saw your phone number. I just . . . I had to hear your voice.'

I may have died. This feels quite possible because he says, 'Are you still there?'

I clear my throat and say a shaky, 'I am, yes. I'm still here.' For a moment my hand goes over my mouth to stop whatever sound that might burst out.

'You know, it's amazing how easily you can find people these days when you decide to,' he says, then adds, playfully, 'But I guess you know that already.'

I am quick to say, 'I didn't go looking for you, Patrick. It was my sister or possibly—'

'Can't you just say it was you?' he says, disarmingly.

I am suddenly hot and place the back of my hand on my forehead. He always had the power to blindside me with his directness and his ability to place an innocent few words on to a charged, higher level. I laugh a little, despite the fact that it's possibly incriminating me.

'Your picture. On your website. I can't stop looking at it. In fact . . . I'm looking at it now.' There is the sound of a smile in his voice.

'Ah . . . my sister took that one.' In our garden. A medium close-up. My dark hair cut into flattering long layers, slightly falling in my eyes. My black-and-white stripy halter-top looking very glam with my two-week-old tan from our holiday to Cyprus. We must have taken hundreds getting me to look – as she insisted – wise and insightful, like someone who you'd trust to make a sound decision about your personal life, yet also a fun girl with her finger on the zeitgeist. 'Bloody cooperate!' she'd said. 'They want Jennifer Aniston-cum-Oprah Winfrey as their matchmaker, not Martha Stewart.'

'It's beautiful. You've changed but in a good way. You suit being in your thirties, if that makes any sense.'

Patrick used to have a way of coming close to intimidating me with something very simple that he'd say, in the sexiest yet most unnerving way, and it now seems as if it's fifteen years ago all over again: nothing's changed. To think he's sitting there looking at my picture is wild.

'Thanks.' I laugh a little. 'Sorry, I . . . This is just so crazy. I think I'm in shock. I don't quite know what to say.'

'Just don't hang up on me, okay?'

As if I would! And he knows it! 'No,' I tell him. 'At least . . . not yet, anyway.'

'Ha,' he says. 'You're as sassy as ever.'

It's a funny word to come out of his mouth. I find myself grinning. There is a moment or two where we can't speak, where the connection that was always there between us fuses again, where we both must register it. Then I ask, 'Where are you? I mean, what far-flung place?'

'Not that far-flung. Toronto. I'm based here now. Or *for now*, I should probably say.'

'Oh. So you don't work overseas anymore then?' I can hear the animation in my voice, as though the butterflies have left my stomach and are playing havoc with my vocal cords.

'Well, yes and no. They pulled me out of the Middle East a few years ago and I've been doing what they call "parachute journalism" since then. They literally drop me in wherever there's a story to be filed, whether that's covering Syria or the World Cup; it can be anywhere, or anything, really.'

I am only half-listening to him, just overcome and made insensible by the sound of his voice. 'I often wondered where you'd be, you know. If any harm had come to you, even if you were still alive. You know you hear in the news, so many journalists . . .' Why am I telling him I've thought he might be dead? But the truth is, whenever Mike and I were watching the news and a foreign report came on, I always half-expected that one day I'd see Patrick's face. And I often wondered if Mike thought that too. If we were both secretly waiting for it. I think I was probably always subconsciously prepping myself for how I was going to react.

'It's okay. I've always been a pretty lucky guy. Although I might have come close a few times.' I can hear the smile in his voice again. 'You needn't have worried, but I'm flattered and touched that you did.'

I can't get over how familiar his voice is to me, even though I only ever heard it for four days. The drawn-out vowels and rounded 'o' of the

Canadian accent. His sibilants like a whisper around my face. Memories of our intimacy filling the space between us, because it was always there; beneath the sex and the closeness with Mike, I would be wanting in the worst way to feel even a fraction of how I felt with Patrick.

A dart, now, of the memory of how well we worked together leaves me holding my breath.

'Are you still there?' he eventually asks.

I chuckle again, nervously. 'I'm still here, I think!'

'You're shocked,' he says. 'You said your family likes to meddle in your personal life . . .'

Patrick never did beat about the bush.

'I'm divorced.' Does he draw a breath of surprise, or am I imagining it? 'Recently,' I add. 'I'm still not even fully used to the idea.'

'I'm sorry it didn't work,' he eventually says. I can almost hear his brain computing the new information. And I compute him computing me. And the incredulity is ever there, skipping along with my heart, that this really is Patrick on the phone. Patrick has rung me.

'And you?' I venture.

'Same,' he says. 'Long time ago.'

He could mean someone other than Anya. So much can happen in fifteen years. And yet somehow, in the concise, slightly humble way he says it, I know he's referring to her. So many questions fill into the silence, and I sense he is aware of that when he says, 'Look, I'm sorry to have just called out of the blue. It probably wasn't fair of me to do this. Thing is, I never saw myself getting up the courage to call you, even though . . .'

'Even though what?' I feel surprisingly reflective and emotional.

'Well, I looked you up about two and a half years ago on the internet. Trips down memory lane . . . But I couldn't find anything on you.'

Two and a half years ago? That would be when I thought I'd seen him in London. What did Jacqui jokingly say about us being on a parallel cosmic track, if you can believe in them?

'I changed my name when I got married.' I think of what Jacqui said about this too.

'I thought that might be why. I still had your mother's address, where I sent that letter to, remember? I thought about trying to contact you again through her. But I didn't know if you were married with a family . . .'

'I'm sure it wouldn't have been a very good idea,' I say, once I've momentarily recovered from my surprise at hearing this, wanting, inexplicably, to shed a tear. Our timing has been all off.

'No. But it still didn't stop me wanting to.'

'You sound like the same Patrick.' I smile.

'I am the same Patrick,' he says.

I try to imagine what would have happened if he had tried to contact me again. What I'd have done. What could I have done if I was already a wife and a mother?

Finally, he says, 'Celine, it's late there and I should probably go. But all I can really say after all this time is it's fantastic to hear your voice. And what's weird is that now we're actually speaking it doesn't feel like fifteen years since we last did.' His voice has gone quiet and I wonder if it's because he's become emotional or if someone else is there.

'I know. You're right,' I say. 'It really doesn't.' I pinch the bridge of my nose, surprising myself with how overcome I am.

'Can I tell you something?' he says, after a moment. 'I mean, I hope you know this already, but when I left you that morning I didn't just walk away and forget. I had to consciously block you out of my thoughts for a very long time. The truth is – and I know we all make mistakes but some of us make bigger ones, with more lasting regrets – I always knew I shouldn't have let you go.'

But you did, I think. The blood seems to rush to my head; I am suddenly swimming in a sea of sadness.

Before I can actually respond, he says, 'Goodnight, Celine.'

SIXTEEN

'Fly there with me!' he said, on our last night.

We were in bed. 'You'll love living in Hong Kong. I'll get you somewhere . . . a hotel at first, maybe.' He suddenly seemed galvanised by possibility and gripped my shoulders. The relief of having landed on a solution was like a physical thing he'd cast off his back.

'What do you mean?' I asked, cautiously excited. 'For how long?' Did he mean a holiday? More than that? It was true that I didn't have a concrete reason to hurry home.

'For however long we want! We don't need to know everything now. We can work that out as we go along.' His eyes, which had been troubled all day, were alive with the idea now.

'So I'll just, what, live in a hotel?' The idea of going with him hammered there along with my heart. But I wasn't clear on the details.

'Yes. At first. Then we can look and maybe find you an apartment somewhere.'

I pondered this, aware that my excitement wasn't taking flight like it probably should have been doing.

Find *me* an apartment?

'But, okay . . . what you said before was that you're either moving out or Anya's moving back to Toronto.'

'Yes,' he said, looking like he didn't follow. He was still on a high from this solution he'd just found for us.

'Then I don't understand. I wouldn't need an apartment of my own. We could live together.' I remember the very optimistic, slightly naïve note in my voice.

But I could almost see the pause in his thoughts. 'Eventually, of course. Yes. That would be the ultimate plan. But I couldn't exactly do that right away . . . Not until she's gone, obviously.'

'Why not?'

He seemed a little exasperated, and I detected the air leaving his balloon. 'I can't look like I've gone to Vietnam, come home with a British tourist, and we're now playing house!'

This stung. 'I'm not sure I understand why that matters, if you're splitting up.'

Surely they were splitting up? He wasn't having second thoughts? My mind was running amok. I wasn't sure what to think now.

'Sorry,' he said, seeming earnest and slightly less jubilant. 'I didn't mean it that way . . . I'm trying really hard to find a way for us to be together, to make it so that you're not just going to go back to England and I'm never going to see you again. But I just . . . I have to end things cleanly with Anya. Like I said before, I owe her that, at the very least. I don't want to be a shit to her. That's not who I am.'

Suddenly he looked caught between a rock and a hard place. I hadn't seen myself as a difficulty in his life.

'I understand,' I said, hearing the grief in my voice, trying not to be dramatic. 'But from what you've just said, I've now got this mental picture of you going back there, to Anya, for however long, and me being in a hotel, like some sort of mistress . . .' It was absurd but I was just being honest. I wasn't feeling prioritised and I felt I deserved to be, even though I knew someone else probably deserved that right too. Plus I would run out of money soon. How was I going to live in Hong Kong, even if I went there with him? How would I be able to work?

'Mistress? God, I don't want a mistress!' He stared at me in genuine exasperation, as though I'd offended everything he stood for. It was a look I could close my eyes and see for years even when I'd almost, frustratingly, forgotten the details of his face. 'If that's how you think I see you – and see myself, for that matter – then you've misunderstood what these few days have been to me, Celine.'

He stood up sharply and it was then that I felt the impossibility of it all.

After a while of me trying to compose myself, I said, 'I just don't see what the problem is. If you love me, and I love you, and your marriage is over, and you both know it is, then I don't see why this has to be so complicated. I think you should be able to tell her the truth, so that you're free to be with me. And if you're not prepared to do that . . .' I didn't really want to give him an ultimatum. 'I just can't see me coming with you and sitting on the sidelines until you sort your situation out with no real guarantee that you're going to. Where would that leave me if you end up staying with her?'

The truth was, it wasn't that I was scared of ending up alone in Hong Kong. I just wanted the great romance of it all. I wanted it to continue how it had started. To be in the bubble. I wanted to stay there forever. This just felt like way too much real life that I hadn't bargained for.

He looked at me, listened closely; I could see him giving it a lot of thought. I sense I had left him slightly lost for an argument. Eventually he sat down on the bed again with his back to me. 'I'd be asking you to put your faith in me, I realise . . .'

His words were left to lie there. But it was the tone of them that told me none of this was going to happen.

The heat of the conversation seemed to fade a little as I could tell neither of us wanted more arguing back and forth to blight what little time we had left. Yet for a while afterwards I could still feel how everything was hanging by a thread, could still sense our brains rattling off in a million directions, still searching for a better solution. I couldn't stand to think that this was our last night and in the morning he would leave. He'd go back to his wife – maybe, or maybe not. I was less convinced he actually was going to leave her now, but perhaps that was just my broken, melodramatic heart speaking. All I could see was myself out there searching for the rest of my life, desperately trying – and probably failing – to feel this again with somebody else.

I was way too young to give myself the good advice that I would later be able to give my daughter. That life is precious; we never know how long we are here for. We should take each day, and everyone who comes by, for what it is – a gift that's meant to be valued and enjoyed in the moment. If we fall in love for four days we should only be glad that we had it, not distraught that we couldn't stretch it to a future we hadn't yet lived. We should trust that loving, learning and letting go are part of living: a beautiful cycle we have to give ourselves up to, that we know will come around again and again.

I remember we went through the motions of eating and drinking rice wine, and the loaded silence between us. Then neither of us could bring ourselves to have sex for the last time, so we just lay there, bare arm next to bare arm. In my side vision I could see the prominent bridge of his nose, his steady blinking.

'What are we going to do?' were his last words before we both went to sleep. But he'd asked that before. I'd given him the only answers I could think of and he'd rejected all of them.

Next morning, he wasn't there when I opened my eyes. I thought he'd snuck off while I was sleeping and I was utterly devastated. *This is how I'll always remember you: as a guy who played at being principled but didn't have the guts to say a proper goodbye!* And then I saw his bag.

He was standing outside staring into the mist. His long body, narrow back, legs a stride apart, his blond, wavy hair. His dilemma was palpable. I could see it. I could feel it. It etched itself into me. And I knew then something that I may have doubted briefly: that as bad as this was for me, it was equally bad for him. I stared at the low mist that hung over everything, hiding the mountains, blanking out our view. Just me and him and this small, primitive place. He turned and looked at me, as if to say, *Yup. I'm still here.*

Back inside, I watched him pack the rest of his stuff. We barely spoke. I remember the quick sounds of him zipping up his bag. That urgent zip seemed to belong to a man who was dying to get the hell out of there. When he stood there with his bag in hand and looked at me in the still-dim early light I could almost feel his relief. In his mind he'd crossed his point of no return. He was on his way back home, to what felt familiar, and safe, and the right thing to do. For now, anyway.

You'll walk out of this door and I'll never see you again, I thought. I couldn't bring my heart to visibly break, so I said a vaguely uncivil, 'Don't look back at me once you walk out of this door. Just promise you won't, because I can promise I won't be looking at you.' How I regretted those words later. How I regretted not following him to Hong Kong and putting all the faith in the world in him. He had asked me to. I was the one who had decided that wasn't enough for me. And I'd done it simply because I wanted to be in a dream world, and I wanted him to be fully in it with me, and he couldn't be.

He paused by the door, rested his head on his forearm, on the wooden frame, like a person going through the worst wrestle with himself.

'Promise?' I said again.

Then he straightened up and said, 'I have to go,' as though telling himself, rather than me.

And he did. And he promised nothing.

SEVENTEEN

James Halton Daly signs and returns my Love Market contract. I ring Trish to let her know, even though it's a bit naughty of me – hardly respecting client confidentiality. She squeals with laughter when I tell her about the Fake Date.

'What's with all the issues all the ex-dates have got?' I say. 'I'm thinking he's the one with issues. Issues-issues!'

'But it's good that he's picky, isn't it? Once he's written them off he doesn't mess around with them. He's a very clean executioner!'

We laugh.

'You like him, don't you?' I pull up a photo of him on my laptop and stare at him again. His aristocratic good looks. The charm that oozes out of him.

She's silent for a second. 'Of course! We're good mates. You know how we met, right? I told you? I was mates with his best friend Andy at uni, who now lives in Newcastle. But since we graduated, whenever James comes up here to see Andy, he and I seem to spend more time together than they do, because Andy's girlfriend always wants to be in tow and that pisses James off. So now, James will tend to phone me and make plans with me, and invite Andy; and if Andy brings his girl, then it's not so bad, since James has me to talk to.'

'He's very attractive, isn't he?' I ask her.

She falls silent for a moment. 'God! I mean he is, in a way. His personality. But do I personally fancy him?' She over-laughs suddenly. 'Don't you think he's a little bit – you know – gay?'

I bring him up in my mind, sitting across from me at the table. 'He's a bit of a Ra Ra Rupert. I particularly liked the popped collar of his tweed jacket.'

She howls. 'Oh God, he didn't pop his collar?'

'He did. Anyway, enough of James. The real reason I called is that I have someone for you. A professional athlete. Football. Premier League. Retired. A knee injury.'

'So he'll be pissed off at life, and in chronic agony. My kind of man.'

'I don't think he's either of those things. He's cute, laid-back, nice Irish accent . . . He's heading up an initiative to send underprivileged kids to football camps in the summer. And he says he's had it with WAG wannabes. He wants somebody interesting and he's more into Netflix than nightclubs.'

'I'm in,' she says.

'But the catch is I want you to go on a real date with him.'

'But I don't do real dates. I told you.'

'But he's initially quite shy. I don't see him doing great in the "hit and run" coffee-shop atmosphere.'

'I'll bear that in mind and won't hold it against him.'

When we ring off I stare for a moment or two at James's signed contract. '*Find me someone as sexy as you, and you might be in for a bonus,*' he'd scribbled on a yellow Post-It note.

Cheeky!

We have a spell of peaceful living. And then we have a flood.

Aimee is standing there with a towel around her, dark-blue varnished toenails sinking into the rug. Water is climbing steadily up the side of the bathtub. 'Turn the tap off!' I screech.

'Duh! I've tried that.'

She's pulled out the plug but the water won't drain. 'It's all your hair clogging it! I've told you about washing your hair in the bath.'

'Sorry,' she says. 'I'll wash it in the sink and clog that up next time.'

I realise we need to switch off the stop tap.

'You'll have to ring your dad,' I tell her.

Pause. Glower. 'Why can't you ring him?'

'Aimee, you'll understand why I can't ring him when you're grown up. Now please, can you call and without telling him why you need the information, just casually ask him where the inside stop tap is?'

She tuts like I'm certifiable. Meanwhile, I start ladling water from the bathtub to the toilet with a bucket. 'Go on!' I scream at her.

'The bath's overflowing and Mum doesn't know where the stop tap is,' I hear her say to her dad. Then a withering look in my direction. An outstretched hand, with the phone in it. 'He wants to talk to you.'

I grab the phone off her. 'Yes, Mike.'

'Have you given any more thought to my proposition?'

'Your . . . ? Can we talk about that later?'

'No,' he says. 'I think we should talk about it now.'

'And if I haven't?'

Pause. 'Better get your wellies out, then.'

I glance at Aimee. 'Hang on. You mean, if I say no, I'm not doing it, then you're not going to tell me where the stop tap is?'

'You're quick.'

I open my mouth, as Aimee rolls her eyes and walks out of the bathroom.

'Mike,' I say, patiently. 'I'm going to ask you this nicely. Please tell me where the stop tap is, before we flood our house.'

'Are you agreeing to find me a girlfriend?'

We have about two inches of room left before the water will be spilling on to the floor. 'Fine!'

'Great. It's in the cupboard under the stairs. You go in there every day to get your shoes. It's got a red handle.'

EIGHTEEN

'Tell me about your life,' he says when I pick up the phone.

I must light up like a thousand 100-watt bulbs. He rang me again!

'My life? Ha! Well . . . clearly, as it's Saturday night and I'm at home alone, I can't really have one.' I am grinning from ear to ear.

'I can't believe that could be true,' he says. 'I, on the other hand, will be going to an all-night party this evening.'

'Really?'

'No,' he says. 'Not really at all. I've been working on research for a book until a few minutes ago and I'll be working on it all night, probably.'

'Book? That sounds exciting.'

'But I'd rather talk to you.'

'Hm . . .' I close my eyes for a second or two, dwelling on the ever so slightly seductive quality in his voice. 'What do you want to know?'

'Well, anything you like. Tell me about a day in the life of Celine Walker, from northern England. I just want to get a picture of you.' He calls me by my maiden name.

I fidget, trying and failing to get into a comfortable position on the couch. 'Well . . . for example, today I went running. I woke up early, had breakfast with my daughter, then Mike – my ex-husband – picked her up and I went running through Tyne Valley park with my sister. Then we had lunch in the sunshine in a pub's beer garden. Then I came home . . . Have you died of boredom yet? I rang my father to see how he was doing. Did two loads of laundry. Opened a bottle of wine and now I'm sitting here. Talking to you.'

I hear him moving around. 'I want to see you. FaceTime or Skype. Which have you got?'

'What? When? Now?'

'No, next month,' he laughs a little. 'Of course now. No time like the present.'

'Oh my . . . I'm not very spontaneous.' I scramble off the couch and run to the mirror, wondering what baloney I can give as an excuse.

'What sort of preparing does it need? You. Me. A computer or a phone . . .'

I peer at myself. My hair long and loose, with all these irritating new layers in it, that would have been washed today had I been going out tonight. My black spaghetti-strapped tank. That at least looks decent. My lips that are a little wine-stained at the edges. 'Another day would be so much better.'

'I can't wait another day.'

'You've waited fifteen years.'

'My point exactly.' I can hear the smile in his voice again. 'Come on. Don't spoil it. Or you're not the girl I know.'

I think of what I've told my female clients. Don't ever put yourself down to a man. Don't imply you're not adequate. Men see what you like about yourself. They see you though their eyes not yours. 'Okay,' I say. 'But I'll need a minute. Best I do it from my desktop.'

'I'll give you five,' he says.

I run to the bathroom, comb my hair, brush my teeth and put on a smear of Aimee's lip gloss – the only thing that's handy.

Then I am staring at the little green button and hearing the ringing tone. Seconds later I am looking at Patrick. Live.

'Oh my gosh!' I press fingers to my lips. I can't believe the stirring of emotion from just seeing his face.

'Surprise,' he says, gently.

And there is a moment where neither of us can do anything but gaze at one another. I feel so incredibly happy-tearful. He looks so much older – like that one recent picture I saw of him – now that I'm no longer seeing him down the path of my memory. The face is fuller, even though he doesn't seem heavier in his body. The hair is still wavy, the blond mellowed a little with grey. But it's the lines around his eyes. Patterns of them, like cracks in china.

'Welcome to fifteen years on,' he says, and smiles.

He is still devastatingly handsome, especially when he smiles.

'God, you're beautiful.' He leans closer as though trying for a better look at me and I flood with self-consciousness. 'You're lovelier than your photo. It doesn't do you justice.'

'That's very kind.'

'Seriously. I can't stop looking at you. I just want to sit here and watch every move of you.'

Memories of our intimacy come rushing back – not that they've been so very far away. How many times have I revisited every last detail in my mind? Recalled just what his kiss or his touch could do to me? The way he seemed to know me? The way he would look so deeply into my eyes as though he never wanted his gaze to be anywhere else?

'I can't believe I'm looking at you,' he says again.

'No. Me too. It's amazing. Though I wasn't sure you'd ring again.'

'Come on,' he cocks his head. 'I don't believe that. You must have known I would.'

I am tongue-tied. I throw up my hands and laugh a little, shrugging. What do you say to somebody after all these years? Everything I can think of is either silly or too serious. I can't do middle ground with Patrick, not even now.

He leans back in his chair – an office chair. He's wearing a dark check shirt and jeans. His shirt is tucked in and I see his narrow waist; he really and truly hasn't changed a lot. I can't stop scouring him with my gaze. 'What did you do today?' I ask.

I see a broad smile. 'Why are you asking that?'

'You asked me.' I feel ridiculous. 'I'm returning it.'

He laughs a little. 'Right . . . Well, I marked some assignments – I've been teaching a course at a local university. Then I spent a lot of time on the internet doing my book research, and then looking into some flights.'

'You obviously travel a lot.' My mind goes back to that time in London. To my conviction that it was him, and then my doubts that came flooding in.

'I do. Yes. A few times a month. And what I wanted to tell you is, I'm actually going to be coming to London soon.'

'What?' I am aware of him monitoring my reaction. 'You mean . . . this is just a coincidence? Or . . . ?' I do a double-take at his expression. 'Why the smile?'

'I don't know. It's just that you always did like to have everything organised and straight in your mind.'

I actually don't remember that about my young self. Unless he is referring to my wanting the straight goods on his marriage. 'Okay. Rephrase. Are you coming for work or pleasure, Mr Shale?'

He crosses his hands at chest level, laces his fingers. 'Work, Ms Walker. But it's going to be a pleasure. I mean, that is, if you'd agree to meet me.'

'Meet you in London?' I process this. 'Yikes! Seriously?'

He laughs. 'Is "Yikes" a yes? Or a "Yikes, no chance in hell"?'

I can't stop smiling. 'How long are you coming for?'

'Oh, a very short stop. I'm on my way to Egypt. Flying in and out of Heathrow. It's in two weeks' time. It should be a direct transfer but

I could squeeze a night, possibly two . . . Think about it,' he says, as I'm sitting here biting my lip and smiling. I'm trying to picture it, and to case my mind for pros and cons. A part of me is a little nervous. It might be oh-so-simple all in a day's work for Patrick but what would it really mean for me if it opened the floodgates of all the old feelings?

'Well, I'm definitely thinking!' I tell him, lightly. In fact, I want to just sit here and do nothing else. I tell him I'd like to chat more but I should probably go, as my daughter will be home any minute. I badly need to end this call before I burst.

'Understand,' he says. Then he slowly shakes his head, his eyes performing another smitten study of me. 'Wait a minute, though . . . Will you do something for me before you go?'

'What?' I laugh with a sudden nervous self-consciousness.

He cocks his head. Still the same endearing mannerisms. The slight tilt of the head when he's about to be a little daring or forward. 'Lift up your hair for me.'

'My hair?' I give him my best mistrusting face.

'From your neck. Like it's pinned up. Like that picture I took of you when you were reading.'

Good heavens . . . The one he snapped when I was sitting in the window chair in his cabin, with my eyes down, reading, completely unaware I was the object of his focus. It was possibly the loveliest photo anyone has ever taken of me. I can't believe he remembers it – or that I even do.

So, even though it seems silly, I lift my hair. I try to do it in a certain unaffected yet slightly suggestive slow motion, raking it up into a hand and turning my chin ever so slightly, exactly as I picture the young me doing in my mind's eye. For a moment I want to close my eyes and just take myself right there again.

'Wow,' he says, quietly.

Just wow.

NINETEEN

I agree to meet Mike at a restaurant where I come to do all my Fake Dates because it's fun, unthreatening, serves great food and you can actually hear your dining partner talk.

The young waiter, a handsome lad in his early twenties, who is often the one who seats me, is at the door when I come in. As soon as he sees me, for some odd reason, he blushes the colour of a Valentine's Day heart. He can't seem to meet my eyes, burbles out some incoherent words, grabs two menus and walks me to Mike's booth, tripping over his feet and looking out of the corner of his eye at mine, in my skyscraper black stilettos.

Mike stands up – eyes going to my shoes too – and I am taken back to our first date. Mike still has that mix of ill-at-ease and disarmed. He might even be wearing the same pair of jeans.

We'd been out together three times before the 'proper date'. The first time, we were feeling out the possibility of going either the romance route or into friendship no-man's land. The second, I drank too much wine and started prattling on about Patrick again. The third time, we were in a very noisy Quayside bar. Mike had talked close to my ear, and I'd been so busy trying to hear him that I was oblivious to any whiff of sexual tension that might have been there. But then I'd started to note the way his eyes would stray from my face to my breasts, and he'd blush. As though he was trying very hard not to look at my body and was inwardly kicking himself for failing. I'd stopped caring about what he was saying, and was more interested in the way that his lips moved as he spoke. A smile would sometimes be on the brink, not quite making itself available to me, but tantalising me with its sexy potential. Then I was homing in on the satisfying sensory things about him: the cleanness of his breath, free from anything unpleasantly foody or artificially pepperminty, his fair, soft skin, and his general overall pleasing masculine smell. A hint of aftershave? Maybe. Or it could have been nice soap. Even his unusual personal style was becoming attractive. I remember trying to engage his eyes in a way that might transmit my thoughts, but seemingly not having much luck. By the time we left the bar, I'd decided I probably wasn't going to see him again; he was being too wishy-washy. But when I got home, I lay there for ages trying to rewrite the night, to make it so he'd just been a little bit more decisive, maybe kissed me. And, unfairly, trying to rewrite him a bit too. If he donated those winkle-pickers to a charity shop, and I took him to Toni & Guy . . .

He called the next morning and asked if I'd like to go for a quick lunch. There was something desperately unsatisfying about it as we sat in an Italian restaurant hurrying down a pizza that had taken an age to arrive. I dropped him off at the BBC building because finally he got around to telling me that his car had broken down, and I wondered if this had been the only reason he'd rung – because he'd wanted a lift. But in a parking spot outside he said: 'Would it be all right if I kissed you? I've spent all this time kicking myself for not doing it last night.'

I leaned in, somewhat relieved. His cold lips met mine, and it was nice. His thumb was stroking along the tops of my collarbones and it all felt very . . .

Like we had company.

I opened one eye to see the BBC security guard's face on the other side of the windshield. I attempted to tell Mike to stop, but he somehow took my moaning as encouragement and revved up his kissing. His hand went to swiftly unbutton my blouse. It had found its way into my bra before he must have sensed something was wrong. And that's when he saw our intruder. The security guard smiled. Mike smiled. Mike got out of the car, sheepishly. And I skidded off before the door was even shut.

After that I didn't hear from him for two weeks. When I could stand the suspense and the cold shoulder no longer, I decided to ring him. 'I'm phoning to tell you that I don't think this is going to work,' I said.

'Is this Celine by any chance?' he said.

'Yes, Mike. This is Celine.'

'I understand,' he said. 'I seem to cock everything up every time we go out, and you're still in love with someone else. And maybe you always will be, or maybe you won't. I don't want to rush you. We can either pick it up in your own good time. Or we can still be friends, and you've got my word that I'll not put pressure on you. Or, of course, you can choose to never see me again. That too. Which is what I'd probably pick. If I were you.'

'Mike, about our kiss . . .'

'Celine, please, if it's okay with you, can we forget about the car episode – if you don't mind?'

'Forget about it?'

'I'd rather not be reminded.'

'I'm sure if that guy told anyone you were feeling up your girlfriend in your lunch hour in the car park no one would believe him anyway.'

'You might be surprised,' he said. 'I think quite a few believed it with no trouble.'

'Huh?'

'The thing was, it got captured on the security cameras. Somebody thought it clever to play a practical joke and the entire staff of the

BBC ended up with it as their screen saver. I'm never going to live it down . . .'

'Nice to meet you,' he says now, snapping me back to the present, looking me over the way he always did: appreciatively. I wonder if he catches the nostalgia in my face. He stands up as the waiter hovers there for a second or two, and reaches to shake my hand.

'Nice to meet me?' Oh yes. I forgot. *You have to treat me like we were never married.*

As we shake hands, a thought just blindsides me: if only this was our first date. If we could rewrite whatever it was we got so wrong. If only there was a magic wand they gave you on your wedding day, so you could undo every subsequent argument, every petty resentment, every tear you caused, every lashed-out, hurtful comment that you didn't even mean.

He is analysing me, cautiously optimistic. 'Mike . . . This is mad.'

'I know,' he says. 'But it's for a good cause. Please stay.'

I am aware of the heat of curiosity from other diners. Mike often attracts attention: the nonconformist look makes him interesting to others. I sit down at our booth, and immediately bury myself in a purple leather-backed menu.

By the servers' station, the young host and our waiter are exchanging smirks, their eyes directed over here. When they catch me looking, they quickly glance away. They have me sussed. Nobody, not even a reasonably attractive, thirty-something female, goes on this many dates with different men. I'm obviously a high-class tart.

'What are you smiling at?' Mike asks me.

'Nothing,' I tell him.

Mike now pretends to study the menu but his eyes keep bobbing up to fix on me. He's made an effort to dress nicely. A new-looking white shirt, a few buttons undone and showing his grey chest hair. A grey blazer that's the same shade as his hair. The drainpipe jeans. Tan winkle-pickers.

'You're analysing me and wondering what you ever saw in me.'

'No I'm not! Why would I do that? This is the first time I've met you, remember?' I narrow my eyes at him and try not to react to the clear amusement in his.

'Somebody once said you should never criticise your husband's faults – because if he didn't have any, he might have found somebody better than you.'

I launch a smile. His eyes twinkle at mine. I go back to perusing the menu again, even though I come here so often I know it off by heart. 'I understand you work in radio,' I humour him.

'Yes,' he quietly charms me. 'I'm the producer of the Jackie Zane show, on Blaze FM.'

'I never listen to it.'

'So that's a conversation stopper right there then.'

'No it's not. It sounds like an interesting job. Do you like it?'

He pretends to think. 'Put it this way, I've done it for twenty years, so I certainly don't *dis*like it. It's been good to me, so I've been loyal back.'

It's true. Mike never cared if he got promoted, made more money; never seemed to mind that he always worked the graveyard shift. When we were happy, I'd admire his ability to be so content. Then, when we were getting on each other's nerves, I'd want to hold it up as evidence of a personal handicap or demerit in his character.

My friend the mischievous waiter arrives and reaches over to make room on the table for a basket of bread. 'Besides, the lifestyle would be hard to give up,' Mike says. 'You know, exotic travel. Penthouses in five cities. The company Ferrari. The chance to eat at a fine restaurant like this; and to meet a woman as beautiful as you, who would have otherwise been way out of my league.'

The waiter places the bread down and a smile has set on his face, like a little boy caught with his finger in the pie. Mike asks him for two gin and tonics. 'Absolutely, sir,' he says, and backs up, looking possessed by an alien.

Mike frowns. 'What's his problem? And why's he calling me "sir"?'

I grin, relaxing into the groove of the light piano jazz, and the wholesomeness of Mike's company that is so familiar to me. 'You know, Mike, we could always skip this Fake Date part and just talk about Aimee or something? If you like.'

'Is there something wrong with Aimee?'

'No.'

'Then we can't skip this part.' The waiter is back surprisingly fast with the drinks, cheeks the colour of plums. Mike continues, 'I'm paying for the full service, remember? That was the deal. Everything that you normally do with a Jim I want done to me. The whole works. No crack or crevice unexplored.'

The waiter freezes momentarily, and then tactfully backs up half a dozen steps, turns, and wonders how fast he can return to his friend.

'That's actually a very nice dress,' Mike's eyes go down the front of me, as he quickly strums his fingers on the table in time to the music.

'You don't have to compliment me.'

'I'm not. It is. It's a good colour on you, with your hair. Red's not normally a colour you wear.'

I unnecessarily look down at myself. 'I got it in the sale.'

'Was it marked down because it was too bright for everybody else?'

'Ha ha.'

His eyes meander over the top half of my body, making me nervous. I snap the menu closed, cross my arms. 'Here's the thing, Mike, about your proposition: I'm not sure I have anyone I can set you up with.'

'Really? I'm having the liver and onions.' Mike snaps his menu closed too. 'So tell me about the person you're going to set me up with.'

Isn't he listening? 'I'm saying, I don't have anyone in mind. And another thing, nobody said you're in. I actually don't let everybody in who wants me, you know. I'm very picky who I do this with.'

The waiter is hovering there with his pad, disbelieving his own good fortune.

'God, he creeps up on you like baldness, doesn't he?' Mike says after the lad manages to take down our order. 'He's as red as a week on the Costa Brava. I think you might have got yourself an admirer.'

'I think it's you. He's after your car.'

He scowls. 'My car? Oh! My Ferrari, you mean.' He chuckles like this is hilarious.

'You'd actually suit a Ferrari, you know.'

'But then I'd be a case of "small bloke, big vehicle" and you know what they say that means.'

'As I was telling you . . .' I beam at him. 'You have to pass this Fake Date first, before I can agree to take you on.'

'Why do I feel I'm already screwed?'

'I don't know, Mike. If that's how you feel, then why are you here?'

We hold eyes. 'I want to fall in love. I miss being in love,' he says. His reproachful gaze cruises over my face. And it strikes me, when he looks at me like this, how much regret is still there. And I want to find somewhere to look other than at his sad, still-loving eyes. I want to. But I am failing miserably.

'Cute versus sexy?' I tap my pen on my notepad, waiting for his answer. We've finished off the wine. Mike has been entertaining me with some of the radio-station sexual-politics stories that I have, admittedly, missed. I note that the upbeat jazz has been replaced with one of my favourite songs – Norah Jones' 'Come Away with Me'. 'I have to have these answers for my personal profile. If you don't want to—'

'No, ask away. What was the question?' He was off listening to the song too. 'Oh yeah . . . Cute is sexy, isn't it? Did you fix the bath tap?'

'I called someone in to do it, yes.'

'To fix a tap? I'd have done it.'

'It's done.' My eyes go back to my notepad. 'Your definition of thin?'

'Kate Moss. I still don't know why you'd pay somebody to fix a tap. How much did he charge?'

'Thirty pounds. Who is a lucky person?'

He tuts. 'The tap man, I'd say. Easy money for some.' He sighs. 'Brad Pitt's a lucky person, if you want to know. Or he was, for a long time . . .' He starts whistling, sits far back in the chair, stretching his arms across the back.

'What's hot?'

'Somebody who argues passionately but knows when to stop. Somebody who laughs a lot, and isn't always searching for things they don't even know if they really want.'

'What makes you laugh a lot?'

'Not a lot these days.'

Am I being hypersensitive? 'What would you have liked to be if you weren't who you are?' I press on.

'Virtually anything that's not a married human being. A dog. Geese are good too. A walking stick. A postage stamp; then I'd get to travel.'

No, I'm not being hypersensitive. Mike is sticking it to me in this ever so slightly passive-aggressive way of his. 'You're not batting high on the compatibility score. I did once have a woman who wanted to be a walking stick, but my geriatric clients were all fighting for her.'

'You haven't really started taking on geriatrics, have you?' he asks. His spot of sullenness has passed.

'No. Not yet. But we're all getting older. We'll all be on my books in thirty years, if we don't get taken soon.'

'Do you want to be taken soon?'

His gaze confronts me. I have to look far across the room, and to struggle to keep the tears back. 'I don't know. I don't think so.'

'That's a shame.' He sits back in the chair, with his legs spread, like a man subconsciously trying to maximise the space he takes up to assert his status, as he does when he's into you. Or, in this case, perhaps just because he's more comfortable this way. 'You deserve to be taken. To be swept off your feet.'

Another Norah song now. Can't they get a bit more current? Seems like we're getting the whole Norah CD. 'Maybe I don't. Maybe I once was and I didn't even know it.'

'Meaning?' he says.

I look into my lap and feel his eyes burning into the top of my head. The waiter comes and saves the moment by asking if we want dessert.

'Why don't you go and find him?' Mike asks, when he leaves again. Mike's magnanimous capacity to care for me makes him selflessly detached at the oddest moments.

The restaurant has cleared out, Newcastle folk now having moved on to bars or clubs. We've been here a long time. Time always used to just disappear when I was with Mike; that's how little he bored me. 'Find who, Mike? And why do you care so much that I find anybody? Can't you just be a normal divorced, bitter, resentful sod of an ex-husband?'

He shrugs. 'Find anybody. Someone who is a vast improvement on what you had.'

'But that would be difficult in many ways.'

'You know, you almost sound like you mean that.'

I have to lower my gaze again. 'I'm sorry,' I tell him, my voice rasping.

He cocks his head. 'What for?'

'Everything left unsaid.'

We sit like this for a while. Then he says, 'The things we painfully find out long after it stops mattering: just because you're in love, doesn't mean you're going to be happy. And just because you're not in love, doesn't mean you're going to be any worse off.'

We study each other until my eyes smart from the raw burn of his gaze.

'You and your Fake Dates,' he says, not bitterly, and I look away through a cast of tears. 'You know, I always imagined that while you were out there dining with your Jims you were secretly hoping for an opportunity to jump ship.'

He always used to call the men 'the Jims'. 'With a belief in me like that, is it any wonder that we're divorced?'

'Why *are* we divorced?' he quickly asks. 'I mean, I know, but I don't know.'

He holds my eyes so grippingly that I am deadlocked there.

I think of him saying to me, 'I can't be with you when I know that I am somehow holding you back.' I had wanted to ask him, *From what?* It seemed he knew – maybe more than I ever did.

'Don't do this, Mike,' I stare at a spot far across the room again. I can feel him monitoring me, his eyes soaking me up.

We sit in silence until the bill comes. The lad watches while Mike puts down the money, says a grudging 'Thanks'. Mike never was a great tipper. I can almost read the young lad's thoughts: *You greedy Ferrari-driving bastard.*

As we walk out, Katie Melua is singing 'My Aphrodisiac Is You'. I reckon we couldn't have picked a better time to leave.

TWENTY

Over lunch I tell Jacqui all about Patrick phoning and about how he's coming to London.

Her mouth seems to have hung open for about ten minutes. Eventually she says, 'Gah! You've been a bit of a dark horse, haven't you? I can't believe you didn't tell me any of this before!'

I feel very shamefaced because I can see by her eyes that she's more stung than she's letting on. 'I know. I'm sorry.' I can't even fully explain it. 'I just . . . I didn't want to get all carried away, which I knew would happen the moment I told you. I just feel I have to tread carefully. I need to protect myself . . .'

She smiles, shakes her head at me. 'I didn't know you had it in you to be such a sneak! But I honestly can't believe you're going to see him again!' She lets out a small squeal that attracts looks from people at the other tables. So this is how I know I'm forgiven.

'Shush! Ha! Well . . . Yes, I do believe I am. Thanks to you!'

She frowns. 'Me?'

I peer at her through narrowed eyes. 'Why would you write nothing, by the way? That's the bit that intrigues me the most. I mean, I can understand you contacting him – I suppose – given the years you've spent dreaming of my love affair and making it your own. But who would send a blank email? Was it just to be more mysterious? Or you didn't want to give the game away that it was someone other than me writing it?'

She laughs, exasperated, but she's blushing madly. 'It wasn't me! I mean, I'm pleased you give me all this credit, though – and I rather wish I had now. But, well . . . I'm not the devious sister! Remember?'

I tut and shake my head in despair.

She still can't stop grinning at me.

'How's the office romance?' I ask her as we climb the steep bank of Grey Street back to her office.

Christian Taylor is the new project manager at Jacqui's firm. He's a dead ringer for Ryan Gosling – or so she tells me – and he always wears a navy Paul Smith suit with a navy shirt, which makes me wonder if he's spent all his money on that one outfit and he's now got nothing else to wear. And Jacqui has a little crush. This would be fine. People are allowed to have crushes on co-workers. But they're not supposed to have them when they're about to get engaged to their live-in boyfriend of five years.

'I have updates,' she says, excitedly. 'We had an incident in the lift.'

'Incident?'

She sees my face. 'No. Not that kind of incident. I wish! Just, well, we were both going down for lunch – not together, of course – but there were all these people in there, all these bodies between us, and yet his eyes were fixed on me. And every time someone moved, blocking us, he'd peek around them, playfully, so he could see me again. So we could continue the eye game. It was so hot. I just wanted to push people aside and ravish him.' She gazes at me with sparkling eyes. The look she always gets when she talks about Christian, yet one I've never seen in the context of Rich.

The hill is steep. I am winded. There is something about this fellow that I don't like, and I don't know why. It's not as though I've even laid eyes on him to formulate a proper impression. 'But what if he's like this with all the girls? Do you really want a man who every other woman wants? Imagine his ego.'

'Well, you can certainly smell the pharomones when he leaves the room.'

'I think the pharaohs are in tombs in Egypt probably smelling very dodgy in their own right, but it's the *pher*omones you're on about.'

She chortles and stops walking and turns to me, all aglow. 'Oh, Celine! Driving home, I sat through a full traffic-light change. And I feel so bad for Rich. I mean, I have this good man who wants to marry me, and I love him, in almost all the right ways. Then there's how much I badly want to kiss Christian, a complete unknown quantity, who flirts with me to the point where it's all I get up for every morning. Rich is about to take me on holiday and I'm sure he's planning to propose, yet I just want to be locked up in a photocopier room – just me and Christian's mouth. Those big succulent lips, the bottom one that looks a little bit split, like Angelina Jolie's.'

'You had me until you mentioned Angelina Jolie.' So many of my male clients cite Angelina as the type of woman they're looking for. It gets tiresome. Although I have as many women who want Daniel Craig. Everyone thinks that paying for it entitles them to someone several degrees out of their league. 'But you'd probably want parts other than just his lips,' I tease.

'I wouldn't! For me, kissing has always been better than sex. A kiss has something ahead of it. Sex has nowhere else to go.'

She gazes at my face with that half-here, half-in-some-romantic-nether-land expression. 'I love that whole time before it actually happens, you know, that second when his face moves in, right before you find out what it's going to be like.' She looks up at the sky and inhales longingly, then smiles at me. 'I'm not the matchmaker in the family, but my theory is, a kiss can determine an awful lot about your compatibility.' I find myself thinking of Patrick again. When I clue back in, she is looking at me like a person who has walked out of a very romantic movie and realised her life doesn't measure up, only she's forgotten it's not actually supposed to.

'Well, as my dad once told me years ago, you don't have to marry someone just because they want to marry you,' I tell her. Then he'd added, *If I'd done that I would have been a bigamist several times over.*

'I know, but it's hard to walk away from someone who loves you. You worry that no one else will be along to love you in the same way.'

'Well, Jacq, people marry for all kinds of reasons. But please don't let that one be yours. I know. Remember, I have some experience of it.'

Something dawns on me. 'Rich isn't unwell again, is he?' I have noticed that her usual sparkle has been missing for a while. I know that Rich has suffered from depression in the past, and it really got Jacqui down in the early days. But he changed his medication some time ago and seems fine now. Or, at least, she never brings it up anymore.

'No, he's fine,' she says flatly. 'It's not that. Not really. To coin a phrase, it's me, not him.'

'So what happens when he whisks you away and proposes?'

She seems to turn frigid. 'I don't know. Part of me wants to stop the holiday so it won't happen. I'm dreading being on that precipice. Where whatever I say might be the wrong thing.'

'Isn't that enough to tell you you shouldn't be marrying him? I mean, listen to yourself!'

'I'm not actually sure I want to marry anyone, to be honest. Do I have to just because everyone else does? Then we'll end up having a baby and I'll never get to do all the things I want to do.'

'Like?' We sit briefly on the steps of Grey's Monument, the tall pillar erected in memory of the former earl and British prime minister who lent his name to an aromatic blend of tea.

'I don't know. But there are things. Just because I can't think of them right now doesn't mean I won't the second I know for sure that I'm not going to be able to do any of them.'

She takes a foot out of her stiletto, and wiggles her toes. There is a red groove across the top. 'Well, if you're with the right person there's nothing you won't be able to do together. Life will be one lovely adventure if you both want it to be. But if you proceed with things at this stage you're going to have a lifetime of regrets. And I think you know that. Do you want that? Or do you think that's even fair to him?'

'I'll take that as good advice, coming from you,' she says.

She forces her shoe back on and we cross the road and head into Fenwick's department store. Jacqui can't end any lunch break without popping into the shops. 'Imagine if he came here,' she says. For a second I think she's talking about lover boy at work popping in to refresh his cologne.

'Who?'

'Patrick, of course.'

'Patrick is not going to come here! Now we're being ridiculous!'

'You're marrying him. I'm not going to have your divorce be all for nothing.'

I'm not sure I like that last remark, even if it's said in humour.

'Do you remember how I used to get rid of you as a kid, when you got on my nerves?' I ask her.

Jacqui's Achilles heel: I discovered it when we were watching the telly and an advert came on with a talking octopus trying to sell an anti-itch remedy. Jacqui took a screaming fit and locked herself in the loo for half an hour. I reckoned she couldn't be afraid of a box of anti-itch cream, so it had to have been the octopus. So I drew a doodle of one and showed it to her. She went into a spasm of screams. After that, all I had to do was wag my pen when I saw her coming with her trying-to-befriend-me routine and she'd leave me in peace.

'I'm about to pull out a pen and paper.'

It seems to be the week for irksome comments from family.

My father has an appointment at the dentist's to get his upper wisdom teeth removed and has asked me to go with him.

'I don't understand,' I tell him in the car. 'If you've had them for most of your life and they're not doing any harm what's the big rush to get them out now?'

He sits in the passenger seat in his navy blazer with the brass buttons, the red handkerchief peeking out of the breast pocket. He looks paler than normal, his hands clenched into fists on his thighs. 'If they're my teeth not yours, then you shouldn't concern yourself about it. We all have dominion over our own mouths.' After a little while of safe silence he says, 'Are you getting back with Mike?'

I glance at him, stunned. 'Why do you ask that? We're divorced.'

'That would never have stopped me getting back with your mother. Not if everything in me was telling me it was the right thing to do.'

I try to picture that messed-up scenario. My parents met when my mother was a pretty nineteen-year-old art student at London's Royal College, and my dad was a thirty-eight-year-old Royal Academician who picked her up in a silver Jaguar, when he could barely afford to pay his rent. Five months later they were married; after nine more, out came me. My father moved us to France to live like the culturally superior expats he saw us as being. Hence the French name that I adapted by removing the accent on the first 'e' because all the kids in school used to poke fun at me. Somehow he sold enough paintings and managed to pay the rent on a small flat in Paris. As one of life's blusterers, he got by trading on the image he had invented for himself, of the suave older artist with his beautiful young wife and muse. And the baby. I always imagine I was paraded like a rather 'in' accessory. Then it was time for me to go to school. My dad's creativity went through a dry patch, and he relocated us to Newcastle where his 'I can't paint' spell turned into a pity trip that lasted forever, and my mother became chronically depressed.

As I grew older, it was clear to me that Anthony, as I came to call him over the years – my token step in the direction of fully disowning him – always needed a posse of new and naïve women. All he would ever say, during our very stiff attempt at ending the cold war between us when I was in my mid-twenties, was that my mother didn't fulfil her end of the bargain. Which means, I think, that she became a bit too much of a real person for him. But I always sensed that they divorced because when the mesmerism of each other wore off, I wasn't enough to make them feel like they had something worth sticking together for.

'Anyway, do you really think people can go back?' I ask him, my mind turning to Patrick. 'If you have something that was almost perfect once with somebody, can you ever recapture it? Would something be lost by even trying?' I'm not sure he's the right person to be asking this of, but he always has some interesting opinions on matters of the heart.

'What has this got to do with my teeth?'

'Not a great deal.'

I am powerfully aware that my father is an old man now, and there comes a time in all our lives when we have to start making amends before we exit this life with one too many regrets on our conscience.

'Love is love,' he says. 'You never stop loving once you've felt it for someone. It just becomes less elevated in the mind because, practically, there's little choice for it to be otherwise. If the person's state of mind hasn't drastically changed, then those feelings never change. Whether it's a good idea to go back is another question.' Then he surprises me by saying, 'You obviously divorced him for a reason.'

I sigh. I can't believe he thought I was talking about Mike!

'Do you believe in The One?' I ask him a little while later, as we're on this topic.

'Of course,' he says. 'I'm a romantic. It's all I'm capable of believing. I think there can be a great many Ones in life, and there should be – as many as possible.'

I'm glad I'm already pulling into a parking space.

'They're far back, so they're hard to brush. And besides, the rest of the teeth are crowded, so once they're gone, the top teeth will finally have room to stretch out.' He slides me a glance. 'To answer your earlier question. You did ask.'

I sit reading a well-worn magazine while he's in the chair. There is a whirring of dental instrument noises, and the dentist's kind and reassuring voice from time to time. A radio quietly plays chart hits. The receptionist makes dinner plans on the phone with her boyfriend.

And then, after about an hour, my father reappears with the dentist and we exchange pleasantries. The receptionist confirms that he knows which mouth rinses he has to do and tells him she'll ring him in a day or two to see how he's getting along.

Outside, I lay a hand on his arm. 'Are you sore?'

From behind his hankie he mumbles oral hieroglyphics.

'Go on then, give me a little look,' I say when we get back into the car.

He waves me away, mumbling a mouthful of invective. And it's only then that I catch a glimpse. His greying, peg-like teeth have gone. In their place is a set of skittle-like creations, the colour of double-churn butter.

'You got dentures!'

He tries to say something.

'What?'

'Hah han hawk.'

'Hah han hawk? Ah! You can't talk!' I chuckle. 'I thought with false ones they were supposed to match them to what your natural colour was. So they look more . . . blended in?' I slide him a look.

'Heep hyr highs on huh hoad,' he growls.

TWENTY-ONE

As part of my initiative to grow my client base, I posted an ad on the bulletin board of an exclusive tennis club in Jesmond. I was contacted by a girl called Jennifer Platt, who works there part-time while she's trying to get a home business off the ground making gourmet meals for Virgin Trains East Coast. What struck me about her was the fact that here was a pretty lady with a brain and ambition who seemed to be the real thing. She said she would never have considered going to an introductions service before; she was only doing so now because she was able to meet me personally first. I've agreed to take her on and waive my fee, mainly because I know she's not well off and I can think of a few men who are going to be interested in her.

We meet in Deb's Tea House in Jesmond, near where she lives.

The first thing she says to me is, 'I'm nervous about getting back out there. It's been so long. I was married for eight years. I don't know how I'm going to cope with someone else's sexual preferences, navigate someone else's body. What if I'm no good?'

Haven't I spent nights wondering the same thing? Dreading stripping off for someone new? Having to adjust to a new pace? Third-date pressure – or is it second now? Wondering if there are new sexual positions that have rendered what Mike and I have done passé.

I can see that Jennifer's temperature has risen just by talking about this so I instantly rule out two of the men who first came to mind for her, because their sexual personalities might be a bit too intimidating.

'Don't ever think in terms of you being inadequate, Jennifer. No man who is lucky enough to be in that position with someone as lovely as you is going to be worrying about your skills or adequacy.'

Wish I could take my own advice.

She smiles. 'You're lovely. That's very kind; thanks.'

'But why not just forget about joining The Love Market for now, and just go out there and have some no-strings fun first. Have you thought about that?'

She's shaking her head before I'm finished. 'I think you can have fun in a committed relationship. I want someone who is going to be around once I've got to know him.'

'If I wasn't a woman I'd want to go out with you myself.'

She laughs. I snap a photo of her for my records. 'So tell me, Jennifer, what are you really looking for in a man?' Sometimes they think I'm testing them, given that I generally ask them this on the phone and then in more detail when we meet. And occasionally I am. Like asking them their age. If you quickly follow the question with, 'What year were you born in?' and they hesitate, you discover one universal truth: that people generally aren't as quick with numbers – or lies – as they might have thought.

'You know, I've never had a particular vision. It always bothers me when friends say, "Oh, he has to be six feet tall, and have all his hair." I mean, it takes more than height and hair to make someone attractive.'

I nod. 'You're brilliant! Maybe you should work for me?'

She blushes. 'Really, he doesn't have to be any one particular thing. Except honest and kind. I like finding qualities that are attractive in people that aren't necessarily the glaringly obvious things.' She scowls. 'Does that make sense?'

'Perfect. And it's a brilliant answer. I wish all my clients were like you! Do you have a single sister or any single friends?'

She beams a smile, sips her tea, a silver signet ring on the middle finger of her right hand. There is something faintly old-fashioned in her gentleness and good manners; although nothing mumsy, by the looks of the curves that seem to be hidden under her clothes.

'If I did match you with a high earner, how would you see your life changing?' I am always curious what they will say to this question. For some, it becomes all about the money. And then that tends to influence how they market themselves to me. More up-sell, less honesty. I am all for impression management. I encourage it on those early dates. Beyond dress and the visual appearance, I urge them to manage their general behaviour, to come off pleasant and assertive, to watch their body language, conceal anxieties and show openness. I beg them to be economical with their life stories and past mistakes and downplay any negatives that might result in them being written off. But when they're dealing with me I like full disclosure right away.

She seems to think about this. 'You know, I'm not sure. I think in the fundamental ways I'd not want to change my life. I'm not sure I'd continue to work at the tennis club. I mean, I don't even know why they gave me the job. I can't even play!' She blushes again. 'No, I'm just kidding. I'm focussed on my goals, on getting the big catering contract and what happens next. *If* I get it, of course. If I meet a man with money, that's nice, but I'm still me, with my own dreams and things I want to accomplish . . .'

I tell her that I'm sure she's going to get her contract for the catering business. I also think I know exactly who I'm going to set her up with.

When I reach for the bill, she insists on buying our tea.

TWENTY-TWO

We have agreed that I am to get the 10.55 train to King's Cross on Friday morning, and Patrick is going to meet me on the platform.

On Friday, however, Aimee has a very bad headache and can't go to school. She complained of it last night but I just gave her a painkiller and imagined she'd sleep it off. When it's still bothering her a little while later, after I've given her a couple more painkillers, I phone Mike at home, even though he'll probably still be sleeping after working until the wee small hours. 'Do you think I should take her to the hospital?'

'For a headache?'

'She looks really awful. And she's just lying around, so lethargic. She seems a bit out of it . . . I'm not happy. What if it's a clot or something connected to her fall?'

'It's not connected to her fall. That was a long time ago.' Pause, while I know he's second-guessing himself. 'But I suppose if you're worried then maybe you should take her.'

When I don't answer he says, 'Want me to come with you?' Then I hear him shuffling around without waiting for any encouragement, probably looking for his jeans and his shoes from under the bed. Sometimes I get the oddest feeling that Mike and I aren't really divorced

– something has just taken him away on a spot of business, but he'll be home again soon.

'Thing is . . .' I don't know quite how to say this. 'I'm actually about to catch a train to London. I was going down for a conference tomorrow.'

He is silent for a moment. 'Ah . . .' he says, as though a penny is dropping. 'Well, I can come over and take her; then you can still go to your conference.'

'You don't mind?'

'Mind? She's my daughter. Of course I don't mind.' He sighs. 'Give me half an hour.'

When I hang up, I think of how earlier she said, 'I don't want to go to school. I just want my mum.' I hadn't heard her say that in a very long time. I'm about to go into her room and tell her that her dad is coming over to take her to hospital but then I realise I can't do it. What if something awful happens when I'm off in London seeing a man I haven't seen since I was twenty-one? 'Dad is coming right over,' I tell her. 'We're both going to take you to the hospital.'

I phone Patrick and explain. We agree I'll get a new ticket and come down tomorrow instead. All being well with Aimee, of course. I'm happy to hear he's disappointed but he seems to totally understand. 'Hey,' he says, before I end the call. 'Don't be upset about it. I'm still going to get to see you. That's the main thing. Even if it's short, I would take it over everything.'

I smile.

We're at the hospital forever. Waiting. For the doctor. For another doctor. For a head scan. For them to read the results. For them to talk, examine her, look over her medical reports, say little and leave us in suspense, walking in and out of rooms, running shoes squeaking on the polished floor. Aimee sits slumped against Mike with her head under his arm, like I'm not there.

They want to know if she has been unusually stressed – anything going on at school or in the family. Mike and I look at one another. Mike tells them about how we have gone through a divorce, in addition to the fact that she lost out in being in a competition that had meant a lot to her. Aimee sits stock-still, with that posture of someone powerfully aware she's being talked about but she knows it's for the right reasons.

The verdict is: everything's fine. It might have just been 'an emotional overload' as the doctor calls it.

'Come on,' Mike says to us. 'Let's go home.'

'Can we go and get something to eat?' Aimee asks, once we're in Mike's car. 'The three of us.' When I glance around at her she is suddenly so much brighter.

She didn't eat breakfast. I'm sure she's starving. I could use a glass of wine. We agree to go to one of our old regulars. I've never come back here since we split up, and I wonder if Mike has, though I suspect he would attach the same sentimentality to our old routines and would probably have avoided it too.

It's full for a Friday late afternoon. Mike goes to the bar and gets Aimee a lemonade, and two glasses of red wine for us. He walks back to our corner table slowly, carrying all three drinks carefully stacked in a triangle up by his chest. 'Should we help him?' I ask Aimee, and he looks up and catches us watching him warily.

'You thought I was going to drop them, didn't you?' He sets them down carefully on our small table. 'Faithless buggers.'

Aimee chuckles. I can't help smiling too. Then she puts her earbuds in and two seconds later is singing 'I'm in love with the shape of you . . .'

At the carvery station the chef loads us up with slices of roast turkey, and we help ourselves to the trimmings. 'Take some veg, Aimee,' Mike tells her.

'I have,' she says. 'Potato.'

'Don't be smart. Take some carrots.'

She frowns. She's not used to Mike telling her off. It's usually me. She walks back to the table, clomping her feet like a herd of pet elephants. Odd. Other than the stroppy attitude, she really does seem fine now, which makes me wonder if this unwell business was some sort of ruse. But then why would she? I watch her tucking into her meat. Definitely a good appetite for somebody who just had us all so worried!

'So you're getting an early train tomorrow then?' Mike asks, just as I am thinking of something Jacqui said: that I'm lucky that Mike and I have managed to remain friends. But have we really? Aimee is the glue that still sticks us together. If we didn't have her, where would that leave us?

'I rebooked myself on to the seven forty-five.'

'Get you there in time, will it?' he says.

I spear a carrot. 'Should do.'

When I glance up at him he is staring at me quizzically and adds, 'For your conference.'

When Aimee finishes off her meal she says, 'Can I order sticky toffee pudding with both the ice cream and the clotted cream on it?'

I narrow my eyes at her. Hm . . . 'I don't know,' I say. 'What if it makes you feel poorly again?'

She shakes her head quickly. 'I don't think it will. I think it'll help. And after that can we maybe go home and rent a movie?'

'Sure,' I say, given I'm not in the mood for doing much else.

'With Dad?' she asks, looking from me to him.

I'm about to protest when Mike says, 'Sorry, love. Can't. I'm working tonight.' Then he sends me a look I can't quite read.

TWENTY-THREE

Patrick is on the platform waiting for me.

I catch sight of him as the train rolls past him, sliding to a stop. The thick, well-cut dark-blond hair. Even a casual olive-coloured jacket, similar to the one I remember him wearing all those years ago. I try to keep my eyes on him as long as possible. Patrick, in the flesh. After all these years. I am woozy with nerves. So sick with anticipation that I have to silently talk myself down from a pleasurable panic attack.

I join the tight trail of bodies waiting to get off. Stepping on to the platform there is a moment where I see him before he sees me, where I get to just consciously observe him, banking every beat of it. His face scouring all the people that pour from the train doors. And then he spots me. Suddenly he is smiling and holding up his hand in a wave, and I just know . . . I am rooted to the spot, the idea that this really is him on a slow burn inside of me. Then he is cutting an urgent path through the crowd. He is beaming, his eyes seeking to maintain contact with mine, as a sea of people bobs in-between us.

Then he is right here. I cup my mouth with a hand. He laughs a little. And then his arms go around me. He hugs me tightly for a crazy long time, as the crowd parts around us. We rock gently on our feet, and I can't get over this feeling – of fitting, of belonging with him, of a click of something between us, an instant falling into place of all the pieces. And I feel like bursting into tears – at the shock, yes; but also at something far more indelible and tragic than shock. At the loss of his boyishness, my youth, and all the years I could have had to love him that I never had. 'You're really here!' I say, in disbelief. Definitely older than the last time we came face to face in person. But just as handsome.

'Yes,' he says, as though he disbelieves it too. He looks deeply into my eyes, cups my face in his hands, briefly, as though he's about to kiss me, but just goes on gazing at me.

So here we are on the King's Cross platform, as people move around us, looking at us: a real-life black-and-white Marc Trautmann photograph. The ticket man leans out of the train door and whistles, overtopping an announcement of a train arrival.

I have to laugh. Because, really, I don't know what I was expecting . . . Us being stiff with one another; me feeling out of my depth. Anything, but not this easiness, this falling away of all the years between then and now. He takes my small suitcase from me. 'Come on, let's get out of here, to eat, or get a drink or something. All right?' He puts an arm around my shoulders and pulls me in to him. 'I can't believe I'm touching you,' he says.

I am struck again by his face – that oddly charming nose, and how dark his eyes are against the fairness of his skin, and how attractive a contrast I find it. Just like all those years ago, I have that same sense of wanting to digest every physical detail of him.

And it seems to go both ways; he can hardly take his eyes off me as we walk. 'This is amazing, you know,' he says, 'amazing.' And when he smiles, the years fall away once more, and he looks so young again. Into the soft April sunshine we go, and Patrick directs us to the taxi line, his hand moving to my waist, where I feel the urgent press of his fingers. 'I think we should go back to the hotel. You drop off your bag, and then we decide what we want to do. How does that sound? I managed to get us adjoining rooms.'

I had given lots of thought to the sleeping arrangements. In the end, realising I didn't quite know how to ask him about them, I decided to just trust him and go with his flow. But I'm pleased he didn't automatically assume we were sharing a bed.

Patrick is staying at the Cadogan Hotel.

'No!' I say, when he tells the taxi driver where to take us. 'Good heavens!'

'What?'

I tell him I was in London two and a half years ago and I thought I saw him coming out of this very hotel. 'We were here for our tenth anniversary. It was in the September.'

'September '14?' he says. Then after a moment, 'I was in London then. Obama had just authorised air strikes against ISIS in Syria. I'd been over there reporting on it. Then on my way back they wanted me to kick around to report on the Scottish referendum. That was . . . the eighteenth I think.'

'My anniversary was the thirteenth. It was a Saturday. We'd just got off a bus. You were coming out of the hotel. You flagged a taxi.' I am almost breathless with suspense, almost as though I am reliving it again.

'Yes. It would have been then, for sure. I stayed at the Cadogan.'

'So it *was* you!' My heart pounds. 'I was so frustrated because I thought it was, then I thought it couldn't have been . . . what were the chances? This sort of thing just doesn't happen.'

I am momentarily speechless as the taxi shuttles down a series of backstreets, and I think of how I ran after his cab that day. 'Patrick, I phoned the hotel! They said they had no guest with your name.'

'We rarely travel under our own names. For security reasons.' He looks as confounded as I feel. 'So you got off a bus with your husband, in the middle of London, and you saw me, of all people, get into a taxi . . .'

I can't tell him how I belted after him. How, if I hadn't seen him, maybe I wouldn't even be divorced now. I think Mike could handle knowing that he was always surer about me than I was about him. He coped with overhearing a conversation between me and Jacqui where I declared the true state of my feelings for him, with finding an old letter that I'd hung on to. But what woman runs after a man she knew for four days a lifetime ago when she's in the middle of a street with her husband? On their tenth anniversary, of all things? Only one who clearly has never let go and probably never will.

'If only I'd seen you,' Patrick says, with an element of sadness and wonderment.

I try to imagine what that would have been like, as I have done probably about a hundred times.

After we reach our destination and I check in and put my overnight case into my room, he suggests we have brunch at a bistro in the neighbourhood. It's a nice afternoon. The streets are a-bustle. People reading newspapers outside cafés; a model-like young woman climbing into a black taxi with her fluffy white dog; a navy-blue Bentley inching out of an ivy-walled, cobbled drive. A gentle thrum of traffic and a red bus marked 'South Kensington' moving past us in the watery yellow sunshine. Patrick's fingers lace through mine.

'You know, a few years ago I got the chance to work for CNN's London bureau,' he says, looking momentarily nostalgic. 'I regret not taking it, in a way. I've always loved big cities. Especially this one.'

'Why didn't you?' I ask, curious to know if he would have even thought of me in the decision process.

'Some internal politics issues. I was currently pretty happy where I was . . .'

And that is where reality and the dream are so different. In the dream, he'd have moved to London just because it would have brought him nearer to me. And he'd have moved heaven and earth to find me once he got there. And yet in real life people don't do these things. We wreak havoc in the name of love, but it's mostly only in our hearts.

We decide on the restaurant on the corner. A French place. Wooden tables and seats. Prints of the Folies Bergère on its two longest walls. We gravitate to a window table, scan a menu, and I order a croque monsieur with frites and Patrick orders steak and eggs. While he takes a phone call, I secretly observe him. I find I can let my eyes settle in a space five or so degrees to the left of him, then have them slide to the right, circling him as though in some bizarre animal-kingdom mating dance, all the while unable to fathom that he's sitting right here. With me.

'When did you leave Asia?' I ask him when he's done and we've settled into two glasses of white wine.

'In 2003. I was pulled out of Hong Kong to go cover the Iraq War. I was based in Baghdad for a very long time. Moved around the Middle East for ten years.'

'And your marriage?' I ask, feeling brave.

He meets my eyes. 'Over before I left Hong Kong.'

So Patrick split up with his wife very soon after we met – just like he said he was going to do. And yet he waited two years before he sent me that letter.

'And you never remarried?' Now that we have opened a door into personal territory, I feel safe venturing in.

His expression falters slightly. 'Not with my lifestyle. Divorce is like a tropical disease among foreign correspondents.'

'But hasn't that been lonely?'

He glances out of the window. 'I've had relationships. Mostly casual. A couple of them long-standing. The job is your life. I was never lonely. I just don't think I'm that guy. But I was aware, at the same time, what I'd missed out on.'

He holds my eyes and there's an expression in his that makes me wonder if he's trying to say he missed out on me.

'What happened to her? To Anya?' I always remembered her name because it sounded so glamorous and I imagined she was too. I held this lasting image of her: a ravaged beauty with raven hair, in a red dress, getting wasted in the bar of the Shangri-La.

The food comes out quickly, but we practically ignore it. 'She moved back to Toronto. She married her psychiatrist, of all people. I believe they've a family now.'

'Does she work in journalism?'

'God, no. I don't think she ever really did. But I'm not in touch with her. Haven't been in years.'

We sit through a few beats of silence and I'm conscious of trying to suppress a sudden surge of emotion. 'Your letter came one week before I was due to marry Mike.' My brows knit with tension bordering on pain.

I feel him stare at me while I gaze at my food.

'You can't imagine what that did. The maelstrom of emotions. The dilemma that caused.' Even saying it is upsetting.

'I'm sorry,' he says. 'I debated whether or not to send it.'

'I still have it.' I keep my eyes down because I can feel the tears forming.

After a long silence, where I sense it's hard for him to speak, he says, 'Even though it was the right thing to do, I still took my marriage breaking up hard. Failure is a big deal for me. Looking back, I see I should have had more sympathy for her but instead I was busy forging ahead with my career. I didn't really have the patience for it . . . After that, there was a part of me that thought I might just not be cut out to be married. Especially not with my career. It's a lot to expect of someone, to just tag along while you go off and pursue your ambition and dreams . . .'

'Well, I can see how it would have affected you. It's not easy to leave a person you've made a promise to be with until you die . . . I know that now. I didn't really know that when I was twenty-one.'

'Well, we're both older and wiser now.' He twiddles the stem of his wineglass. 'I shouldn't have waited two years. That was a huge mistake. I don't know why I did.' He looks frustrated and rather sorrowful.

'Like you said, you weren't ready to rush into something else.' I understand, and yet I don't understand. We could have taken it slowly. I don't know how, exactly, but somehow!

'If you'd replied, God knows what I'd have done – maybe I subconsciously knew I needed that test. But I suppose we'll never know . . .'

I nod slowly, contemplating the concept of a test. Me being it. Patrick surprising himself with a shift in priorities, or confirming to himself what he already knew. And us both finding out at the expense of Mike. Mike, who, in a way, never fully had me and lost whatever of me that he did have.

Now we're on the topic I have to say what's troubled me for a long time. 'You know, the thing was, there really wasn't any call to action in the letter . . . I mean, you sent me your article that the editor said had too much of you in it – but you didn't write anything to go along with it. If you'd asked any questions, told me anything about your current situation – anything that was designed to open a door, that might indicate we weren't over in your mind – but there was nothing.' I shrug.

'I think my return address was on there,' he says. And he's right. It was. 'But I know what you mean.' He sighs, frustrated. 'I wasn't exactly encouraging . . . I can't really explain what I was intending . . .' He smiles, benignly, and I can tell that it's as hard for him to exhume this as it is for me. 'Can we change the subject?' he asks, with a slight plea.

We eat, converting to safer topics like Aimee and the events of yesterday, my dad, my life in the interim years. And the more we talk, and the more we discover how easy it is, the last time we met could have been just yesterday, not fifteen years ago. My mind is only one small skip from this sense of having been cheated out of a future with him. Paths taken and those not. Why are the 'not's so hard to live with?

'I wouldn't mind some fresh air,' I tell him.

He pays the bill and we leave. He takes hold of my hand as we walk down the high street and it reminds me so much of how he took my hand that first day in Vietnam that I inwardly smile. Our conversation bobs around, yet all roads somehow wander back to the same point. I sense that, at the heart of him, it's important he feels I understand this. 'You know, even just seeing you like this – if nothing else happens between us, just exactly what we're doing now – this is something I would never trade for the world.' He squeezes my hand. 'I made mistakes, and I wish I could undo so much of what I've done in my life, but I just want you to know that if you'd been forgettable I'd have forgotten you. If I wasn't still curious about you, I wouldn't have found myself re-routing here with hardly a minute's thought put into the decision, just for the chance to see you again.'

A flock of birds flap their wings in my stomach. 'Re-routing?'

'I usually fly direct – Toronto to Cairo. I had to shuffle some plans around, make some sneaky changes.'

'I thought it was all part of business!'

He slides me a playful glance. 'For me, there's only this business.'

It's on an out-of-the-way bench in Kensington Palace Gardens, a couple of hours later, that he kisses me. Patrick's kiss, exactly like all those years ago, like a homecoming. Patrick's skin, softer with age, as my fingers touch his cheek. Our hearts are hammering when we eventually pull apart.

'You married so quickly,' he says, and it startles me how he brings this up out of the blue. 'Two years . . . I mean . . . Damn.' He shakes his head in dismay. 'Why did you have to marry so quickly?'

I have a sense he is back to thinking about that letter.

I can tell it's not really anything he expects an answer to. But I want to answer it. For Mike's sake. 'I met someone good. Someone who adored me. I was hurt – badly – and with Mike I knew I never would be again. And I loved him. It was different, but fortunately I had the good sense to see that people like Mike don't come around every day.'

He says nothing because so much between us now feels already understood.

Instead, he kisses me again. It's like an auto-thing. An instinct. I can't look at him without wanting to kiss him. I had warned myself to take this slowly. There may or may not be a kiss, I'd thought. Anything more might be too much at this stage – if this even is a stage. I certainly wasn't going to be an old flame he'd helicoptered in between terminal changes at Heathrow. But right now when he says, 'Do you want to go back to the hotel?' there really is only one answer.

I set my bag down on a chair, in a dimly lit room that feels more soundless than quiet, and tug off his jacket. We don't speak as our faces move together, eyes locked until we can look at one another no more.

I am aware of the flourish of his jacket falling to the floor. Of feet scuffing along a carpet to a bed, two bodies landing as one. The unusual sensation of someone heavier than Mike on top of me. He is taller, broader, different altogether than Mike. The whiff of unfamiliar deodorant as he quickly peels off his T-shirt with a static crackle. My hands slide up the sides of his body where I used to be able to walk my fingers along his ribs. The soft padding on top of the muscle. My nose in his hair. The scent of his shampoo as he lowers his head to blaze kisses down my neck.

Familiarising myself with Patrick's body after all these years is like going away on holiday and sleeping in a strange bed. That first night of finding out how a new pillow fits, a new duvet settles around you. The texture of new sheets, a fabric softener you're not used to. The sad realisation somewhere that you're more comfortable in this bed than you ever were in yours at home.

Patrick's eyes lock into mine as he slides his hands down the back of my jeans, lifting my bottom. His nose up and down my neck, stopping in places, absorbing the smell and feel and taste of me. I am his strange bed.

I tug at his belt as he reaches for the button of my jeans. Then I'm lifting my bottom again for him, as he struggles to get them off, my little white knickers coming down with the effort. The sexy peel-down of clothes against skin. All this frustrated by the fact that he now has to contend with the fiddly buckles of my sandals. A small laugh from me, while he pulls at shoes, brushing his lips along the insides of my knees and looking up at the view of my crotch. 'Success,' he says, flinging the shoes behind him; one of them bounces off a piece of furniture. I tug at his jeans. Then he takes the soles of my feet in the palms of his hands, as though his hands are stirrups, clam-shelling my legs, opening them to put himself in them, then closing them around his back.

I have missed how we work.

The tears run down my cheeks as he enters me. He kisses them away. I don't have to tell him why they're there. I remember how occasionally I would be emotional as Mike made love to me, but for different reasons: because I couldn't force myself to feel what I wanted to feel. And that felt like I was cheating both of us. As I clasp on to Patrick, and more tears run down, he dries them up, dotting me with kisses.

We are quick. He groans when he comes, then he groans when I do, staying inside me, his fingers paused now between my legs, where he has been touching me, to make it happen for me, just like he remembers how.

Our hearts hammer again as we pant there for a while. I wonder what I've felt like to him. I move my hands to the top of his head, clasping it between them, his nose pressed into my forehead, thinking I hope he likes the woman over the girl.

I read a study about the elusive thing of physical attraction. Somewhere in our early lives we are supposed to imprint in our minds our idea of the perfect face for us. We don't realise we've done it, or even remember what it was that influenced our preference, but when we see it again later, we know. I thought it a very lovely idea.

I am kissing the perfect face.

TWENTY-FOUR

'Well, there's definitely no doubt about the chemistry still being there,' he says, with his familiar cheeky humour. He props himself up on an elbow to look down at my face on the pillow.

His handsomeness, even after sex with him, is still almost mesmerising to me. 'Ah-ha! You'd had your doubts then!'

'No.' He grins. 'I thought you might have.'

'Actually, I thought we were going to be an utter lost cause.'

He tugs on my hair, as though laughing at my silly joke is secondary to just staring at me. He lifts strands of it, pulls it through his fingers; even this is déjà vu. This is fifteen years ago. 'You were always wise. And impulsive. And believed everything was possible. It was quite the magnetic combination.'

'Well, we're certainly repeating the impulsive part!' I stare at the ceiling, feeling rag-doll loose in my limbs. 'My intention wasn't to hop into bed. I thought we'd be better served by getting to know each other a little more first.'

He kisses my shoulder. 'That was us getting to know each other.'

I run a finger down his nose. The nose I loved: long and fine-boned, with quite the pronounced bridge that gives his face a certain appealing, aristocratic imperfection. 'Had a feeling you'd say that.'

'So tell me about this crazy job of yours,' he says, later. The same serious expression that I remember. The intense dark eyes – if you were going to search him for flaws – just a fraction too close together, but perhaps noticeable only to someone who was a student of facial bio-metrics. He gazes at me as though he's getting a fix from my face. Then his uber-intense expression launches into a smile, and an unforgotten longing fills me.

'I don't know why men always think what I do for a living is funny.'

'I don't think it's funny. The journalist in me just wonders how you made the leap from meeting me in the famously romantic Love Market, and having a short, albeit very intense relationship, to going home and deciding to enter the matchmaking business. I mean, it would make more sense if ours had been a story with a better ending.'

My eyes can't stop consuming him. There is still something about this that feels like it can't be happening. 'It really didn't have anything to do with meeting you. And I didn't decide anything. It was just a fluke.'

I tell him about the trajectory. About some of my clients, which makes him laugh.

'It must seem unbelievably superficial, given what you do for a living.'

'Yes,' he says, shocking me, and I laugh.

'Oh well, at least you're honest.'

'No. I'm joking. I don't think it's superficial at all. Being respon-sible for somebody's happiness and the biggest personal decision they will make in their lives is hardly something to be taken lightly.' I feel the scrutiny of his gaze on my skin, gently awakening nerve endings. 'I think I'd rather have my job than yours. Any day.'

I reach up and kiss him.

'Do you want to go out for a walk?' he asks.

'No,' I say. 'Why would I want to go for a walk?'

We make love again. When I get up and go to the toilet I stare at my flushed face in the mirror and try, pointlessly, to make some order out of my hair. Then, when I come back to the bedroom, he has pulled on his T-shirt and is propped up with a pillow, tinkering with his phone. 'Just got to answer some emails,' he mutters, without looking up.

I stand still in the doorway watching him while he busies on. And all I can think is this: I could have been married to him all these years. This could have been our life. We could have been on holiday and this could be the most natural thing in the world, me coming out of the bathroom and him lying here, tinkering with his phone, on our bed.

When we do eventually go out for a walk, through some quiet public gardens, my mobile rings. 'Ah!' I say to Patrick. 'Kim. World's nuttiest client.' I had sent her on a date with Ralph Caswell, a fifty-one-year-old divorced dentist. This must be the State of the Nation report. If I don't pick up, she'll ring back until I do. I know it's a bit naughty but I click her on to speakerphone. And, true to form . . .

'Everything was going fine, until he came back from the toilet!'

I glance at Patrick's wide eyes.

'It wasn't until he'd sat down again and put his napkin back on his knee that I saw it. It was suspended there between his nose hairs like an anaemic spider in a web. It actually glistened, like a bead of dew.'

I beam a smile at him.

'It was moving in and out with his breathing. Like it had a mind and a central nervous system. I spent the entire meal riveted to it, waiting for the moment when it was going to fall into his food.'

Patrick hides his face in his hands in mock exasperation.

'Kim,' I say, when she's done, taking her off speakerphone. 'Look, I'm in London right now. On business. How about we sit down when I get back and we have a glass of wine and a proper chat?'

'About my refund?'

'If you like. Or just about how things are going in general.'

'They're not going very well, are they? I'd rather talk about my refund.'

'I realise that. And I promise that if, after we've chatted, you still want a refund, I'll give it to you.'

'Can I have that in writing?' she says.

Patrick nods furiously.

We hang up. 'I think I'd rather have your job too,' I say.

TWENTY-FIVE

It's our first morning and already our last.

I am powerfully aware that because of Aimee being unwell I was robbed of a day, which is all the more precious when you have only two. Patrick has to be on the late-afternoon flight to Cairo. I have already told him that I don't want to do awkward goodbyes or have to watch him leave with his suitcase. It's too reminiscent of the last time we met, and I just don't want to relive that. We agree we will say goodbye in public and each return separately to the hotel to collect our luggage.

We wander down Queen's Gate, ducking into Hyde Park and following the path all the way to High Street Kensington, where we have coffee and eggs Benedict at Caffè Concerto.

'They've offered me a job in Toronto, anchoring the nightly news,' he says. 'They've given me six weeks to decide if I'm signing the contract.'

'Wow.' I want to sound happy for him. 'That sounds very glamorous indeed. You're going to be on the TV every day? The face of the news?'

'That's the general plan.'

He sounds unenthused. I scrutinise his broad shoulders in his pale-mauve shirt, his lovely, lightly tanned hands. 'What's to decide? Don't you want it?'

He gives a friendly nod to the waiter, who scoops our plates away. 'I should. Since I pulled out of the Middle East I've been kind of spinning my wheels, doing a bit of lecturing at college, trying to get the book started, waiting for assignments but not getting the same fulfilment from the work anymore. I spent years in one of the deadliest spots in the world for the foreign press; so, if I'm going to leave all that behind me mentally, this couldn't be a better opportunity. The network wants someone who can interview and ask all the tough questions. They think I'm it.'

'That's fantastic.' I stare at his hands again, slightly mesmerised by them. Hands that won't touch me intimately again, given that we've checked out of our hotel and he's leaving so soon. Will they touch me again, ever? 'I mean . . . Isn't it?'

'Maybe. But I'm not sure I know how to be on the other side. My entire career has been standing there in the hotspots of conflict. I've spent my life reporting breaking news and trying to find a way to add the context, thriving on the pure adrenalin of it. I've been part of a team of people, Celine – reporters, TV crews, photographers, not just those from the AP but from bureaux all over the world, back in the heyday, before the bureaux started falling like dominos. These people's idea of relaxing is jamming into a high-risk bar in Baghdad to talk shop, debrief, bounce around ideas that might help us all broaden our understanding of the complex stories we're immersed in. This has been my life. I don't know how to have a home, in a city, how to go into an office, sit in a chair and speak into a camera day after day after day. Even though, yes, they'd be paying me three times my current salary to do it. And I'm probably going to live to see my old age.'

'But surely your life's more important than some adrenalin rush?'

'Try telling an alcoholic that his liver is more important than his vodka.' He smiles distantly, bringing his eyes back to mine. He pays the bill and we leave.

As we're walking through the park, taking a moment to stand at Round Pond and admire some swans in graceful sleep, he says, rather urgently, 'Tell me about Mike.' His thumb briefly rubs the palm of my hand. 'I wanted to ask you earlier . . . I know you've told me some things, but, I guess . . . I'm sorry; maybe it's wrong for me to ask.'

I think for a while, staring across the pond into the trees, conscious of the sun warming my face, the feeling of his fingers around my hand. 'Mike's a great guy. He hasn't got a bad side. He's a great father, a good provider, and he was a good husband.' I stare at the pebbles and splotches of bird droppings on the ground immediately ahead. 'And he deserved to be married to someone who had no doubts.'

I look at him now and we hold eyes. I can't voice the words *I wasn't in love with him*. It seems an unnecessary detail and an unkind betrayal.

He puts his arm around me and pulls me in to him. 'You and I wouldn't have had doubts. If I'd been able to marry you back then.'

'We have the benefit of not knowing.' I tuck into him.

We watch some dogs playing off-lead, one of them friskily trampling over ornamental flowerbeds, and the couples out walking, enjoying their park on this beautiful London morning. And we gaze at one another with longing and indulgence. The way two people do who are quite enthralled with each other and have no one they have to hide it from.

'What are we going to do?' he asks me. It's like déjà vu again.

'I honestly don't know.' I have been waiting for this. I've just had a moment where I caught myself being aware that I'm too happy. Always a bad sign. 'A part of me always believed that if I ever did meet you again you could never live up to my fantasies. So this is all rather shocking, that you actually are living up to them.'

He drags me out of the path of a family of geese who seem to be on a mission to peck my feet and sweeps me into a kiss.

'What we need is some perspective on this,' he says, a moment or two later, looking flushed. 'A reality check. The fact is, neither of us is married. So theoretically, anything is possible. You live in the north-east of England, and I live, for now anyway, in Toronto. Admittedly, a small but fixable problem.'

'Fixable how?'

'I haven't got to that part yet. I'm at the perspective stage, not the clarity stage. But what I always find is you never have one without the other, so I'm just waiting for the solution to hit me.'

Like he was back in that cabin all those years ago.

'What I think is going to happen is, you're going to go home to your beautiful Canada, accept your fabulous job and become an overnight sex symbol for the entire female Canadian population. And I—'

I can't say the words *I'll never see you again.* 'We'll email, keep in touch, see each other when you pass through London . . .'

'No,' he says, stopping on sun-dappled ground under the canopy of a huge plane tree. He faces me, gripping me by the shoulders. 'I don't want that.'

'Hang on; I haven't finished. I was going to add "until it gradually fizzles out".'

'It's not going to fizzle out.' He pulls me in to him swiftly as he leans back against the tree and I rest my face on his chest, hearing the quickening of his heart. 'Years ago I made the decision I made because I felt I was in an impossible situation. But, really, looking back, it wasn't that impossible. I should have fought harder to find a way to keep what we had. Instead of my mind being so full of what I couldn't do, it should have been full of what I *could*.' He rests his chin on the top of my head. 'I'm not sure what I can promise you right this very second – because, as I said, I don't have an instant solution – but I can tell you that occasionally getting together while we're both living different lives doesn't feel like it can possibly be enough now.' We both look up at the same time, eyes meeting in complete seriousness. 'It's either all or nothing,' he says, and drops a kiss on me. 'And I think we have to find a way to make it all.'

TWENTY-SIX

'It was fantastic,' I tell Jacqui over drinks. 'The mature Patrick is a fantastic thing . . . The years have definitely given him so much more than they've taken.'

Her eyes brim with tears, which makes me love her even more than I already do, if that's possible. My face bursts into a smile. 'Look at you!'

'Sorry,' she says. 'It's the love affair of the century.'

'Well, the century is still young; and really, it's got more going against it than for it, I feel. Because I've been hurt in the past I have to be very level-headed where Patrick is concerned. I can't go on wanting what's not gettable. I can't do it anymore.'

'Well, don't write him off just yet.' Jacqui hates anyone touting hard reality. 'Those were some pretty strong words he said about how he feels.'

I don't really want to say any more on this, in case I'm jinxing it. 'We'll see,' I add, noncommittally. And then, 'How are things with Christian?'

'Same,' she brightens. 'Crazy flirting. But he's not really an initiative-taker, I notice. I'm thinking if he's not going to be the one to step it up then maybe I should.'

'No, don't do that! He knows you're interested. And while this is all great, have you given any more thought to what you're going to do about, you know, that other man in your life – Rich?'

She gives me that look that says, *Do we have to go there?*

As I'm walking home I check emails. The first is from Kim.

I'm assuming you're back now . . .

God, woman!

The next is from Sandra Mansell, my quiet-spoken spa-owner client, whose photo my father had a thing for.

Dear Celine,

Had a lovely time last night. Although it was NOT what I expected! Your father is an extremely adorable, charismatic man, and SO interesting! If only he were forty years younger! Please thank him again for a lovely evening. I was very flattered.

Sandra

Father? Evening? Flattered?

I ring my father.

'Hey,' he starts singing, 'did I happen to meet the most beautiful girl in the world? And if I did, was she called Sandra? Sandra . . .'

'Anthony!' I growl. 'What on earth is going on? How did you end up spending the evening with one of my clients?'

'Just dinner. Not the entire evening. Though it wasn't through lack of trying.'

'You took Sandra to dinner?' I have to sit down but there's nowhere to sit.

'Well, she didn't exactly go out with *me*. She went out with a six-foot-tall, thirty-eight-year-old paediatrician from Jesmond who wants children, loves foreign holidays, country walks, Nebbiolo and Michelin-star dining.'

It takes a moment for the penny to drop. 'Hang on, you set this up? Pretended you were one of my clients? You posed as a doctor?' I'm so stunned I think I must be still asleep and having a nightmare. 'But how?'

'Well, I didn't exactly set it up. It was your trusty assistant, Freddy, who phoned her and told her about the date.'

'Who's Freddy?'

'Nice fellow. A little long in the tooth to still be in the workforce. But he's got a nose for a match made in heaven.'

'Wait, you're saying that *you* posed as the assistant I don't have, and then you set yourself up with a client?'

'And she's thinking of sitting for me. I told her that the planes of her face make her the ideal model.'

'Oh, God help me!' I hold on to my head like it's about to blow off. I bet he wasn't looking at her face. 'I don't believe this. How many others have you done this with, Dad?'

'None,' he says, disdainfully. 'But now you're giving me ideas.'

When I hang up, I fly off an email to Sandra.

I am so sorry! I am so embarrassed! I can't believe he'd do something like that! I don't even know how he got your contact information!!! This is terrible! Please accept my apology!!

Then I reread it, delete all the exclamation marks, and send.

Two minutes later she types back:

> Had a wonderful time with him!!! No need at all to
> be embarrassed! As I said, he was utterly charming,
> and knowing someone would go to those lengths
> to meet me really gives me hope!

Well, I suppose that's one way of looking at it.

TWENTY-SEVEN

Patrick phones every night before I go to bed and we talk for about an hour, sometimes two. I'd be lying if I said I don't wake up looking forward to this, and that it's hard to focus on work at times. But focus I must. I email Trish to make sure she's going to show up for her coffee date with Liam Docherty, the ex-footballer. Then I receive this from James Halton Daly.

> Know that Rome wasn't built in a day, but am fossilising waiting for the list of lovelies you are setting me up with . . .

All communication with James makes me sit here and smile. But he's right: I am dragging my heels a little. I'm not sure why. I pull up his digital photo again and stare at it, thinking of our amusing conversation, his terrific sense of fun and humour . . .

I could set him up with Petra, who owns a hair salon in Newcastle and is very attractive in a high-maintenance way. Perhaps too much so? There's Elaine Thompson, who runs a travel agency. She's worldly, interesting, but five years older than James. Not brilliant if he does secretly want kids. I have a bunch of others who just wouldn't be on his intellectual level. I could see him getting really turned off by Lorraine McNaughty's lack of self-confidence and by Julia Forrest's talkativeness. Diane Bookington isn't a bad one. I reread her profile, and the notes I made on her. She works in marketing for the Northern Sinfonia, is certainly attractive, well educated, dignified . . . I stare at her photo now, and then go back to James's. They'd certainly look fine together. I can't think of a reason *not* to match them. Well, only one that keeps floating around in my head . . .

Thursday is a powerhouse day. It starts with Aimee stomping around the kitchen in the new cork-heeled shoes her dad bought for her, grunting incoherent replies when I tell her she's going to be late for school. I frantically check stuff off the to-do list so I can clear time for Patrick, as we've agreed to speak earlier because he's flying again tomorrow morning and has a lot to do.

I also ring Kim on the off-chance that she'll meet me for lunch. So we do. She orders a Pinot Grigio spritzer and sinks it quickly.

'I just don't think I can do it. I've spent the best years of my life trying to meet someone and it just never works out. I'm so tired of getting my hopes up, only to repeat the same disappointments.'

The waitress comes to take our order. Kim petulantly says she wants 'nothing' and then calls her back and changes that to a chicken salad. The salad arrives; she comments that it's swimming in dressing. She sends it back and knocks off a second spritzer while I tuck into my lamb burger. 'Kim, there are things we can't control and things we can. You should try to remember that of all the matches I've sent you, not one of them didn't like you. It was you who didn't like them.'

Her cheeks turn the same shade as the fiery under-tip of her nose. 'What was there to like? If I'm paying for a professional service, I should be able to meet better men than I would find walking down the street.'

Just what they all think! When Kim signed on with me, she came up with a wish list of what she wanted. Right down to her completely shameless declaration that he should have 'a tanned complexion but not be a foreigner', had to be six feet or more, with 'bulging biceps but not steroid-type ones', have all his hair, and have no hard skin on his feet. On top of that he had to earn more than £80,000 a year. I had four people who matched her ideals – although, admittedly, I took a gamble on their feet. I introduced her to all of them and she still found stuff wrong with them.

'I think I know what the problem is,' I tell her.

She tries to drain her glass even though it's empty, and says a sceptical, 'Oh?'

'I think it's possible that, deep down, you don't want to meet someone.'

She doesn't instantly jump to contradict me, so I press on. 'You know, all through my teens I had acne. I bought every kind of cream with no success. When it finally cleared up of its own accord, you'd think I'd have been overjoyed. But I actually missed it. I missed not having something to be constantly trying to get rid of.'

She scowls. 'How is this relevant to me?'

'Well, you've got into such a habit of trying to meet someone and it not working, that you'd actually be a bit lost if you met someone and it worked. You've made unsuccessful dating a habit, and in your own way, you're happy with that.'

She does a small, shocked laugh. 'Why would I be paying you, then?'

'To feed the habit.'

I watch her and she won't meet my eyes.

'There are such things as the perfect pair of shoes. Or the perfect haircut. There is no such thing as the perfect human being.'

She picks up her fork and helps herself to a couple of chips off my plate. 'I really do want to meet someone. I have some problems I'm trying to work through. With your help. Unless of course, you want to give up on me.'

'No,' I say. 'I don't give up on people. So please don't give up on me.'

Next, in my powerhouse day, I phone Mike to give him the good news. 'I have someone I think you might like to meet.'

I wonder if my decision to set him up with lovely Jennifer Platt is motivated by my own guilt about Patrick. I tell him a bit about her.

'Right,' he says. 'Okay. Well, when am I going to get to meet her?'

My usual practice is to give the woman the man's number and let her make the first contact. I used to do it the other way around because the most successful relationships tend to be the ones that maintain a degree of respect for the traditional roles for the sexes. Then I had one situation where the man wouldn't accept rejection and became a nuisance. As with most aspects of this business, I've learned through trial and error. But, after all, this is Mike. 'I'm going to make one quick call to her and then if she agrees to the date I'll email you her phone number.'

'Great,' he says. 'Can't wait. Maybe I'll see if she's free tomorrow.'

I try to ignore the *can't wait* that I feel might have been said for my benefit. Then I ring Jennifer. 'I have a very lovely man for you to meet,' I tell her.

I neglect to add that he's my ex-husband.

Imagining your ex in bed with someone else is the strangest thing. Mike and I weren't great in that department right away. It took time, love and practice. But we grew together, sexually, over the years. And I realised that sex without lust could still be lovely. I didn't have to desire Mike in the heart-slamming sense of the word to care about him, to enjoy his body, and to feel horribly empty at the thought of him not sleeping beside me at the end of each day. I told myself I'd arrived at love a whole other way; the journey was different but not 'less'. And there were times when I actually believed it.

Can I picture Mike with another woman, after so many years of being with me? Jennifer gaining the benefits of Mike's experience, both in and out of bed? Mike's love and devotion? His goodness? His steadiness? His there-ness?

No. But picturing him without someone hurts more.

TWENTY-EIGHT

'How free are you two weekends from now?' Patrick's call feels like it's coming in the middle of the night. When I squint at the clock I see it's actually almost 7 a.m. and I've come dangerously close to oversleeping.

'Free?'

'To get your ex to watch your daughter? Friday and Saturday? Possibly Sunday?'

'Well . . .' I scramble to think. 'I'd say very. Aimee stays with Mike that weekend.'

'Perfect,' he says. 'Got to rush. Check your email.'

He hangs up and I'm left sitting here on the end of the bed wondering if the call was a figment of my imagination. Nonetheless, I check my email.

As it's loading, a text comes in from Trish.

Nice-looking bloke. Shy for a footie? Problem though – I was first in line to order, and he told me that he'd buy the coffee because he'd managed to find a parking spot for free!! He's an ex-footballer!! Why would it even be on his radar that the spot came free???!!!

I type back:

Could he have been joking? Can't see him being afraid of paying a few quid to park his car!

Then again, I recall our Fake Date. When the bill came he scrutinised it and then remarked how he didn't remember either of us having ordered an orange juice.

She responds:

Oh, he DEF wasn't joking!! Extremely serious in fact! SO sad! But still don't think he's for me. Slightly intellectually challenged?

And I thought he was quite bright. For a footie.

'I'm going to Paris!' I tell Jacqui as she walks in our door right as I'm struggling into my running shoes.

'What?'

'He's sent me a ticket! He's going to be there covering the French presidential election so he thought I could join him at the hotel for two nights. He said he's going to be busy but any time we can scrape together is better than none.'

'You lucky duck,' she says. There is something in her face that says, *I wish that could be me.*

On Saturday morning Mike comes to get Aimee.

'How was the date?' I ask him, as he stands on the doorstep, refusing my offer to come in. I'm fully expecting him to say, *I haven't really had time to get around to that yet!*

But his eyes glance down the front of my Primark denim dress and he says, 'I like her. She's a very nice, genuine person, isn't she? Pretty too.'

I want to ask him if he's planning on seeing her again but he says, 'How was London?'

I frown. Why's he asking about that? 'That feels like ages ago.'

'Conference was good, then?' His eyes sweep around my face like the second hand of a clock – too much scrutiny for comfort.

'Fine, I suppose. For a conference.' I have to look away. Lies have never sat well with me; and even though I don't owe him any account of what I do, fluffing the truth still feels kinder than being completely honest. 'Oh, I wanted to ask you a favour. In a couple of weeks' time, when you're due to have Aimee again, would you mind very much if she spends the Friday at yours as well as Saturday?'

I'm waiting for him to say, *Going somewhere?* and I haven't really prepared what my response will be to that, but instead he says, 'Of course. In fact, I've got a few days off work so why doesn't she stay three nights and I'll take her to school Monday morning. You can just pick her up at the end of the day?'

'Okay,' I tell him. 'I'm fine with that if she is. Thanks.'

Aimee clonks downstairs in her new platform wedges, saving us from having to say any more. She throws her arms around her dad and smacks a kiss on him.

'Have fun,' I tell them both, and watch them walking down the garden path together. Sometimes it still feels so odd to me that we are functioning as separate units, dealing with the logistics of sleepovers and schedules, attempting to make our new definition of family work. When I close the door, I don't feel as peppy as I did before he knocked.

To make matters worse, my email pings, and when I look I see it's Jennifer.

I really like Mike! What a terrific guy! Can't wait to see him again!

Very pleased! I respond, wondering why I'm just the tiniest bit disappointed.

TWENTY-NINE

Because he has to attend a press breakfast on Friday morning, Patrick gives me his hotel's address and suggests I cab there from the airport. He's staying in Le Marais, which I only really know about through a spot of frantic googling. This is only the second time I've been to Paris. Mike doesn't like cities, so our holidays were always somewhere beachy and warm. My first time was with a school trip when I was around Aimee's age. All I remember is that it rained, we toured Versailles, I took some lovely pictures of Sacré-Cœur and ate a very runny omelette.

It's gloriously sunny and warm when my cab pulls up outside the lovely new Art Deco hotel. Patrick's room – ours, I take delight in thinking – is compact for the size of its bed, but is redeemed by high ceilings and a vast window that opens on to a walk-out balcony, with lots of light bouncing off crisp, high-thread-count linen. His small carry-on suitcase sits on a rack in the corner, a navy-blue T-shirt spilling out – I lift it carefully and have a peek at the stuff underneath: neatly folded socks, underwear, a perfectly rolled navy-and-pink-striped tie, a notepad and pen. In the agreeably large bathroom, his toiletries are laid out on the slab of white marble. I examine the pale shavings of hair on the blade of his Mach3 razor, take the lid off his deodorant and smell it, the scent of lemon and spice carrying me back to a few short weeks ago, making the small space suddenly fill with the memory of him. Just as I'm doing this, my phone rings.

'You're here!' he says.

'You'd better believe it! The room's gorgeous. I love it.'

'Man! I so wish I was there right now.'

I smile. 'How's your meeting? How's the president? Stressed?'

He laughs. 'Not sure how he's feeling but I'm feeling pretty good. I'm on my way over there now. Just going to grab a cab . . . How about we meet in Place des Vosges? Do you know it? It's just around the corner from the hotel. You can ask at the front desk if you like . . . Late lunch?' He names a restaurant. 'Best steak tartare in town.'

'Sold,' I say.

We sit outside in a patch of sunlight with a carafe of wine, his hand holding mine across the tiny table. It occurs to me that this sense of being about to burst out of myself just with the nearness of him will never grow old. And when I smile without reason, and he performs a slow take of my face, I have a feeling he knows it.

We talk about the buzz that's going on in the city this weekend. I enjoy hearing about his work, getting a picture of him other than the one I see. He tells me about the implications of the election that will take place on Sunday. When our food arrives, we're reluctant to break hands. I'm suddenly aware of two beautifully dressed French ladies walking towards us. They stop right where we're sitting and gabble something in French, and I realise they're shamelessly talking about us.

'You're famous!' I say, when they continue on.

'I doubt that very much. I think they were saying they've just seen a movie star and the lucky guy who's with her.'

'Very droll.'

The steak tartare is not quite what I was expecting. 'You hate it,' he says, when he cottons on that I'm not exactly tucking in.

'Hate's a strong word. Let's put it this way . . . I bequeath the raw beef to you.' I slide the plate in his direction.

'Some things never change,' he says and I know he's remembering the cow-intestine soup we had in Vietnam. To be kind, he gives me his basket of pommes frites with mayonnaise.

After sharing a piece of tarte Tatin with ice cream – of which he grants me the lion's share – followed by coffee, he pays the bill (having turned down my offer to get it) and suggests we walk off our food. We wander around the square, stopping to peer in shop windows, standing for a moment when we both must catch our reflections in the glass at the same time. A tall, fit, fair-headed fellow in casual pants and a shirt, and me – a good deal shorter, in an A-line denim skirt and sleeveless white blouse. There is barely a sliver of daylight between our arms. 'Hang on,' I say, untangling my fingers from his, and reaching into my bag. 'The perfect opportunity for a selfie . . .' I pull out my phone and snap our reflection. It doesn't come out very well but I still rather like it.

'I kept all the photos I took of you in Vietnam,' he says.

I grin now. 'Really? Or you could be making this up. How am I to know?'

'I'm not. I have all of them. I know exactly where they are.'

'In a shoebox at the back of the wardrobe?'

'No. In my desk drawer in a big manila envelope.'

I think he must be serious. 'You did take a lot.'

'Forty-three.'

I slap a hand over my mouth. 'You counted!'

'Have them memorised.'

I cock my head. 'This I definitely don't believe, but I love it anyway.'

I remember a few of them; I recall him shooting me to the point where I wasn't even aware he was doing it anymore. 'It's funny but no one had made me feel beautiful before you took my photo,' I tell him.

'It probably dates back to my dad refusing to paint my portrait when I was a teenager. All I knew was he was more than happy to paint every other female. I think I must have spent my young teenage years believing I had two heads.'

'What a crime,' he says, semi-seriously.

We join hands again and move on in silence and I am so powerfully aware of the light, warm grip of his fingers, the rhythm of our stride, how physically right I feel with him – how we fit in a way that can't be designed, only discovered – and the unexpected and very lovely sense of peace that brings. I love how I see other women looking him over – perhaps French ladies are a little forward this way – and how they then look at me with a certain competitive admiration. I love this sense I have of being *his*.

And yet, something is keeping me grounded. This eternal question. Can we ever be more than the sum of two glorious weekends? In theory, we can. I feel like I'm in a hurry to get to the finish line before I've even run the race. I have this unabating need to know and yet the fear of asking. 'What gave you the idea to book me a ticket?' I say, after a while, perhaps hedging around it. We emerge from the serenity of the square on to one of the bustling meandering streets of the Marais and it's a bit like cracking open champagne when you've just sunk a mellow martini.

'Come on!' The way he looks at me says, *Do you even have to ask?* 'How could I possibly be in Paris knowing you were just a leap over the water and I wasn't going to get to see you?' He stops and looks at me as though he might want to declare something bigger but is tentative.

'But it's only two days. Barely.'

'It would have been worth it if it had only been two minutes,' he says, putting his arms around me.

Before I can think any more about 'could-have-beens' or tomorrows, he dips his head and kisses me. Despite not being overly comfortable with public displays of passion, the feel of his mouth exploring mine obliterates all consciousness of time and place. 'I couldn't do that if you hadn't come here, now, could I?'

'How very true.' I smile at him. 'And what a loss that would have been.'

He moves to go but I stand here, at the end of our outstretched arms. 'What else would you not be able to do to me if I hadn't flown here?' I give him a small tug in the direction of our hotel.

'Tell me about your other relationships,' I venture, gently, on Saturday morning, as we lie there with the balcony doors open, the sounds of the street below pleasantly wafting in.

'What do you want to know?'

My ear rests against his heart.

'Who they were.'

'Well . . .' He appears to think. 'I dated a couple of journalists—'

'You have a thing for journalists.'

'Not really. I'm just surrounded by a lot of them.'

'Go on.'

He raises an arm and our palms join and we lock fingers. 'There was someone briefly from the US Embassy when I was posted in the Middle East.'

'You said a couple of them were long-standing.'

'Did I?' He sounds playful. 'Oh yes.'

'You're uncomfortable.'

'Why do you say that?'

'The scant responses. It's what men do when they don't want to talk about something.'

'I forgot you have the inside track. In your line of work . . .' His brings his arm to rest across my pelvis, my hand still in his. 'No, you're right. Two of them were quite serious. I was with Giuliana for four years. She was a lawyer in Toronto. We both kept our own places, led pretty well our own lives from Monday to Friday. She had no designs to ever be married or have kids. She was very independent, which I liked.'

'What happened?'

'Nothing really. I mean, no sort of defining event . . . I think we worked really well for a time, but then we became a bit of a lazy habit. We were probably so hell-bent on not wanting much from each other that after a while there wasn't really a strong enough reason to stay together.'

That's right, I think. People want ties. Even those who claim they don't still long for the loose lines of demarcation that tell us we must be special, might even be loved.

'Whose idea was it to split?'

He seems to think. 'Both. Maybe a bit more me, but both really . . .'

'And what about the other long-standing one?'

He laughs a little. I realise I'm grilling him. 'Robyn. She was in the movie business in LA. A set decorator. I saw her for almost three years. But it was very off and on.'

I sit up, look down at him. 'Because of the distance?'

'That was part of it.'

'You were having a long-distance relationship and it didn't work out.' *And you consider that one of your more long-standing ones.*

He places an index finger under my chin and draws it back so I have to look at his face. 'It was mainly sexual. We met, we had fun until it became too much effort. She met somebody else and married him.'

'So is that, in a way, what this is? We'll be great until we become too much effort?'

He looks at me and I'm pleased to see a note of surprise in his eyes. 'Is that what you think we are? A transatlantic fling?'

He stops me from answering by kissing me.

Patrick has to work part of the day, so I do a spot of sightseeing. Then after a lovely dinner a short cab ride away from where we're staying I pop back to the hotel to change into flat shoes and we go out and walk the streets of Paris by night. We walk forever, his hand holding mine. 'Fifteen thousand steps on my counter!' I tell him, when we come to the Seine and dangle our upper bodies over the wall to watch lights bob their golden reflection on the water. 'And those were just since dinner!'

'And if you count all the steps we've taken in bed . . .'

I smile and he reaches for me and pulls me into his arms, hugs me tightly.

By the time we get back to the hotel it feels like another deliriously long day – for both of us. I lie in the spoon of him, his chin resting in the curve where my neck meets my shoulder, his breath making rhythmic little draughts on my skin. Until I've no idea which one of us falls asleep first.

And on Sunday morning, when I'm to fly home, this is how I leave him: sleeping. As my taxi shuttles quickly through the backstreets of Paris I think back to the last time I saw him fifteen years ago when he packed his bags and I watched as he walked out of the door. That awful sight it took years to quell the memory of.

Though the circumstances are slightly different, it still feels better to be the leaver than the left.

THIRTY

The house Mike moved into a couple of months ago, after he left the flat he'd rented when we first split up, isn't much from the outside: a brick Victorian mid-terrace in West Jesmond, just a short walk from the Metro stop.

'Have you met your neighbours yet?' I ask him, nodding next door. 'What are they like?'

He pulls a face. 'A bunch of tossers really. Or, he is. Got uptight about my weeds coming through his fence. And it's not actually weeds. It's climbing wisteria. So much for what he knows about gardening.'

It takes me back to the wind chimes. Our old neighbour and Mike had a vendetta. Pat liked to hang wind chimes off his patio, which was fine until it was a windy night and you were trying to sleep. Instead of being direct and telling Pat that they were bothering us, Mike tried to subtly bring up the topic and the fact that he was a light sleeper. Still the chimes chimed on. So one day, when Pat was at work, Mike took them down. Pat thought they'd been stolen and bought new ones. Mike waited until he was out, and took those ones down too. When Pat brought up the subject of his mysteriously vanishing wind chimes, Mike admitted that he was the culprit – that Pat had failed to get all his hints about how they were bothering him. This pissed Pat off. So he bought two sets. Now the chimes chimed in clanging disharmony. Mike decided: okay, let's see how you feel about heavy-metal music at six o'clock on a Saturday morning. The nonsense only ended when he noticed Pat's 'For Sale' sign had gone up. I presume his moving had nothing to do with us – but I wouldn't like to bet money on it.

Mike has on a tight white T-shirt with his black drainpipe jeans. He looks like he might not have shaved in a day or two – like he's taking the whole 'few days off work' thing quite literally. Unlike most men, he's always at his most appealing when he's done absolutely nothing with himself. It's a look that somehow suits him.

'Aimee,' I shout past him up the stairs. She was only supposed to be popping up there to collect her overnight bag. When there's no answer, Mike says, 'Look, will you come in? There's something I want to talk to you about.'

I gaze past him down the skinny, dark passageway, into the house that I can already tell has none of the home comforts he's used to. Then I follow him inside.

'Is it about Aimee?' I ask.

He meets my eyes. 'No.'

He leads me into the living room, which is boxy and devoid of redeeming features except for a seldom-used fireplace. He's bought an uninspiring brown-leather sofa – a cheaper-looking version of the one we picked together for our place – and an oversized chair. There is a coffee table, and a brass mirror hung above the fireplace. A wilted plant sits on the sill of the curtainless bay window.

'It's Jennifer I wanted to ask you about,' he says, turning to face me. 'I've some more days off coming up . . . thought I might take a little break somewhere and wondered if I should ask her if she wants to come. Not sure if it's too soon . . . I'd like to, but I don't want to come on too strong. I'm not sure what the etiquette for these things is.'

'Oh,' I say, turning slightly tongue-tied.

'What do you think I should do?'

I notice he seems to have lost the little paunch he developed in his late thirties; he's reed thin now, like Mick Jagger.

'When is keen too keen?' he presses.

I am inexplicably exasperated. 'Well, I . . . I thought you'd only taken her out once?'

'No,' he says. 'It's been a little more than that.' He glances over the denim dress I'm wearing again.

'Well, only you know how well you're hitting it off . . .'

'Thanks,' he says, as though I've imparted vital wisdom. Then he nods at the door. 'Come on, I'll show you the rest of the place. It's not Buckingham Palace but you might as well have a look.'

In the hall he gestures for me to walk ahead of him up the stairs. I really don't want a guided tour, but it seems I've no choice. As I mount the stairs, I'm aware of him following close behind.

'This is my room,' he says, squeezing past me on the tiny landing and pushing open a door. I take one step into the room and then he edges around me so I'm hemmed in there. It's just a room with a chest of drawers and a bed in it. Only the bed is unmade. On both sides. Mike always sleeps on the left. Has Jennifer been staying over? Is this what this is all about – the questions about a holiday and the tour of his bedroom?

'Sorry it's a mess,' he says. I am again conscious of how close to each other we are standing.

'It's fine,' I tell him, feeling my face burn up. I turn around, hoping he'll move, but he continues to stand there, blocking me, our faces only inches apart. A complex energy passes between us. 'Please,' I say, wanting to shut down my mind and the picture I now have of Mike immersing himself happily between Jennifer's legs and, at the same time, wondering why it should bother me – it's more than a mite hypocritical. 'Can I get past, please?' I say.

His gaze is level with my throat. He moves barely half a foot; just enough for me to brush past him, out of the suffocating confines of his bedroom and on to the small landing again. My heart is racing.

'The bathroom,' he says, pushing open another door. Then, 'This is Aimee's room.'

It's clear he's given Aimee the best room. It has a beige-painted ceiling, slanted on both sides to make a V-shape above her bed, and a small window. The bed is a double, with a dark-green eiderdown on it and a collection of fetching patchwork pillows. Aimee sits primly on the end of it.

'What's the matter?' Mike and I both say together when we realise she's in tears.

'I don't want to go home. I don't want to stay here. I want us to be a family! I don't want two homes. I want one home with all of us in it.'

I sit on the carpet by her legs, letting my head rest beside her knee, in its holey pink leggings with the denim shorts on top. Mike stands there, watching us, like a man who is first on the scene of an accident and doesn't know what to do. Sometimes, just when I think she's finally accepted the situation, I will be blindsided by these dramatic displays of longing for our old life. I want to sit her down and repeat how we're still a family and how we have to try to move on from this, but I can't make her feel what I want her to feel because it's convenient for me: she has to get there in her own good time. I must tread so carefully because I know in years to come that Aimee will remember today, and this feeling of being split between two people. Like I remember. The anger I harboured for years at my parents – towards my dad for having to have other women, and towards my mum for not forgiving him and just getting him to come back. My wishes were born of a simple, naïve heart. I just wanted them back together again. I didn't care how, or what they had to relinquish in the process.

Seeing her like this, *I* suddenly ache for our old life back too. It would make so many things simpler. Haven't I done to my daughter the one thing I promised myself I never would: failed her as a parent, as I always felt I had been failed as a child?

'How about if she stays tonight?' Mike says.

'No! I want us all to stay!' Aimee says.

'Aimee, we can't all stay!' I want to hug her but can tell her anger is mainly directed at me. 'What about Norman, darling? We can't leave him on his own. There'll be nobody to let him out.'

'I forgot about Norman,' she says, softer now.

I reach and stroke the top of her warm little head. 'Look, I'm happy to go home and see to him, if you want to stay here with your dad. Just for tonight.'

'It's okay,' she says, after a while. 'I want to come home with you.' She glances at her dad and I follow her eyes. 'Only because we have to see to Norman,' she adds.

Mike is standing there looking rebuffed, and tries to snap out of it by giving a typical-Mike resigned shrug.

In the car she says nothing. But I am aware of her every breath, her every tiny sniffle. Her hands are locked together in her lap. She sits barely moving a muscle. At the traffic lights I look at my own eyes in the rear-view mirror and just see oceans of confusion.

THIRTY-ONE

'I've got a date for you!' I say to Trish on the phone. 'Believe it or not his name is James. And I'm not going to tell you any more, except that he's perfect for you.'

'Seriously?' She sounds excited. 'His name is James? Ha! Is he going to be able to afford to fill a parking meter?'

'Several parking meters.'

She laughs. 'Well I won't be able to go out with him for a little while. I just booked two weeks in Cyprus! I leave tomorrow!'

'Not to worry,' I say. 'I'm sure he'll be happy he waited once he meets you.'

'Speaking of James, have you been in touch with *my* James? Do you have anyone for him yet?'

'I have, yes. I think he's going to really like her but I don't want to say any more. Client confidentiality and all that.'

'Of course.' She sounds disappointed. 'Well, that's great, then! I'll look forward to hearing all about it.' She is definitely deflated. 'Anyway, why am I talking about James? Let's get back to this other James! Way more important!'

When I come back home I see the post has been. There's a large manila envelope addressed to me. I pull out a bundle of what look like 5" x 7" photographs with a piece of paper wrapped around them.

Because you didn't believe me, he has written.

Forty-three of them. Though I guessed that before I counted.

I am spellbound, staring at my younger self. He captured me there in so many wonderful moments I'd almost forgotten. Me that day when we went out in the jeep he'd hired. Me in various places we ate. Me in his cabin. Me looking at him taking the photo as though to say, *Oh not another one!* Me entirely lost in my own world. Most of them are black-and-whites, the odd few in colour. I sit on my bed and lay them all out on the duvet and it's like going back in time.

But there's one in particular I can't stop staring at. It's of me in my little wet jean jacket, and I recognise the location immediately. The café in Hanoi, that first time we met when he had been tinkering with his camera, completely ignoring me.

But clearly not.

I am sipping my egg-yolk coffee.

THIRTY-TWO

'I'm here,' he says.

'And I'm here. Sitting at my desk wading through a mountain of unpaid bills and other domestic maintenance.' I stuff the phone under my chin so I can work and talk.

'Could you take a break?'

'To FaceTime?'

'No. To come pick me up.'

'What?' I must have missed something he said. 'What do you mean?'

'I'm here. At Newcastle airport.'

I laugh. 'Terribly funny. And a bit cruel, actually!' Gosh, if only he were! 'Those pictures were astonishing, by the way. Especially one of them . . . I can't believe you sent me your whole stash.'

'Copies,' he says. 'I would never part with the original ones . . . But back to you coming to get me.'

I laugh. Then it dawns on me that he really is being serious.

And so, Patrick stands in my little oak-beamed living room, absorbing every last crack and crag on the pale-lemon walls. His eyes travel over the tall stone fireplace, over piles of magazines on the pine linen chest in front of the window, the aged green-velour cushions against the dark-brown leather sofa, the lemon and cream drapes, Aimee's shoes in the middle of the floor, an empty wineglass on an end table that I missed in my tidying up. I had expected we'd go straight to his hotel but he seemed to really want to see my home. 'Are you thinking of putting in an offer?' I ask him.

'It's beautiful.'

'It's old. It needs a lot of work.' His eyes comb over my kitchen, somewhere we did renovate when we moved in. Mike bought DIY books and learned how to put down dark-honey wood flooring, install white marble countertops and change the wall and base units to oak. I painted the walls a brighter yellow than the living room, and sewed white roman blinds for the three windows.

I put the kettle on and he seems to get lost in the view of the giant wilderness of moss green and heather that goes on endlessly beyond our back garden.

'It's like *Wuthering Heights*,' he says.

'But I don't want to live in a novel written in the 1800s. Besides, you should try being here in the heart of winter. Endless rain and fog.'

'Do you remember the mist in Vietnam?'

I smile. 'Yes. But that was beautiful.' Our gazes fuse together. 'Did you ever go back? I meant to ask you.'

He shakes his head. 'I thought about it. Maybe to make a documentary. But Sa Pa has changed a lot since we were there. The Love Market has gradually become more and more commercial – a show for tourists.' He shrugs then says. 'Who's this?' as the cat staggers in.

'Norman. He's really Mike's cat. He's old and he thought it best to leave him here for Aimee.'

He bends to pet him, and then looks up, his eyes going straight to the picture of Mike and me next to the one of me and Aimee. 'Who does Aimee look like?'

'My mother, actually. I have a portrait that my dad did of her when they first met and were very much in love. Aimee is the image of her.'

He goes on studying the picture, asking some questions about my daughter. But I wonder if it's really Aimee he's looking at, or if it's Mike. 'Does your mother live nearby?'

I tell him about how she was diagnosed with cancer and hadn't told me. How I learned she was dying just three months before she did.

'You weren't close, were you? I think I remember you telling me.'

I shake my head. 'She never seemed to have much time for me. There was always a Dad drama . . . Even when they were divorced she seemed more interested in what he was doing than in me . . .' I shrug. 'I held out hope that she might rally and be a good grandmother to Aimee. But she was living in York with her third husband when Aimee was little. It's not far away, but she rarely came to see us and never seemed to get any great joy from us visiting her.' I don't tell him that I bumped into my mother and Donald when Aimee was about three. It was in Marks & Spencer's café in Newcastle. They'd come to the city but hadn't let us know.

He ponders me. 'Your dad?'

I smile. 'Good. He's a character! He and Aimee go out painting sometimes. They go to the beach and he shows her how to capture the angle of the waves, and the change in colour and the movement of the sea. She was pleased as punch the other day. He had bought new colours for her. She kept walking around repeating their names: Prussian blue, cerulean blue and titanium white.' I smile and pour boiling water on the teabags. 'Didn't you ever want kids?' I'm glad Aimee is going to the radio station for a couple of hours tonight with Mike – to be 'an assistant to the assistant producer', as Mike called it.

He glances at her photo again. 'It wouldn't have been fair, with my life. But I never especially wanted to have a family, no. But then things happen to you that make you wonder how sure you are about what you do and don't want . . .' He pulls a chair out from under the table and sits down, and it takes me a moment to fully process the fact that he's sitting here in my kitchen. 'A few years ago we filmed a piece on an orphanage in Sarajevo – what had happened to the so-called "rape babies", kids born of women who were sexually assaulted by Serbian soldiers. These kids were largely unacknowledged by the state. We brought them candy and toys so they wouldn't be too intimidated by a bunch of guys coming in with all this equipment, which they were at first. But by the time we were ready to go, they were clinging to us and telling us they loved us. They wanted us to take them home. One of them, a little girl of about four, was calling a nine-year-old her mother.' He shakes his head. 'And here was I, doing my work and walking away. All I was really doing was broadcasting their story to sell news, to keep the network's ratings where they wanted them. I could try to convince myself that awareness is key to change, but it's not. Actions are key to change. I used to believe in what I did wholeheartedly. I used to believe my news stories could change the world . . .' He shakes his head again. 'But there was no good that I could have possibly done for that child. Even if I'd wanted to, you can't adopt them. Bosnians have very strong feelings against removing Bosnian children from their homeland.'

'You were thinking of adopting one of them?'

'The little one who was calling her sister her mother – and the older child too, of course. I couldn't get either of them out of my head for a very long time.'

He looks at me as though he's probably said way more than he intended. 'How's that tea coming?'

After I pour us our tea, I log on to my computer, and find the video blog of him in Afghanistan. He is sitting in a white vest and jeans, on his blue sleeping bag, in a tent, drinking from a paper cup, looking extremely gorgeous.

He comes and stands behind me. 'That was in Helmand province. It was somebody's idea of a good segment for the public to see what we look like when the camera isn't trained on us. People seem to think being a foreign correspondent is glamorous, yet look at us – a bunch of smelly guys shacked up together in a tent in the middle of nowhere. I'd just filed a piece on the Taliban for the ten o'clock news. I'd gotten a good interview. It was a great day. Brent in the picture there was editing it.' He points to a big-bellied, hard-lived man in a white vest on the screen. 'I was drinking cold coffee and I'd been awake all night because these guys snored so damned much . . .' He huffs a laugh.

'So that was a great day?'

'Yes. Actually it was. When you're there it all becomes about the story. It's like being in a room full of heroin addicts. All they can think of is the drug. If they're not shooting up, they're stalking around, working on where to get their next fix.'

'That's your bed you're sitting on,' I say, fascinated. 'Where you slept.'

'I told you it's not luxurious, even in civilised posts. The networks cut back; they don't have the big budgets anymore. So much of the news is reported by stringers who carry their own cameras and do it all themselves. We're the old brigade. A dying breed.' I look up at him. He rubs a hand over his mouth, stares at himself on the screen.

'You really miss it.' Now his reservations about the news-anchor job make sense.

He drags his gaze away from the screen. 'There were good times, for sure. But now so much is at stake reporting a story. As a journalist you're supposed to be a witness, an impartial observer of the conflict. But in the Middle East you don't observe it; you become part of it. Sometimes you don't know what side you're on.' His eyes have drifted to a place that only he can see. 'So what else have you got on me?' he says.

'Nothing else in my MI6 file.'

He smiles, then I can see his mind wandering off. 'You know, when we were in Paris and we were talking about the letter I sent? Well, I meant to say – to stress – how much I regretted not telling you I'd got divorced, and somehow making it clearer . . .'

'We shouldn't keep revisiting this,' I say. 'What's done is done . . . So, you know what? Let's not.'

He rests his hand on the back of my neck, runs his thumb along the bottom of my hairline. 'Yes. Our timing has been off all along.'

Hadn't I recently had the same thought?

His voice from my computer filters into the momentary silence between us, incongruously.

'Can we get rid of that?' he asks.

In his hotel room – because I'm not entirely comfortable with the idea of us being intimate in my home that was once Mike's too – Patrick makes love to me tenderly.

'Were you ever in love with Anya?' I ask, as we lie there afterwards. I'd wanted to ask this in Paris, when we were talking about the girl-friends, but it had seemed like too much. 'You must have been, once.'

He strokes my bare arm. 'At the time I believe I thought I was. I mean, I did marry her . . . I think a lot of the appeal initially was my competitive instinct. All my life I'd done well at everything – sport, exams, scholarships. She was just an extension of that for me, I think. If that makes any sense.' He kisses the top of my head. 'Aside from the fiery temper, she was perfect on paper. You'd have matched us. She was bright, passionate, beautiful . . . But I just kept feeling I'd got some-thing too easily that I hadn't wanted badly enough in the first place. And that's kind of how I'd always felt about a lot of things when I was growing up. I got things whether or not I wanted them.' He looks reflective. 'It sounds crazy now, saying that about myself. Maybe I was just a little too reckless then. Something in me was unstoppable, and yet there were times when, clearly, I should have stopped myself.' He seems to go on pondering, then adds, 'I think when you're in love with some-one, it repositions how you've felt about everybody else you've met.'

I lie there blinking, wondering exactly what he means by this.

THIRTY-THREE

This weekend is not technically Mike's turn to have Aimee, but on Friday night I phone him and ask if it's okay if she stays. He tells me he's got plans with Jennifer but if I am fine with it, maybe this would be a good time for Aimee and Jennifer to meet. This wasn't what I had in mind. Now I feel a bit caught between a rock and a hard place. If Mike doesn't take her for the weekend, I can't spend that much time with Patrick. I'm definitely not ready for Patrick to meet Aimee. Similarly, there is a part of me that doesn't want Patrick to meet anyone in my family; I'd prefer to just keep him for myself a little while longer.

Reluctantly, I tell Mike that's fine.

'Great, then,' he says, flatly, after a curious hesitation.

After spending the night with him in his hotel room, Patrick and I go for a long leisurely lunch down at Newcastle's lovely Quayside. We sit on a patio overlooking the river, dipping focaccia bread into a pool of olive oil, then sharing smoked salmon and cream-of-leek pasta and green salad. It's a warm day. Patrick appraises everything around us and then smiles at me when he sees me watching him. 'Tell me about growing up here,' he says. 'I want to know what your life was like.'

'Well that'll take all of five minutes,' I say.

Later in the afternoon we drive to Swallowship Woods for a walk. We lean over the bridge to watch the River Tyne jump and froth over the rock bed while I fill him in on some of the history of this area. He marvels at the tall redwood trees and the occasional kingfisher and speckled thrush that hop across our path.

I'm just putting the kettle on back at the house, and Patrick is in the loo, when I hear the front door. By the time I venture down our passageway, my father is walking in. I hadn't thought to lock it.

'Dad!' My face must fall. 'What are you doing here?'

'I thought I'd come and see my daughter and granddaughter.'

'Aimee's with Mike. I thought today was your life-drawing class?'

'Not anymore,' he runs a hand through his thick, snow-white hair. 'If you must know, I was asked to leave.' He pulls out a chair and plonks himself down, as though he's here to stay.

'Leave?' I watch him pull out a cloth handkerchief from the breast pocket of his jacket, blow his nose, fold the hankie, and put it back. 'Why were you asked to leave, Anthony?'

'For making the models feel uncomfortable.'

I gawp at him. 'You got kicked out of the life-drawing class?'

He sighs. 'The trouble with England is that everybody's too uptight. Women are afraid to show their sensuality, and men are afraid to be throbbing male beings. This sort of thing would never happen in France or Italy. A harmless comment about a woman's body.' He takes from his pocket the same hankie that he blew his nose in, and wipes it across his brow. 'Teesh!'

'But we're not in France or Italy!'

He throws up his hands. 'Well, what can I say? More fool us.'

I scrutinise him. 'So what did you say? To the models? To warrant being thrown out?'

'Model – singular. And it was nothing. I commented on a particular part of her anatomy, that's all.'

This is getting worse by the minute. 'Which part?'

He pulls out a piece of paper. It's a drawing of a small-breasted woman's narrow-hipped body. Between the V at the top of her legs is a wild and wiry crotch.

'It was positively forest-like. I've never seen one like it before. It almost looked like it might be inhabited. I worried that if I got too close I'd be attacked by a band of pygmies.' He smiles to himself. 'But then the idea became quite appealing.'

'Anthony!' I shove his drawing at him. 'You're leaving. Right now.'

As I'm helping him to the door, Patrick emerges from the toilet.

'Hi,' he says, and beams a smile.

THIRTY-FOUR

We have driven to the coast. It's not the best day, weather-wise, but we have managed a walk on the virtually untouched expanse of buttermilk sand that makes up a portion of the region's thirty-nine miles of coastline designated an Area of Outstanding Natural Beauty. Because Patrick seems so fascinated with local history, I have told him about Grace Darling, the girl with the windswept hair who lived in lighthouses and bravely risked her life to rescue shipwrecked men. I drive us to a place for dinner where they serve the best Holy Island mussels I've ever tasted. We get lost again in the food and the wine and our easy ability to talk about pretty much anything.

Then Patrick says, 'Hey, I've been thinking . . . How would you feel about maybe coming to Canada? I know the school holidays are still a little way off but maybe you and Aimee could come stay with me? I could show you Toronto. Then we could go to Muskoka. I have a small cabin up there on the lake. I inherited it when my dad died and it doesn't get used very often. It could probably stand a clean-up, but it's right on the water. We could go fishing, boating, have barbecues. Aimee can see wolves and moose and white-tailed deer and black bears. The real Canada. She could bring her painting supplies . . .'

'Gosh,' I say. 'I mean, it's a lovely idea . . . How long would we come for, do you think?'

'Well, a proper amount of time, not just a flying visit. Maybe a month?'

'A month!' That certainly takes things out of romantic-weekend territory. A part of me wants to jump at it, but the doubts are ticking away. 'That's a long time for a twelve-year-old to be away from home. Their attention span isn't that great . . .' It's a long time for her to not see her dad, too, but I don't voice this. When I see disappointment in his eyes I try to lighten things. 'How could you stand us for that long, anyway?' I am partly serious. It's one thing to go from a few weekends together to the entire summer, playing house with a near-teenager.

'I think it would be a good test. It'd be an adventure. For all of us.'

He has used the test word before in a similar context. I'm not sure what I make of it. 'It's a lovely idea . . . I'm not sure, to be honest. Don't know if Aimee would want that.' She can barely tolerate Mike and me being in separate houses. How do I introduce her to, of all people, my long-lost love Patrick and expect her to stay with him?

'You could ask.'

'I could.'

'Does that mean you will?'

I smile. 'Yes. When I feel the time is right. I will.'

He looks happy again.

'Let me in!' Jacqui barrels past me into the house the moment I open the door.

Patrick is sitting in the garden having a beer. I have come in to get us two more.

I follow her into my kitchen. 'What's happened?'

191

'I told Rich I needed to take a walk. He's been smothering me all weekend. I haven't had the chance to . . .' She buries her face in her hands, and growls.

'What on earth is wrong?' I haven't seen her like this before.

'I have no idea how I'm going to go back to work tomorrow!' She is nearly breathless. 'So on Friday night we had "going away" drinks in the office, you know, because Cyril is moving to the Frankfurt office . . . I had about three glasses of champagne; so did he, and the whole time, from when I walked into that boardroom, he never once took his eyes off me.'

'Cyril?'

She tuts. 'Not Cyril, for God's sake! Christian! Who else would I be talking about?'

Oh, thank God! I was horrified she was after two blokes now!

'Celine, it was so unbelievably charged. It was total hardcore flirting. Unlike anything I've ever felt before.' She shakes her head, snivels, sits down opposite me at the kitchen table. 'Anyway, I went out to the toilet at one point and he watched me walk out of the room, and I was sure he was going to follow. My heart was hammering in the loo. I was so sure he was going to walk in and something was going to happen right there . . . Anyway,' she snivels again, 'he didn't follow me in. So when I came out, I walked back into the boardroom where everyone was, and he'd disappeared!'

She wipes under her eyes, where her mascara is running. 'I got another glass of champers and went on a little walkabout. So I went down the corridor that leads to his office, and his door was open, and his little desk light was on . . . There was no one around, so I walked in.' She hides her face in her hands again and squeals. 'He was sitting at his desk. Not really doing anything. Just sitting there, like he was thinking. So he looked up. I closed his door, threw myself up against it, fixed him with my most vixen-like look, and said . . . "Come and get me."'

A tiny laugh bursts out of me. Until I realise she's serious. 'God,' I say. 'You said, "Come and get me"?' *Please, no!* I try not to react quite as horrified as I feel, for her sake. 'What did he do?'

'Well, that's the thing: he just looked at me, and said in a very firm, unamused voice, almost like he was feeling threatened, "Please open my door."'

Her eyes glass over with tears. She stares, vacantly, as though picturing it all again. 'He was looking at me as though I was some sort of contemptible person. Then he just got up and said, "Please step aside" – and he opened his door himself.' She scowls, shakes her head. 'I was mortified, Celine. I wanted to die right there.'

'"Please step aside"?' I repeat. 'Oh, what a wanker!' I knew I didn't like him.

'As soon as he'd got his door open, he seemed so relieved. Like I'd been about to attack him or something; it was so weird – so *unmanly.* Then he just stood there, sort of like the meeting was over and now it was time for me to go. He looked very, very uncomfortable, and so cold all of a sudden – pathologically cold.'

'Oh Jacq!' In all the years I've known her, my sister has never made a fool of herself over a man. I just can't picture this at all, or really make sense of why it happened. 'What did you do?'

'I didn't know what to say. So I blabbed something stupid about how all I really meant was "come and get me *another drink*". I just made it worse.'

I pull a taut smile. 'Oh.'

'It was terrible! A part of me was so ashamed, and the other part was furious that he'd embarrass me like that – even though I know, technically, it was me who was embarrassing.' She wipes away tears. 'It was the way he just stood there, as though he was so superior. I am not kidding, he was like a completely different person. Then I blabbed something about how I wasn't getting on with my boyfriend, and I was going through a hard time with my family, and a close friend had just died, and I didn't know what had come over me.'

'Who died?'

'No one. But I had to say something.' She stares at me through glassy eyes. 'I even burst into tears – about this dead person – and then he said, "Well, I'm sorry about your loss." The pompous, self-righteous prick! He sounded like he was some sort of psychologist and I was off my rocker.' Her teary brown eyes flash venom. 'So I said, "Well, er, I'd better go back to the party" – and as I walked out, he was already picking up his briefcase to go home. Just like that! So I just walked out of there, walked back to my own office, stood there dying a thousand deaths, and then I got my bag and went home to my fiancé.'

'I don't believe it!' I say. 'What kind of utter loser . . . ?' I rub a hand over my mouth, feeling such fury on her behalf. My heart ticks wildly for a few moments. Then I say, 'Well, Jacq, think of it this way: there's obviously something wrong with him. No real man would behave like that. He clearly got some pleasure out of leading you on and then embarrassing you.'

She looks right at me, 'But why, Celine?'

'Because he's sick! Or he's got problems. Confidence problems. Sexual problems. Who knows . . . Maybe he's got a really tiny penis . . . Jacqui, there's only one thing to do. Forget it. Put it behind you where it belongs. He's not worth another second of your thoughts. Go home to your boyfriend, then sit down with him and have a good talk about your feelings. This behaviour… it's a cry for help. You don't want to get married. So for God's sake just tell Rich how you feel.'

She snivels, looking a tad brighter. 'Thanks.' She shakes her head. 'But I can't go home to Rich – these last two nights have been horrible! I mean I would have had sex with Christian right there if he'd wanted.'

'But you didn't.' I pat her shoulder. 'Everybody does something stupid once in their life, Jacqui. No sense in making it more than what it was. And you should absolutely go into work and hold your head up high! He's the one who should be afraid of showing his face! The prat!'

'Please can I stay here tonight?'

I am taken aback. As is she – by my hesitation.

'I can sleep in the spare room. Just for a few nights.'

I grimace. 'It's not entirely convenient.'

She frowns again, looking wounded and confused. And then we look up and Patrick is standing there holding an empty crisps dish and a beer glass.

'Oh,' she says, her face falling.

'Hi,' he smiles and sets the empties down. 'You must be Celine's sister.'

She recovers quickly, shoots me a loaded, bitterly disappointed glance. 'No. I am definitely not her sister . . . I must be someone else.'

'Well, hi, someone else,' he says.

She reaches out to return his handshake. 'And I'm guessing you must be Patrick.' She glares at me again, quickly. I am going to have a tremendous amount of crawling to do to make this up to her.

'Look,' Patrick lays a hand on my shoulder. 'I think I'm gonna take a cab back to the hotel.'

'You don't have to,' Jacqui says. 'I was just leaving.'

'No,' he says. 'I've got some things to do anyway.'

He kisses me, and then looks at Jacqui. 'It was nice meeting you briefly. One day I'm going to have to thank you properly.'

'Thank me?' she frowns.

'I believe you were instrumental in all of this somehow.' His eyes leave her and settle briefly in a lingering, meaningful way, on me. Then he says, 'And Celine's right: the guy sounds like a complete jackass. Definitely challenged in the manhood department.'

THIRTY-FIVE

Saying goodbye is awful. This time I man up and drive him to Newcastle airport. 'Don't forget about summer,' he says – his parting words as he waves to me before going through security.

'I won't,' I say, feeling frustrated. Our time together is always too short. It's become the story of our lives.

I meet Jennifer Platt in Costa Coffee opposite the Theatre Royal. She has just been to a meeting with Virgin Trains and excitedly tells me that the head of catering has agreed to hear her proposal.

'I really, really, really like Mike!' she says, when I return with two coffees and a muffin for us to share. 'I never thought I would meet someone this fast. And it's going so well!'

I dive into my coffee before replying. 'Actually, the most successful matches were lukewarm about each other the first time they met. Generally the average person goes on dates with three different candidates before she meets the one she'll have a few dates with and end up going to bed with.'

Her gaze slides out of the window and back. I can tell she's trying to be restrained about the whole thing but deep down she's glowing like a 100-watt light bulb. 'Mike's interesting, he's mature and sensible; he's very down to earth. He's not crude, like some who make you feel more like a buddy than a lady. He's actually funny too! I always laugh at the little things he comes out with! And he listens to you. He seemed fascinated with my business idea, although I might have talked his ears off about it.' She tinkles a laugh. 'We really hit it off from the moment we met.' Her eyes are iridescent with new love. 'After that first date, I barely got home before he rang me, and we talked for another two hours! And now I've met Aimee . . . and she's utterly adorable.'

'Thanks,' I say. 'And you don't think it's odd that he's my ex-husband?' Mike will obviously have told her.

'No. Not at all. In a way this is why I feel I can say so much about him to you – because, well, you know him, don't you? You'll understand.'

'You're probably wondering why, if he's so fantastic, we're divorced.' I try a laugh.

She tries the same. 'No! I don't believe in judging people. I mean, the only two people who really know what their marriage is like are the two that are in it, aren't they?'

Why is she so fabulous? And how did she manage to get massive natural breasts on such a petite frame?

'Well, I don't know what he might have told you . . .'

'Nothing! Honestly, he never got into any specific details about his marriage. When you meet someone, you don't want to bring out all your old baggage, do you? Certainly not in the early stages.'

I nod, trying to swallow the idea of me being old baggage.

'Same as myself; I rarely talk about my divorce. Because just when I think I'm doing fine now and I'm all right, I don't want someone to sit there looking for chinks in my armour, or then I'll probably start acting like I'm not all right, if you know what I mean.'

'I never asked you why it didn't work . . .' Because something about her just made me take her at face value. But now I am brimming with curiosity.

'It's all right. I don't mind saying.' She looks at me with a certain reconciled expression. 'It was an affair. Not especially original. I remember thinking that there was so much I should be feeling – anger, jealousy, sadness – yet all I felt was an overwhelming disgust. Disgust at myself for not suspecting, and disgust that he could be with her and then come home and be with me, sometimes in the same night, as I'm pretty sure happened. It seemed monstrous.' She wrinkles up her nose, and I notice she's got a rather big freckle on the edge of her top lip, that looks like a crumb she needs to dust off. I can see Mike becoming enamoured with that freckle the way he used to fixate on the small mole on the inside of my elbow. 'But once I made him leave I was determined not to let his actions ruin my own self-image. His decision to screw around was a reflection on him, not on me. I had to keep reminding myself of that. So that's one of the reasons I didn't want to talk about it with Mike before we knew each other really well. I don't want anybody thinking I've been shaped at all by what he did.'

I drink some of the coffee I now don't want and stare out at the dashing, neoclassical façade of the Theatre Royal opposite, one of Jacqui's favourite buildings in the city, thinking, *She's a bit goody-goody, isn't she?* Then I feel bad for the catty thought. She's lovely. She's better for him than I ever was.

Suddenly she reaches a hand and briefly lays it on the back of mine. 'You're obviously a very good person, wanting to set him up with someone else and see him happy.'

Tears inexplicably burn in the back of my eyes. I look across the road, turning my head slightly so she won't see. When I can speak, I say, 'It was his idea that I took him on as a client. I didn't want to tell you I was married to him, you know, in case you thought I had no one else to offer so I just touted my ex around.'

She laughs. 'Tout your ex around! That's funny!' She cuts the muffin down the middle for us. 'I hope that it's not awkward in any way for you, you know, if Mike and I . . .' She pushes the muffin around the plate with her knife, while I hang in anticipation. 'I can certainly promise you that if we do work out in the long run, I will never try to be a second mother to Aimee. I just hope we can have a lovely relationship if that happens.'

I shake my head a little too enthusiastically. 'It's not awkward for me in the slightest.' I wonder if Mike knows she's already seeing herself as Aimee's second mum. 'I took you on to help you find someone. And you were quite right: I want nothing more than for Mike to be happy.'

We smile together, holding eyes, and in one synchronised move our fingers go out to claim our respective halves of the muffin, and they touch. It's almost as though we are shaking hands.

It's only when we have parted ways at Grey's Monument – she's about to go into Waterstone's, and I am about to trot down the steps of the Metro to go home – that I remember something. I hesitate there, one foot poised to keep on going, but then I shout back at her.

For a second I think she hasn't heard me but then she turns.

I am already walking over to her, digging in my handbag. 'I forgot, I brought this with me . . .' I hold out a folded-up piece of paper. 'I intended to give it to you, but, well, anyway . . . It's not a lot.' She takes it, looking curious. 'It's just some stuff I wrote about Mike when I was considering taking him on as a client – some questions I made myself answer about him to remind me of all his good points.' I give her a smile. 'I thought that perhaps you might like to have it.'

As it exchanges hands, a shift seems to occur in me. It's too late to take it back. It's gone now. Like Mike, or so it seems, it's hers now, not mine.

THIRTY-SIX

'To love and other mistakes.' I raise a glass of wine to Jacqui across the pub table. We've not been out for a drink in ages. 'And to you one day forgiving me for not bringing you in on Patrick . . .'

She tilts her head. 'There's nothing to forgive. I mean – there is – but let's just say you've made up for that particular crime in many other ways.'

I smile.

'How's Christian these days?' I ask.

She sighs. 'Oh, I see him around the office. He'll be very formal and say, "Good morning, Jacqui." Like he's my geography teacher or something.'

'He's worried word's got out. He thinks everybody's laughing at him and wondering about the size of his pecker.'

'I think I need to get away from here. Newcastle's not exactly the centre of the architectural-design universe, is it?'

'But I thought you liked your job? I've never once heard you complain about it. I mean, you complain, but in a happy way.'

'I kept thinking I was all right for now. But maybe now has expired. I do a lot of glorified administrative work, really. I mean, when I saw myself getting into architecture as a career, it was the creative side I was attracted to. If I'd known I'd be endlessly dealing with sexist contractors and cranky engineers, and basically being some kind of middleman, then I'd have gone and got a masters degree in something else.'

'But everyone has to pay their dues.'

She stabs an index finger into her chest. 'I'm owed a refund.' She looks at me quite seriously. 'Don't you sometimes wish you'd been born stupid, ugly and smelly so that no one will want you; you'll never get a boyfriend?'

'Born smelly,' I grin. 'Now there's an interesting idea.'

'I envy people with simple lives!'

'I don't know anyone with a simple life, Jacq.'

We order a couple more glasses of wine.

'You don't seem yourself,' she says, after a time. 'What's up?'

'I don't know,' I tell her. 'It's this Patrick thing.'

'This Patrick thing?' She scowls. 'That's a strange way to describe your second chance with the love of your life!'

'It feels odd now that he's been here and seen my life. It's like I'm starting to see him in it, and picture him being a part of all this, and yet how can that happen? He lives in another country, Jacq. On another continent. He's got commitments keeping him there. A crazy demanding job.'

'Those are, admittedly, obstacles.'

'"Obstacles" are his parents don't like me. His dog likes to sleep between us on the bed . . .' I tell her. 'He's forty-three and he's never really and truly committed to anyone in his life, except for a brief marriage when he was young.'

'So?'

'His career is his world. He likes to do spontaneous things like send me a ticket to Paris for only two days, or surprise me with a visit to my home town! He's a free spirit . . . Does that sound like a man who is going to commit to a divorcee with a daughter who lives across the world?'

'My! You really are a Debbie Downer today, aren't you?' She can't seem to stop staring at me like she's seeing a completely different person.

I tell her about how he wants us to go there for a chunk of the school holidays.

'But that's fantastic! Just tell him you need to keep it to two weeks, if you've got concerns . . .' She's frowning. She doesn't see the problem like I see it, which makes me wonder if I am making something out of nothing.

I sigh. 'I'm not trying to be negative. But in some ways I'm just not sure you sending that silly blank email was such a great idea. I know you meant well, and I love you for your good intentions, but a part of me can't help but think that if we'd been going to work we'd have worked fifteen years ago. There's no such thing as picking up where we left off. Life doesn't work that way. And the complications are still there. They're just different ones.'

'If everybody thought like that there'd be no second chances. But I really do wish you'd stop going on about that email. It's like by having everybody say I sent it I'm starting to believe I actually did!'

I don't really want to argue this one back and forth.

'Look,' she says. 'He came here to your home to see your life. My guess is he came prepared to meet your family too – though you decided not to tell any of us about him. That doesn't sound like someone who just wants to be a spontaneous free spirit. And just because he's had relationships that didn't end up working out doesn't mean that was all his doing and his fault . . .'

'But we can't just go on doing more of the same. What's to come back for? Really? More walking around London? More endless fantastic sex? More strange encounters with my peculiar family members?'

'I'd take more sex, and less of the peculiar family members!'

'No you wouldn't. You once said sex has nowhere else to go, and maybe in this case you were actually right.'

'Don't be silly! I didn't mean it even close to that way!' She stares at me and I try not to look at her. 'Besides, I think you're forgetting the obvious.'

'And that is?'

'He's in love with you.'

I wag a finger at her. 'Ah, but he's never actually said it.'

'Some things don't have to be said.'

'Not all the time. But they should be, once.'

'So what does he really think of us lot, then?' She changes the subject because she probably realises I am right about this. 'I mean, there's your old man, who molests models, then there's me, who is about to get engaged and who attempts but fails to molest a co-worker. And we both seem to gravitate to your house to tell you what disasters we are, at any time of the day or night, not really caring whether we've been invited. Actually preferring that we haven't because it somehow adds to our drama.'

I beam. 'At least he knows who we really are. What he'd be taking on. Not that he is going to take us on.' Rita Ora is singing 'Your Song' and I have to shout over the music.

'Are you sure you're over Mike?'

The question stops me cold. I'm about to say my doubts about Patrick have nothing to do with Mike, but what comes out is something born of a lot of reflection lately. 'Can anyone ever be over the person they were married to? Unless that person really hurt them badly and they're just desperate to block them out? I know him more than I know any other human being. Even more than I know myself, I sometimes think.'

'Ah . . .' she says, as though a light has just come on in her head. And I don't like what I think that *Ah* means.

I'm just pulling up in front of the house when my phone rings.

'Hi!' he says, sounding happy.

'Where are you?' I ask him.

'At my desk, in my apartment, staring out of the window, unable to stop thinking about you . . .'

He's back in Canada. And life moves on. And again everything feels more impossible than possible.

'Ah . . .' I say.

'I don't know what I thought about until my mind started going automatically to you.'

'That's nice.' I smile. 'You've just created the perfect five-second soundbite. You should be proud.'

He laughs. 'Anyway, just wanted to say . . . hi, I suppose.' He sounds a little crestfallen, suddenly. 'And I also wanted to tell you something I probably should have said a very long time ago.'

'Oh?'

'I wanted to say I love you.'

I bite down on my bottom lip. Did he hear Jacqui and me talking? I am totally overcome.

'Are you still there?' he asks.

'I'm still here,' I say.

I'm just about to say it back when he jumps in. 'Damn. A call. Got to take this. Really sorry! Shoot . . .' I can hear his frustration.

'Okay, then,' I say, hating the limpness of my response, how the lovely spell of the moment unfortunately got broken. Because Patrick has to go again.

But he's not gone, is he? I remind myself. Not when he leaves me with those words.

THIRTY-SEVEN

Time seems to fly. And then it's Father's Day. My dad is bringing his mysterious girlfriend, Anthea. I casually asked Mike if he wanted to bring Jennifer, fully expecting he'd say no, but that backfired somewhat. Jacqui is coming along too, but by herself.

I'm just bashing a piece of garlic and some ginger in my mortar to make a dressing to toss over the watercress salad that I'm serving with the grilled salmon, when I get a FaceTime call.

'Hi.' Patrick's eternally handsome face fills the screen of my iPhone.

I wipe a sticky hand down the front of my apron, glad Aimee is in the shower. 'Hi to you indeed!'

'God, I miss you.'

'I bet you say that to all the girls.'

'But to you I actually mean it.'

'Ha ha.'

'What are you doing? You look like you're cooking.'

'Yeah, it's Father's Day and I'm having my dad over with the girl-friend he sees when he's not molesting models.'

'I wish I was there.' The dampened note of his voice.

'So what have you been up to?' I ask him, brightly, perching on a chair and holding the phone so he can see me at a less awkward angle.

'Oh, organising my office and a few other things. I'm working on an outline for my book on the Middle East.'

'Ah! You're back to that! Excellent.'

'Finally. Though I don't have much to show for my efforts. You could say I've been distracted.'

'Have you?' I smile, hearing Aimee shutting off the shower.

'Every time I sit down to think about the Taliban I end up thinking about you.'

'I wonder what that says about me?'

He laughs. 'Anyway, I wanted to tell you something – the reason why I rang . . . I've decided to take the job.'

I stare at the oblongs of salmon lying on foil on the grilling tray.

'I won't be starting before Christmas, which is a long way off . . . It's a good opportunity for me to establish myself somewhere. I'm thinking I can work on my book at the same time, and maybe it won't be such a bad life . . .'

I clear my throat, aware that it doesn't seem like I was factored into his decision at all. 'Congratulations,' I tell him, hearing the fallen note in my voice. What else was I hoping he was going to say? 'I'm sure it'll be a great life,' I stand up again, momentarily walking away from the phone so he can't see me.

'I gave it a lot of thought,' I hear him saying. He is probably stuck staring at my ceiling. 'I didn't really see what the other options were.' He sounds like he's explaining himself.

'Of course.' I force a smile into my voice. What was I even thinking his other options were? That he was going to give up his life and move to northern England? It never would have worked. Because it was never meant to. Stupid!

I come back to the phone. 'You know my dad and Mike should be here soon.'

'Mike?'

'Well, it is Father's Day.'

'Oh,' he says. 'Of course.' Do I detect a beat of disappointment? After a while he says, 'I don't suppose you've given any more thought to August?'

'Not a lot,' I say. 'But I will.'

'You promised.'

I tell him I have to go or I'll burn my food.

Mike and Jennifer arrive first. My mood is striking a bum note. Opening my door and seeing them both standing there like a couple is so bizarre that they must see the involuntary shockwave before I have a chance to put on a smile. 'Hi,' I say, brightly, but it's too late. Mike's eyes have so many mixed messages in them that it's unbearable for me to look.

'Come in,' I say, noting that Jennifer is very mod today, in faded, low-rise jeans, wedge sandals – the kind that Aimee would covet – and a sleeveless cotton floral top. She has her longish brown hair pulled back into a messy ponytail.

'For you,' she says, presenting me with an armful of flowers. 'Just a little thank you for – well, among other things – inviting me to your lovely home. It was a really unexpected but lovely invitation.'

'Glass of wine?' I ask, quickly turning and trotting down the passageway.

My father and Anthea arrive about two minutes after. When I open the door, I'm completely unprepared to see my dad alongside a very old-fashioned, middle-aged woman. She has dyed dark-brown hair that shows off about two inches of white roots. And in the unusually large gap between her top lip and her nose is a moustache Charlie Chaplin would have been proud of.

'This is Anthea,' my dad says, unnecessarily. Anthea and I go to shake hands, and I ignore the fact that my dad is measuring me for my reaction.

'Hello, Anthea,' I say, trying not to focus on the pea-sized wart on the side of her head up by her eye.

Mike puts new batteries in the smoke alarm that has recently started tweeting all day as though we are living under the same roof as a family of bad-tempered sparrows. I keep an eye on the salmon grilling. And Anthea – who actually seems really nice – chats away with Jennifer. Aimee shows my dad her progress on the seascape she's been working on. It seems like art has replaced her interest in gymnastics now. I'm just glad to see her passionate about something again.

Jacqui arrives in an emerald-green strapless sundress, smelling fresh and bearing red and white wine. When she sets eyes on Anthea, her smile takes on a cunning quality and she keeps trying to catch my eye, so I have to avoid looking at her.

'You're looking very lovely, as usual,' my dad says to Jacqui. Then he turns to me. 'Jennifer is something, isn't she?'

'And she's with Mike!'

He glances around. 'Yes. Where is he? If I can't see him, he doesn't exist.'

'It's done, I think.' I pry two flakes of fish apart with a knife and fork. Mike is suddenly standing unnervingly close to me.

'Yep,' he says. 'You definitely want it out now, or it'll be dry.'

'Thanks. For telling me what I already know.' I smile. Mike always used to mock my cooking. And while I honestly don't think it's terrible, and it definitely has improved since he moved out – necessity being the mother of invention, I have to admit that he was the chef in the family. I pop the tray on top of the oven, and then give my salad dressing a final vigorous shake before tipping it into the bowl.

'I'd better get a bib,' he says. 'That looks oily.'

'Excuse me,' I slide past him to turn off the oven. I am still on a downer over Patrick's video call and it's taking a massive effort to go through the motions of this meal when, really, all I'd like to do is open the front door and send them all home.

Norman comes mewing into the kitchen. Mike picks him up and cuddles him. 'My old lad. How have you been, eh? Do you miss your old man?'

I turn and catch Mike looking at me.

The meal goes down well. I have pulled out the drop-leaf on the table, and we sit with the back door open, hearing the birds in the garden. 'We should have eaten outside,' I say, wishing I'd thought to set up the picnic table.

'It might be cold to eat out,' Anthea says. 'It's warm while you're walking around, but not so great to sit in.' She holds my eyes and I try very hard not to let mine drop to her top lip, to what I've noticed are three or four extremely long hairs among the downier ones.

My father keeps us all entertained. Anthea sits next to him like a fixture, with the unexcitable air of someone much older and more jaded than she probably is. She's not the most feminine of souls, and I'm not trying to be cruel. It's just a shock to see the disparity between what my father used to be able to get in the women department and what he gets now. He told me she has been divorced for twenty years. Now, given that my dad is in his mid-seventies and she can't be more than sixty, I should be having a very hard time imagining what she sees in him. Yet it's more the other way round. And I can tell by the glances she's shooting me that Jacqui is having the same thought. I put their relationship down to an unlikely companionship. Curiosity satisfied on that score, I move on to Mike and Jennifer. My gaze shifts surreptitiously between them, and then to her large breasts, which seem to be a whole other person in themselves. They almost can't be real. Yet I can't see her being the type to go for implants. When she moves an inch closer to say something in his ear, they're a fascinating buffer between her and his arm. I'm sure this isn't lost on him.

'I remember she wore a pea-green chiffon dress . . .' My dad is in the throes of one of his stories, wandering down the dissolute alleyways of his past, searching for a brief imbuement of the man he was – the man who drank absinthe on Paris's Left Bank, locking heads with the literary intelligentsia, arguing Henri Matisse over Pablo Picasso and transforming into iconic creations young models who all invariably became girlfriends. But none more so than this one he's talking about. Very soon he's going to say that her pea-green eyes matched the pea-green dress that she then let float off her to the paint-splattered wooden floorboards – or at least that was the version I heard. The stories have been known to change. How many times have I heard my dad's nostalgic embroidery? His tales are like supermarket-brand wine: they go down pleasantly enough in the absence of anything better to fit the occasion. Somehow you get so used to them that your life would be a much worse existence without them.

By the time he painted this particular girl, he was mentally finished with my mother. I understand now what I never understood growing up. My mother was his love affair in London. By the time they got to Paris, and I had come along, he was seeing her in a different role. That's why she never comes up in his stories of that time. My father was addicted to falling in love; as fast as he fell out of it, he had to fall back in. It was the only way he could live.

A curious thought strikes me. Was Patrick just my love affair in Vietnam? Consigned to a part of my growing up that had craved something epic happening to my heart? Am I also addicted to the idea of being in love? My dad looks at me, as though reading the thoughts that are rattling through my head. Truth is, I probably made peace with my old man a long time ago, even though I may have fought it. I am probably more like him than I care to admit.

When I put out dessert, Mike says, 'Oh God, it's tiramisu.' He winks at Jacqui. 'She's made this before.' He nudges me. 'Remember?'

'It nearly killed us!' Aimee recoils. 'We were on the toilet for days from those dodgy raw eggs!' Then she says, 'Like when we went to Spain and Mum came back thinking she could make paella. She put . . .' she looks at me. 'What was it, Mum? Tell the story!'

I shake my head, accepting that I must make myself look ridiculous to entertain the table; it's the price of playing host. 'Saffron was too expensive. I got creative and decided to use turmeric to turn the rice yellow. Only when I went into the cupboard looking for it, I accidently picked up the cayenne pepper instead.'

Everybody laughs. Mike just sits and stares at me, looking hollow with nostalgia.

'Anyway, the eggs are practically right out of the chicken in this one.' I peel my eyes away from my ex-husband's.

'Still . . .' Mike says, digging a spoon into the white topping. 'We'd all feel safer if you try it first.' He scoops out a heap of it and directs the spoon to my mouth. There is a moment where everyone seems to become hyper-aware of this gesture. Nonetheless, I wrap my lips around the spoon. A bit of mascarpone sticks to the corner of my mouth. He catches it with his finger before it falls on to my clothes, then licks it.

'It looks very good.' Jennifer is the first to break the strange spell.

The intimacy of Mike's gesture has taken the wind out of me. 'And I'm still alive, so I think we can all tuck in,' I manage to say.

After we eat and are pleasantly narcotised by more of my dad's stories, Aimee and Mike playing Wii boxing.

'Your turn now,' Mike says, sometime later, catching me reflecting on family gatherings of the past. When we were a family. He's holding out the Wiimote.

'No!' I flap him away with a hand. 'I'm rubbish at it.'

'Come on, you just have to hit me. Surely it'll not be that hard.'

'You'd be surprised. The intention might flourish but the hand falters.' I grin. I notice Jacqui is beaming a smile but her eyes are measuring Jennifer closely for her reaction. 'All right!' I finally take the thing off him. 'One game.'

He slaughters me in seconds. 'Come on,' he laughs. 'I'm actually letting you beat me!'

I aim the thing at the screen and go mad, no clue what I'm doing.

'You're knocking yourself out!' he says. 'Remember, you're the red.'

'Oh yeah!' I laugh. 'I forgot!' I am determined to lay him out now. I discover a knack for the right high jab and land him a good one.

The women say, 'Whooh!'

'Nice one!' Mike tells me. 'Try doing a big uppercut now. One of these!' He socks the little red *me* right on the chin.

'Ouch!' Aimee chuckles from the floor where she's sitting cross-legged. 'Victory!'

'That wasn't fair! You were distracting me by talking!'

'Oh, that's what it was!' Mike says. 'We just thought you were totally crap.'

Jennifer and Anthea protest, playfully: that kind of comment isn't called for.

'Look, if you turn the Wiimote inwards like this to cover your face . . .' Mike comes to show me, but I suddenly think, *Oh! I know what he means now about a big uppercut!* So I uppercut like there's no tomorrow, and make contact with his cheek.

'Ow!' he says, as the others fold up laughing. And then, 'Bugger!' and then, 'All right. I think you've won. You play dirty.'

I instinctively go to touch him, thinking, *Heavens, maybe I have hurt him!*

'Ooh, are you all right?' Anthea becomes excessively giddy and starts making a strange barking laugh.

I notice she has a manly way of sitting, with her legs spread, and because I've had three glasses of wine I have to hide my face in my hands and stifle a laugh.

When I look up again, Mike clearly thinks I'm laughing about his cheek. So he makes a big play of touching it.

'Are you okay?' I ask.

'I'll survive. If you can fetch me a bucket for the blood, and a needle and thread.'

'I'm sorry,' I tell him, feeling terrible for hitting him and for laughing at Anthea. I glance at my father, who is watching me as though he's on to me. I can't help my giggles suddenly. When I look back at Mike he's watching me steadily. There is so much warmth and love and pain in that expression. Once I'm aware of it I can't let go of it.

My laughter tapers off. We hold eyes, and for a while neither of us can stop.

My dad and Anthea are the first to leave. As Anthea goes to the toilet my father pulls out an envelope from the inner pocket of his blazer, and shoves it at me. 'Now you've finished wetting yourself laughing over my girlfriend, please give this to Sandra.'

'Sandra? Oh my God!' I can't believe this! 'Dad! When is enough enough?'

'It's never enough!' he says, desperately. 'Please . . .' he implores. 'I really need you to just give it to her.' His eyes are combing my face like his life depends on my saying yes. Anthea appears suddenly. I take the envelope from him and put it in my jeans pocket.

Anthea thanks me and says she's had a lovely day. She gives me a rib-cracking hug that's enough to send me off for an X-ray.

At the door, Jennifer unknots a creased pink cardigan from around the straps of her handbag, and slips it across her shoulders. As she reaches to pull it around herself, the fabric between the buttons of her shirt gapes and I get a private view of a canyon of cleavage. Mike must see too, because his cheeks flush when we make eye contact.

'Good heavens!' I suddenly notice: 'Mike, I think you've got a bruise!' Instinctively I go to touch his cheek but stop myself.

'Oh, she's right, you do!' Jennifer cups her mouth, hiding a smile. And then she gently dabs a middle finger on the bruise as though testing to see if he finds it painful.

'Sorry,' I tell him again. 'How will you explain that at work?'

'I'll just tell people my ex-wife punched me. What else?'

'While we were playing Wii!'

'I might selectively leave that bit out.'

'Goodnight,' I say, again. They thank me again. Jennifer gives me a snuggle, her pillowy bazookas pressing against me.

Q: What made me love him?

A: Because Mike's not slick, isn't a game-player, has no agenda, isn't in competition with you, isn't ever possessive. Mike loves you limitlessly. When he commits he goes all the way. He is in your corner, and he lets you know it all those times you need him to. Mike is guileless; he's not vain, nor is he ever ashamed of himself.

Q: What do I admire about him?

A: All of the above. Plus, he doesn't need to impress anyone. He's had better job offers, chances to make more money, but sticks with what makes him happiest. Mike is not a patsy, nor is he afraid to stand up for a principle. He will throw a teenager off a train if the lad swears at him. He'll report a bus driver for not waiting for the senior who was hurrying to the stop with her hand out. Mike is what you'd want your little boy to be, if you had a son.

Q: What does he do to make me feel good?

A: Makes me laugh. Forgives me. Doesn't take me too seriously, especially when I'm taking myself too seriously. Will tickle me to sleep. Will push me to get out of the house on a day when I don't feel like going anywhere. Will never let me feel sorry for myself unless it's for a good reason. And then only for five minutes. Encourages me always. Tells me I am beautiful. Often.

Q: What do I miss most?

It was the last question but I didn't jot this one down. The answer, since it only recently came to me, just floats around somewhere in my mind . . .

A: How we had a fit, even though it's taken divorce for me to reflect and to realise this. It may not have been perfect. I didn't set out looking for perfect from him in the first place, so I don't know why I was so disappointed. It certainly wasn't the extreme of square peg in round hole. It was what it was.

We were better than I gave us credit for.

THIRTY-EIGHT

After Aimee and I watch two episodes of a new show on Netflix, I tell her that I've been seeing Patrick – casually – and that he has invited us to Canada.

By the time I get to the bit about me having got in touch with him and that we've been corresponding, she is already rolling her eyes. 'Mum, I already know that you went to see him in London.'

I gawp at her. 'How do you know that? Did Aunt Jacqui say something?'

'Not really. She said you'd gone to see an old friend.'

'I really did go for a conference!'

She gives me that look again. 'Please! Besides, there's FaceTime. His phone number in your contacts. Area code 416 . . .'

I study her waif-like upper body, with its vest under the T-shirt, the tiny mounds of breasts, her indigo toenails. Since she kissed Rachel's boyfriend, she hasn't really talked about boys anymore. Except to tell me that Rachel is still in love with Edward from *Twilight* – but he's from a decade ago and Aimee thinks he's lame.

'Well, I told him you wouldn't want to go. That you'd have no interest in seeing a big, exciting Canadian city. You won't want to go to the Canadian lakes and see black bears and wolves, and go boating, and have picnics and barbecues. You'd far rather just hang out at boring old home for the summer, with me and your dad and all your fantastic best friends who are now back in your life.'

'Why'd you tell him that?' She stares at me like I'm from outer space.

I remember when I went to Greece with my father and 'my Marie', as he called her – the one he had left my mother for. I was Aimee's age. At first, the idea of going seemed morally repugnant. But a part of me thought: *Hm, I've never been to Greece before . . .* And that one detail was about the only positive of the entire experience.

I remember sitting in a fish tavern, *my Marie* in her bikini top, dragging on a cigarette in a way that said she knew secrets about life that I would never know. She was twenty-seven to my dad's fifty-one. The most gorgeous thing I'd ever seen, and I suddenly couldn't fathom what she saw in my dad. Until this holiday, I'd esteemed my father to be greater than great. Even his dumping us was something that people like him – who were too good for the rest of us – did. Yet here he was in his acrylic jumper, with his furrowed forehead, and his tall stories I'd heard a million times before. From the other side of a plate of fried calamari, I watched his hand sneak a fondle of her side-breast. I remember her laughing once, and my dad possibly forgetting I was there – the shock of his tongue sliding in and out of her mouth, and my huge relief when she brushed him off to smoke another fag.

I was never going to fall in love. I was never going to kiss like that. If you took those two small details out of life, everything else felt like it was going to be manageable.

Somehow I will have to orchestrate this trip carefully. I refuse to ever leave my daughter with that warped view of love.

I send Patrick an email telling him that it looks like a visit to Canada might be possible after all. That I'll start looking for tickets for two weeks at the end of August.

THIRTY-NINE

A writer for *Hers* magazine wants to interview me. She has contacted me through my website, after one of my very first clients apparently recommended me to her. She says she's doing a piece on 'Modern Love' and plans to explore international online franchises like Match.com and DatingDirect, and then the smaller boutiques like myself. She says she's intrigued by the name – The Love Market – and wonders if she might phone me for a chat.

I google the mag and find it's got a circulation of 350,000. I could never afford that sort of advertising value. I might just have found a way to grow my business. Or, rather, it has found me.

No sooner do I type back, Yes! I'd love to chat than she rings me.

'We talked nearly an hour!' I tell Jacqui, down at the pub, settling into an aged-velvet corner seat surrounded by oak-beamed walls lined with brass horseshoes and plaques that say things like 'Good Food. Good Fun. Good Friends.' 'Right off she wanted to know how I came up with the name The Love Market, so of course I told her all about the Love Market in Sa Pa, how I went there, how I met Patrick . . . She was fascinated. By the time we rang off, she knew the whole story of how you ended up playing matchmaker and bringing him back into my life. So she wants to interview us.'

'Do you think Patrick will be game?' she asks.

I clutch my half-pint of Guinness. 'No! She doesn't want to interview Patrick. She wants to interview you!'

'Me?' She looks astonished.

'She said that since we chatted the focus of her article was going to change. She wants to make it a more personal, romantic story. She loves the whole angle of how a successful matchmaker is unsuccessful in her own love life, until her sister does a bit of matchmaking and reunites her with her lost love.'

'Well . . . that does sound like a jolly story, but don't you think it's a bit personal? The whole of the country getting to read about how you had sex with a married man, then thought about him all the time you were married to Mike, and then two minutes after you're divorced he's back in your life again?'

I stare into the froth on my drink. 'I didn't see it that way.'

But of course now I do.

'I don't have to tell her all the intimate details . . .' I'm a bit hurt. I'd never really thought of myself as having had sex with a married man. Not after I'd asked him the question about whether she too knew they were splitting up. When I first kissed Patrick I trusted he'd been honest, so I didn't feel I was taking what was somebody else's.

'Jacq, I'm doing this because I need to earn more money. I have to think of Aimee's future. And – frankly – my own.'

'Sorry, I know. You're right. It just seems odd, them writing all about your private life. And I just think when Mike reads it, it's going to be like rubbing his nose in the whole Patrick thing. Have you considered how he's going to feel?'

Admittedly it hadn't occurred to me. Some of the wind leaves my sails. 'Jacq, we all have to move on. We're divorced. This is a terrific business opportunity. And, anyway, he's dating Jennifer now, isn't he?'

'That's completely different. I think he's dating Jennifer to get at you.'

'Why would it get at me?' I gawk at her. 'And he wouldn't do that. He's not a user.' She just looks at me and says nothing. 'Look, Jacq, I realise I'm going to have to tell him about Patrick soon, given that we're going to Canada. Or the minute Aimee knows I've bought the tickets she's going to tell him, and I don't want it coming from her.'

She cocks her head. 'Surely that's not why you don't seem excited about going?'

'Who says I'm not excited?'

'I don't know. You don't seem to be. Not massively.'

I open my mouth to speak, but I'm bereft of words. I take a drink instead.

'Do the right thing,' she says. 'Tell him now.'

FORTY

'You matched me with James!' Trish is almost squealing. 'Not just any James, but *my* James! You even told me you were matching me with James and I didn't even realise! How thick am I?'

'If your James had been called Jasper I'd have said you should never have been a lawyer.'

She chuckles. 'But how did you know to do it?'

'I just knew. On the Fake Date he kept going on about how fantastic you were, and it was as though he compared everyone else to you and found them lacking. And then there was the way you worked overtime to convince me that you weren't attracted to him.'

'Me?' she chortles dirtily. 'I did that?'

'You did that! And then there was something else. You seemed to really, really care about him. Something about you lightened and brightened when you talked about him.'

She falls quiet. Then says, 'Argh!'

'So how did it go?' I ask her. 'Your date?'

'Oh my God . . .' She sounds emotional. 'Do you want to know how shocked I was? I mean, there I was; I arrive at the restaurant and I see James sitting at a table in the corner. And I'm like . . . *Hang on, what's he doing here?* And he looks up and we both look at each other and then I think, *James? James!* And I say, "What are you doing here?" And he says, "I'm meeting a girl called Patricia!"' She chortles. 'The last time anyone called me Patricia was when I was baptised. I'd almost forgotten that's my real name.'

'I had a feeling that if I told him he was meeting a girl called Trish, it would have given the game away.'

She chortles again. 'Oh, Celine, it was amazing! We actually had a date! A real date! And we didn't even have to try. That's what was so wonderful. It just evolved so naturally. Like it had always been meant to be.'

I hear some background shuffling, and then, 'Celine!' James's voice. Presumably James has spent the night.

'Has anybody ever told you you're quite clever at your job?' he says to me, clearly taking the phone away from her. 'But the thing is, there are a few problems with this. One is she's a lawyer and, as you know, I never date lawyers – never have and never will; they're absolutely despicable, argumentative, uncompromising people. Two, she's got issues about sleeping with one of her best friends, as well as some other foibles that I can see being quite problematic in the long term . . . Ouch! She's just bashed me with a feather pillow. See what I mean? And three, I'm really quite in love with her.'

When I hang up, I sit down on the end of my bed and think about the pair of them. That's how true love is supposed to go. Why can't it be this easy for me?

In the week, I phone Kim and break some good news. 'I have another match for you. He's in the music business. Lives up here but flies down to London. He's got a flat down there.'

Andrew Flemming is the type of man Kim should be drawn to – an Ideas man, who has an atypical career, is at the top of his game, is incredibly interesting and entertaining and not at all bad-looking.

'He's thirty-nine,' I tell her. 'And he's not opposed to meeting a woman in her mid-forties. I'm going to aim for next Thursday night if that works with you. But I have to tell you: if you don't like him, I have an awful lot of women who will.'

'Hm,' she says. 'I'm going to try really hard not to blow it.'

I then phone Andrew and tell him I am setting him up with a very pretty public-relations executive. Being in the music industry, Andrew is used to dealing with 'characters'. And I have to remember that none of the men I have sent her out with have disliked her. Yet.

FORTY-ONE

I'm tidying my room and folding my jeans when I find my dad's letter to Sandra in the pocket. I had forgotten that I was supposed to give it to her. I sit down on the end of the bed. He has sealed it with a shiny silver sticker, round like a bright ten-pence piece. I'm worried about what might be in it, so I open it and read:

> Beautiful Sandra . . .
> There is absolutely no truth to the rumour that, following her intensive search to find love, Sandra will now fly away with Anthony to spend a fabulous two weeks in the Maldives . . .
>
> In truth, I write this to thank you for your company at dinner. If you ever wish to go out again, to continue our conversation, you have only to let me know. But failing this ever materialising, I hope I can captivate you on an entirely different level. The offer to paint you is one I did not make lightly. So rarely am I moved by my subjects these days that I cannot help but think you and I can somehow benefit each other.

If you would agree to sit for me, I shall repeat to
you here my phone number: (0191) 542-1265.
Yours, Ancient Anthony

Ancient Anthony!

I go downstairs, find another envelope to put the letter in, and pop
out to the post office.

When I come back I have an email from Lindsay Walsh, the journalist at *Hers.*

Dear Celine,

Have you had a chance to speak with your sister?
When is a good time for me to phone? Prefer
sometime this week.

LW

'There isn't a good time,' Jacqui says, when I ring her. 'I'm extremely
busy at work. I don't think I'm going to be able to do it, Celine.'

I park on the edge of my sofa cushion, and stare at the space
between my feet. 'You know, stop me any time and tell me I'm wrong,
but I'm getting the impression you don't want to do this for me.' It's
the first time I've ever been a bit disappointed in her.

Silence. Then, 'Well, you're right, in a way. I don't want to be
involved in the article, Celine, if you must know.'

I pluck at the threads of my cut-off jean shorts, trying to remember
that she's got a right to say no, if she's not comfortable with the whole
thing – even if she's spoiling things for me. But I still can't resist saying, 'But you *are* the article – I mean, part of it. The best part, actually.
The whole angle for the story is how there are two matchmakers in

the family! Without you, Patrick wouldn't be back in my life and the journalist wouldn't have such a great story.'

She sighs heavily. I am so confused by her reaction that it gives me a sudden headache. 'I just don't get it,' I tell her. 'It's hardly a big deal. I really don't know why you're being like this . . .'

'Okay, then let me tell you why,' she says. She sounds exasperated. 'It's because it's not me they should be interviewing! I wasn't supposed to say anything but I've obviously got no choice now, have I?'

I am confused.

'It wasn't me who got you back in touch with Patrick.'

'So it *was* Aimee?' I knew it!

'No,' she says. 'It was Mike.'

FORTY-TWO

'Mike?'

I laugh. A short burst of disbelief. 'Did you say it was Mike?'

'Yes. Mike emailed Patrick. I'm sorry. I wasn't supposed to tell you. He asked me not to. That's why I let you just go on believing it was me.'

'Hang on . . .' I stand then sit back down again. 'Are you being serious? I mean, you can't be . . .' When she doesn't answer I say, 'My God, you are!' I try to get my head around this. 'Mike emailed Patrick? But . . . how? The email was sent from my computer. My desktop . . . Mike never . . .'

'Had access? Yes he did. When you went to Manchester to meet that client of yours and he came over. Remember?'

'No!' But then the cloud lifts, and I do remember something. Didn't he tell me that he took them out to dinner? I was peeved they were spending time together.

'He came to pick us up. I invited him in because he was a bit early and Aimee as usual had been having a clothing crisis, and wasn't quite ready. He was downstairs. I was upstairs with Aimee, helping her rootle through her wardrobe. While we were up there he went on your computer.'

'What for?'

'Not to snoop. He said he wanted to check something on the internet. He said he'd logged out of something and then wanted to log back in so he went into "History" and then he saw all these pages – endless pages of stuff on Patrick.'

Mike hates using his phone to do anything other than text and make calls. Probably because he needs glasses and has been holding off on getting them for way too long. So it makes sense he'd have used my computer. We always used to share one. We had no secrets.

'He went fishing in my *history*?' I feel so violated.

'No! I don't think it was like that at all! It was purely by accident. You know Mike . . .'

He wouldn't go fishing. It's not his style.

'Anyway, you've got a twelve-year-old daughter. If you don't want people to see stuff you've been looking at you should clear it! I mean, what if you'd been looking at porn?'

'Huh? Why would I look at porn?'

'I don't know! People do funny stuff when they get lonely.'

Good heavens! She's starting to sound like my father. 'So, hang on – he knows Patrick and I met? That I went to Paris? That he's been up here? That he's been in our house?'

'Not everything,' she says quickly. 'But some of it. That cat's out of the bag, I'd say.'

'Oh my gosh! I don't believe this.' I don't know what to say. How have I been the last to know this?

'I only told him the bare bones. He actually didn't want to know anything more. I didn't have the impression it was a topic he wanted to talk about, to be honest. He'd just done what he'd done and that was it.'

'But why would he even tell you he'd done it? That's the bit I don't understand.' My brain is scrambling to make sense of it.

'He didn't, really. But when you started saying it was me, then I started to want to know who the heck it was! I truly thought it was Aimee at first, but she told her dad we were trying to pin this on her and she was all upset, so he owned up – to me anyway. So I sort of got saddled with it.' Then she adds, 'Until now. And your damned article.'

'This is crazy.'

'He's known your whole marriage. He's known he wasn't really the one you wanted. I think Mike has known a lot more than you've ever given him credit for, even without him overhearing us drunkenly talking about love and how you were never in it with him, and seeing you do a mad stampede after a taxi in the middle of London. He's not an idiot. And my guess is he finally got tired of being taken for one.'

She's not saying anything I don't know. And yet I am still stunned to hear the truth played back to me. Was it always that obvious? I feel so desperately regretful and sad.

I look at his photo on the shelf above the table. His eyes staring at me, the way they always are, whether he's a photo or he's in the flesh. What man would try to set up his ex-wife with the man she'd always loved? The one who got away? Who would do that?

I believe I'm just pondering this but I must have asked it out loud because Jacqui says, 'Probably the type you don't really want to lose.'

FORTY-THREE

We arrange to meet in one of our old local pubs at the far end of Tyne Green Park. To get him to come I told him I need to talk to him about Aimee. It's a dark day but dry when I set out. But by the time I am halfway along the riverside trail it starts throwing it down. In my haste to leave the house, with all this rattling around in my head, I didn't bring an umbrella. I try to hurry along but it's hard to walk on a wet dirty path in flip-flops; they keep sticking and making small noises like trapped birds.

Within moments my toes are caked in muck, and my white dirndl skirt soaked. But then my mobile rings.

'Where are you?' he says. 'I'm at the pub.'

'I'm nearly there,' I tell him, trying to walk a little faster. 'I decided to walk instead of drive. But I didn't bring a brolly.' I push back hair that's dripping styling product into my eyes, making them sting. I usually run this park, so have no perception of the time it takes to actually just walk it. For some odd reason I remember Aimee getting lost in here when she was about five years old. One minute she was there, then we bumped into a neighbour and got chatting, and when I looked, she was gone. We split up and took two different directions. I can still remember my feet pounding the grass, my heart hammering like I was going to die if we didn't find her – what if someone had taken her? – my head dizzy from dodging trees and trying to watch my step. How I was calling for her and thinking, *What if I can't find her? If she just disappears? If I never see her again?* Then, completely unexpectedly, Mike came round the corner smiling. He was carrying her in his arms.

'I'll come and meet you,' he says now.

'No. I'm not far. There's no sense in us both getting wet,' I say, but he has already hung up.

I go and find a tree that offers at least a bit of shelter. My eyes are burning like mad. I mop at them with my wet sleeve, but that just mops up my running mascara. I close them but when I open them again Mike is standing right there, about fifty feet away, on the gravel path. A lone figure against a background of tall trees, cold river and iron rain.

He has on his light-blue skinny jeans with his white running shoes and his old beige blazer thrown on top of a white open-necked dress shirt that he hasn't bothered tucking in, as though he threw it on quickly. He is holding his huge black Blaze FM umbrella.

'You're drenched,' he says. 'You're going to catch your death.'

As I walk up to him he holds out his umbrella for me to come under. The rain almost perforates the nylon above our heads. He looks pale, and traumatised somehow. His eyes comb over my dripping-wet hair, over my face, and he wipes mascara from my under-eyes with his thumb. He smells of fresh air. There are beads of rain in the quiff of his hair.

'Mike,' I say, hugging my arms about my body. Not that I am cold; it's warm rain. There's no way I can go into a pub looking like this.

'What's wrong?' he asks.

For a moment I can't go on, can't look at him. A family of starlings fly back and forth between two trees. There is gravel in my flip-flops, small stones sticking to the soles of my feet. Then I meet his eyes. 'Why did you email Patrick?'

His expression doesn't change much. But in the dark clarity of his face I suddenly see him in a way that maybe I never have: as someone with feelings I've underestimated; someone who is capable of being irredeemably hurt. 'Oh,' he says. 'So she told you. Well, I suppose I shouldn't be surprised.'

'She did. But not for the reasons you might think.' I don't feel like getting into the magazine-article thing now. I am shivering, suddenly, and just crave to be dry, to be moved back in time, or forward – to be anywhere except in the *now*. 'But why, Mike? What on earth made you do it?'

The rain is pelting on top of the umbrella. Beyond our cover, it seems to slide down in sheets, riddling the calm grey surface of the river like a hail of bullets. He stares through it, and doesn't speak for what feels like a very long time. Then he says, 'You and I didn't work, but that doesn't mean I don't want you to be happy.'

He meets my gaze, and the bareness of his honesty makes my eyes brim with tears.

'I knew you'd go on wondering about him, and doing nothing about it. So I decided to do it for you.'

Hot tears roll down my face. They're bolstered by a sob. I don't mean to cry – I don't even know why I am crying. Mike watches me steadily but without huge pity or any other emotion. Then he balances his umbrella handle in the crook of his arm and wiggles his jacket off, then gives it to me. 'Here. Take it.'

I pull it around me. It's warm from his body; I could just paint myself right into it. 'I mean, don't get me wrong, it's not like I set out to do it. It wasn't my great mission . . . I was on the computer, saw his name connected to some college, clicked on it and there was his email address.' He shrugs. 'I have no idea what made me do it. I just thought, *Put it out there; see what happens. If he bites, he bites* . . . I didn't exactly want to say anything to him, so I just fired off a blank email knowing he'd see your name and he could take the rest from there.'

I can't stop shaking my head. Part of me thought he was going to say that none of it was true.

'You know he came to London . . .'

His cheeks flush: that look I know so well – the Mike-getting-pissed-off look. 'I'm really not interested,' he says. 'In fact, it's the last thing I want to hear about.' He gazes right into my eyes with an air of finality. 'I hope it works out for you. But do I have any desire to know anything about him or what you're both doing?' He shrugs. 'None.'

I process this.

'Don't feel bad,' he says. 'Neither of us is a bad person. It's not your fault any more than it's mine. You tried to make it work, I know that. You couldn't help being in love with somebody else any more than I could help being in love with you. We're both people who tend to reach for things that are somehow a bit far out of our grasp.'

It takes me a while to be able to speak because I'm ashamed that I must have allowed my state of mind to be so obvious all those years. But he's got something wrong. 'Did you really always think I wanted to be with him all the time that I was with you? Because that's not true.' No human being could live their life endlessly wishing they had chosen someone else. Life is for living and you just get on with it.

'No, maybe not all the time. But enough of the time. I think you wished I'd been him. You had this ongoing thing for him. Most people would have snapped out of it, but you never did.' He pulls a resigned smile. 'I actually happen to think our marriage was a lot better than what you made it out to be in your own mind. But I suppose I always knew something was wrong, deep down. That you weren't really happy.' His face has flushed now. His hair is flattened with the rain.

'What you heard me say to Jacqui . . . we'd both had too much wine.'

We'd been curled up at opposite ends of my couch. I'd said, *I love Mike but I was never in love with him. And sometimes – God – the sad waste of that is more than I can take.*

He'd been standing in the doorway. We hadn't heard him come in. Two days later he threw the shoe across the room and broke his mother's ornament.

'It wasn't that,' he says. 'Not *just* that. Most people don't have these outbursts, do they? When their husband finds them crying for what seems like no reason, and then they say they're not happy.'

'That was many, many years ago. I was in my twenties! And it only happened – what? Twice?'

'But all the same . . .'

I do remember that terrible restlessness that was in me at the time. It started shortly after we got married and silently grew like a cancer. I just wanted to feel more! I wanted to feel that frenzy, that electrifying, unstoppable rush of lust and in-love-ness, when I was kissing him, when he touched me. It was like craving a highly addictive drug that I should never have tried in the first place. And then I had Aimee and had other things to think about. Then I found myself in my thirties. And something in me settled itself. It was almost a relief, like a fever finally breaking.

I wipe tears away. At least my eyes aren't stinging anymore.

'For a long time I thought that if I was good to you in all the right ways I could change that,' he says. 'But then, well, I had to take the blinders off eventually, didn't I?'

I look at this man standing here in the rain, this human being who I happened to meet quite randomly when I was so broken, when I'd felt I'd lived an emotional lifetime in the span of a few short days. This man who taught me to trust again. Who knows more about me, in more meaningful and intimate ways, than any other living soul: certainly more than Patrick, if I'm being honest. What was the point of it all? What's he going to do with all this knowledge and understanding of me he has acquired now? Wasn't it just a wasted education in another human being? If our marriage had been a mistake, then it should have ended earlier, before there was the expectation that the longer it went on, the longer it would go on. It's like putting yourself through years of training and entering a race you have no hope of winning.

'I'm so sorry, Mike.' I look at his lean shoulders under the shirt. The goosebumps on his neck like chicken skin. His chest hair poking out; I remember how I would lie in bed and nestle into it, feeling, if not exactly what I wanted, then definitely loved and safe. 'It's not enough. Not nearly enough. But I am. Truly sorry.'

I bow my head and feel his eyes burning into the top of my skull. When he speaks, his voice bears a heaviness of heart, with the faintest hint of reproach, which I can tell he is trying to suppress. 'You know, it would be a shame if you never found what you were looking for. And who knows, maybe you and this bloke were right for each other. Just because you hardly knew him . . . I feel like I've known you all my life and that didn't exactly help us, did it?'

I grasp myself around the waist again, as though I am caving in on myself. I look at him, and then can't look at him. Because his composure is almost unbearable.

And still we stand here, and the rain pounds the ground around us. I look away, staring across the river until my eyes burn.

'Don't cry,' he says, quietly. 'You should be happy. You can have what you always wanted. How many people are in that position? Eh?'

'But what if—' We meet eyes through the screen of my tears. 'What if there's been a mistake?' My voice comes out in a whisper.

His eyes scope my face again, and I can see the disarray of him: like a person wrestling with the desire to try, yet again, to believe in something he just can't. 'There's no such thing as mistakes, Celine. We all make our decisions for the right reasons at the time.'

He tightens his grasp on the umbrella handle, while he watches more tears spring from me. 'You have to think of us as a season,' he says. 'We came to an end, but life moves on.'

And then something odd occurs. While he is studying me, there is a moment where his expression changes, the steel front falls away, and

I see a look that used to be there years ago, before I'd given him too much reason to view me differently. He smiles – a sad and yet still loving smile. Then his face moves closer to mine, and, spontaneously, mine to his. His hand goes to my waist inside his borrowed blazer, the umbrella faltering overhead, his fingers gripping the wet cotton of my cardigan. Then he kisses me. At first, a tentative granting of lips meeting lips – Mike's kiss feels new again, after Patrick. Then it's as though we are both inspired by the familiar. The umbrella drops from his hand. The rain is like needles on our heads. Mike's grip on my waist intensifies, his fingers burrowing under light layers of material to find bare skin. His touch has an oddly exhilarating effect. These same hands that have been on my body so many times that I'd told myself I couldn't feel them. Now I feel them as though they're different hands.

And it's almost like all those years ago, in the car. A small flame fans somewhere inside me, like it could become something if I let it, if I stopped telling myself, *Ah, but it isn't burning brightly enough!*

We are getting soaked, but he doesn't seem to mind. The kiss goes on, making unexpected strides through my consciousness. He is the first to pull away. His hair is plastered to his head. He smiles with his eyes and his gaze doesn't once move from mine as he sets about tucking my T-shirt back into my skirt and carefully doing up the two buttons on my cardigan. Like you might wrap up a present that you're going to re-gift.

'Hm,' we both say together.

FORTY-FOUR

'I'm not going to marry Rich.' We are devouring jacket potatoes and salad in a café in Eldon Square in Jacqui's lunch break.

I set down my knife and fork, fold my arms, and study her for a moment or two. 'You're not? Wait, I'm too stunned to speak.'

She chuckles. 'All right! So it was a foregone conclusion. That's why you're in the business. Because you know things about people that they don't know about themselves.'

'In your case it hardly required supernatural powers.'

'Maybe not . . . I suppose I've always known I couldn't go through with it. The Christian thing, awful as it was, probably had to happen to make me see sense – or to show me that I'm just way too immature and juvenile to considering adult things like marriage.'

'Have you told him?'

She nods. 'He took it quite well. He said half the time he felt we were roommates anyway. I think he realises he's got a lot of stuff to deal with about himself before he commits to a life with someone.' She rakes the flesh out of her potato, and then unwraps a small patty of butter and scrapes it on there with a knife. I watch her draw it around the potato until it melts. 'So we're going to sell the flat. But in the meantime I have to move out and rent somewhere. But I wondered if I could move in with you, just for a month or so, because I'd like to take my time to look around.'

'Of course. Aimee will be thrilled. You can stay as long as you like.'

She blows me a kiss across the table, and then eyes her potato again, as though she's suddenly gone off it. 'There's another reason, though, why I don't want to go buying somewhere just yet.' She looks up at me, with her chin tucked, sheepishly. 'I've actually applied for a job. To work for Foster & Partners, in London.'

Now I really am floored. 'In London?' I gasp. Sir Norman Foster is the famous architect who designed the North-East's premier music venue, Sage Gateshead, among other things. I know how much she admires his company's work.

'There's no guarantee I'll get it. In fact, it's highly unlikely, so I'm trying hard not to get too excited.'

I scrutinise her. 'Jacq, you graduated uni with a first. Your current firm practically kidnapped you to get you. I can't imagine there'd be too many people more qualified.'

'Oh, you'd be surprised. They're fishing in a very big pool. It's not a sure thing.'

'You know, I always sensed your restlessness was about more than just you fancying someone else,' I tell her, dousing my own potato in butter now. 'I'm not sure you're really ready to be married to anyone. I think you've got personal goals to achieve first. Maybe you have to have a life you love before a love you love.'

She smiles. 'That's nice. And true. And if I get a job offer in New York I want to be able to take it, without feeling I'm tied. And, if I'm being honest, I'm a happy, upbeat person and I found living with someone with depression very hard. I have to admit it. But I'd only say that to you, because I realise it makes me sound so selfish and horrible.'

I shake my head. 'No, it doesn't. I'm very sorry for him and I hope he meets someone who will love him and accept how he is, but I think you did the right thing. It's scary letting someone who loves you go, Jacq – you once said that to me. But what I should have said is that something always comes along to replace what's gone. It's a bit like digging a hole. You shovel all the soil out, but the earth around it falls in and fills some of it back up again.'

She smiles. 'I like that idea.'

I nod, feeling wistful for a moment. 'Me too.'

FORTY-FIVE

Aimee and I are off to Canada.

Aimee stays at Mike's the night before we fly. I haven't talked to Mike since I told him about Patrick's invitation. It's only when he drops her off at our house that we come face to face for the first time since we kissed. 'Hi,' he says flatly, seeming to look everywhere but into my eyes.

'Thanks for driving her,' I tell him. Given that our flight leaves shortly after noon, it would have been a bit of a rush if I'd had to go pick her up and then drive to the airport.

He nods. Now his eyes do meet mine and he looks at me with almost disturbingly hard focus. I think he's going to say something dramatic, but he just says, 'Will you phone Jacqui to tell her you got there safely?'

'Of course.' I let out a sly breath. 'Rather than pay for roaming I was planning to buy Aimee an old-fashioned calling card so she can ring you as much as she wants. I'm sure she'll have lots to tell you.'

'Whatever you want,' he says. 'So long as I know you got there all right.'

'Do you like my new Sketchers?' Aimee darts to the door, lifts a foot to show me her new pink and brown leather running shoes. 'I'm travelling in them.'

Amazingly, she seems unperturbed by the idea of getting to know Patrick, as though it just goes with the territory if she's to have her holiday in Canada. 'Black bears live until they're twenty-three,' she told me the other day. 'I was looking on the internet. I would have thought they'd live longer. Like elephants.'

'I told you, you shouldn't wear new shoes to fly in,' Mike says, uncharacteristically gruff with her. 'Your feet swell in the air. It's a long time to sit in pain.'

Aimee looks from her dad to me for help. 'I'm sure it'll be fine,' I tell him. 'I think it's only older people who suffer from that. Not someone Aimee's age.'

'Well, take some Elastoplasts,' he says. Then, to me, 'I should go. Have a safe flight.' And then, as a bit of a throwaway line, read by an actor who is not quite talented enough to be entirely convincing, 'Enjoy yourself.'

We arrive at 6 p.m. local time. As we proceed through the exit doors into the arrivals hall, I spot him right away, and whatever doubts I've harboured about coming here just disappear. He waves, his face breaking into a big smile.

I can tell he wants to hug me but catches himself in the awkwardness of the moment. Instead, he gives me a quick kiss on the cheek and makes a point of introducing himself to Aimee, who is standing stiffly at my side.

A muggy heat hits us outside, as well as the bluest sky with gleaming sunshine. Patrick directs us around wheelie suitcases, past orange taxis and crawling black stretch limos, through the horns and shouts and the shrill whistle of the uniformed parking commissionaire. My first thought is that everything is bigger: cars, buildings, paths; an immediate outpouring of freedom and space. He leads us to his car, talking animatedly, one hand still on my back, and the other carrying Aimee's suitcase. In a short-sleeved pale-blue sports shirt and faded jeans, he looks fit and lean and tanned. And I wonder how many times, for Aimee's sake, I'm going to have to catch myself before I reach to attack him with kisses.

And then we are bulleting along the highway, Patrick still chatting from the front seat – about our flight, the weather, about what he's got lined up for us to do – and Aimee intently observing the vast size of Canada from out of the back window.

His home is a condominium in an area of the city called Yorkville. It has two concierges at the gate, one of whom valet-parks his navy-blue Volvo SUV. His unit is way up on the thirtieth floor. 'I don't think I've ever been in a building as tall as this.' Aimee stares at all the floor numbers that light up as we ride the lift. 'Not very good if you're scared of heights.'

'I actually don't care for heights,' he tells her. 'I just try not to look out of the window.'

She blushes and a little smile plays there.

As he swipes his door with a key-card I am struck by how unreal it feels to be standing here anticipating walking into the place where Patrick lives.

'Welcome,' he says, pushing open the door for us.

I walk in, surprised how magazine-interior it is. 'It's all white!' I laugh.

'Hey, not my doing. The person I'm renting from is an interior designer.'

I am drawn to the massive windows behind the white leather couch that overlook a busy intersection of streets. 'Cool!' Aimee says, coming to look too – high-end stores like Tiffany right below, glass buildings that reflect the sky, broad avenues disappearing in all directions. 'That's Lake Ontario,' he says, standing right behind us, pointing ahead as far as the eye can see. 'And that is Yonge Street.' He points left. 'Some say the longest street in the world.'

'In the *world* or in Canada?' Aimee quizzes him.

'It used to be in the *Guinness Book of World Records*. They wrongly said it was more than eleven hundred miles long but it's actually around fifty-three, I think.'

'*Fifty-three?*' Aimee gawps at him.

He smiles. 'We'll walk it tomorrow.'

'*All* of it?'

He laughs now. 'No. Just the bit that takes us from here down to the lakeshore. Maybe a mile.'

'Phew!' she says, looking to me. 'Otherwise I really will need those Elastoplasts.'

'Hungry?' He glances at his watch. 'We could go for dinner.'

We are hungry, or at least ready for a proper-sized, satisfying meal. 'Come on,' he says. 'It'll be good to get some fresh air. You can unpack when we come back. Let's hit a patio in Yorkville and soak up some sun.'

We go back down in the lift and walk for about ten minutes until we come to a lively area of bars, boutiques and outdoor restaurants that feels instantly European, set one block in from the main street. Patrick leads us down a narrow walkway, to one of the less busy patio restaurants in a tiled courtyard that is decked with plant pots spilling colours.

We sit down at a chrome table in the sun. Patrick orders a bottle of Prosecco, and a cranberry and soda for Aimee, which he suggests after the waitress says they don't serve ginger beer. I order chicken with linguine Alfredo, Aimee orders fish and chips, and Patrick an ahi-tuna salad with a side of yam fries. The Prosecco is sparkly and refreshing. Aimee holds my flute up to the sun and peers at the pale golden bubbles. Patrick sits back in his seat, wearing his sunglasses that prevent me from seeing his eyes, his mouth twitching into a pleased smile every time I look at him. We are as much a novelty to him as all this is to us.

When our food arrives, Aimee is so stunned by the portion size that she gets her phone out and takes a picture of each of our plates, which amuses Patrick. 'Mum! That's not a portion of pasta, it's a whole box! I'm going to send it to Dad.'

It's true about the size of the food. My enormous oval plate is loaded up with a heap of buttery noodles, and what appear to be two grilled chicken breasts on the top. 'God, I'll never eat all this,' I tell Patrick, laughing. 'My protein allowance for the entire month!'

'Welcome to North America,' he says.

When we finish all we can manage, it's after ten, which, with the five-hour time difference, is the middle of the night for us. We walk back slowly, taking a slightly longer route along another narrow street that's full of expensive boutiques, which leads on to a main, tree-lined thoroughfare. Aimee totters on ahead of us in her new running shoes and white footless tights with a brightly coloured sundress over the top. And from time to time, when she's not looking, Patrick takes hold of my hand and squeezes it before releasing me again.

I spot his building on the corner. When we get upstairs I watch Aimee brush her teeth and then she falls semi-clothed into bed. 'Cool,' she says enthusiastically when he shows her the view from her bedroom window. But she's too tired to show much interest for long.

With the blinds open and the city lights streaming in, Patrick and I stand there in his bedroom, illuminated in stripes of white light, kissing, joining foreheads and taking stock of the fact that, somehow, we're together again.

The next few days are a whirlwind through Patrick's itinerary. A whisk up to the top of the CN Tower, one of the tallest buildings in the world, where we eat a very expensive lunch. Then we take the ferry across to Toronto Island and have steaks for dinner on the park's communal barbecue. In bustling Chinatown, Aimee is repulsed by the sight of whole fish lying on the 'sidewalk' in the sunshine. Temperatures are over ninety, so a trip to the Eaton Centre is a pleasant escape. Aimee is enthralled by the oasis of clothes shops that offer something different from what we have back home. When Patrick discovers her interest in shoes, we end up ditching Black Creek Pioneer Village for the Bata Shoe Museum. When he tells her it houses more than 12,000 exhibits, Aimee nearly squeals. Two hours in there is clearly not Patrick's idea of a great way to spend the morning, but Aimee's fascination with the History of Western Fashion, and her rabid delight over a pair of leather platform Oxfords, circa 1973, is almost worth Patrick's pain.

'You can draw. You love shoes. Seems to me you should become a shoe designer,' he tells her, looking through his rear-view mirror when we're on our way home.

She turns very still while I can practically see her little brain processing this. Then she gawks at me, wide-eyed. 'That's totally what I'm going to do!' She reaches into her bag and pulls out a pencil and sketch pad. Patrick and I smile.

All that, plus Greek food on the Danforth, and a rather romantic dinner for three in Toronto's Distillery District: we are almost worn out by the time Patrick hauls us to Niagara Falls. But Aimee's excitement reaches new levels when we don ridiculous plastic rainwear and take the *Maid of the Mist* boat ride to the foot of the falls to watch six million cubic feet of water fall over its crest, the equivalent of thirteen storeys, above our heads. Patrick tells her the tale of the woman who was the first to go over the falls in a barrel in 1901, and of other subsequent stunts that haven't proven as successful, and Aimee looks at him, part disbelieving, part like she just might want to run out and try it herself.

As our time together inches on, I find it easier to hold Patrick's hand, accept his arm around my shoulders. Our quiet passion for one another doesn't need to be hidden so much anymore. Aimee doesn't seem to really notice it.

And of course I can't help but compare this to holidays with Mike. How, in the early years of our marriage when we'd go to France or Italy, we would inevitably find ourselves confronted with all these lovey-dovey Europeans who are so demonstrative with each other in public. And Mike would say, 'Why aren't we like that?' And there was really no answer. None I could voice. Because the truth would hurt too much: *I am not in love. And I can't make myself be.* But as the years went on I realised that's not how everyone behaves anyway. Whether you kiss or hold hands when you walk down the street is not an indication of anything. Sometimes the most outwardly affectionate people are the ones dying the most dismal death inside.

The photos I snap of Aimee driving back from the shoe museum show a girl who is as happy as I've seen her in a very long time. And I know that she's had a rough time with Mike and me splitting up, but I see more positive than negative ahead for us. I was so happy when she thrust a sketch of 'John Lennon's "Beatle Boot" crossed with an English leather pump circa 1925' over Patrick's shoulder. 'I think I've found my new career,' she said, with the enthusiasm of the old Aimee.

On Tuesday she phones Mike on my calling card, while we pull over for a snack on the drive to Patrick's cabin up at Muskoka. She chats animatedly on the payphone, while Patrick and I sit and watch her from a nearby picnic bench. When she gets off the phone, I recognise that slightly subdued look – the homesick face, the very one I'm sure I must have had that time my dad took me to Greece with his girlfriend.

The cabin is far more impressive than Patrick has led us to believe. Right on the edge of Lake Muskoka, and a small sand beach, it sits in its own private jewel-sized hideaway among tall trees. We crunch gravel past a small storage shed and then a snowmobile shed to a 'change house', as he calls it, that's as close to the lake as you can get without stepping in. 'My dad built this for my sister and me to towel off in, and to dry the dog,' he laughs. 'My dad must have seen us as little animals in our own right, but for us, our time in this place was all we really wanted from summer. We'd look forward all year to coming here.'

He unlocks the change house to reveal not at all what I am expecting. A tiny room with a single bed in it, with a cream eiderdown; there's a pine side table and a sink in the corner with a small, frameless, cracked mirror above it. 'The guest cabin,' he says, looking at Aimee. 'Your own private suite while you're here, if you'd like it. Or you can stay in the main house; it's up to you.'

'But what about the bears, though?' she asks him, slightly hesitant.

'No bears,' he says. 'Except when you go to the toilet.'

Her eyes widen. 'Where's the toilet?'

He indicates a wooden shed right next door. 'Don't worry, I'll teach you to use a gun before nightfall.' He smiles at me, but I've time to see her jaw drop. I give him a look that says, *Okay, I think the joke has backfired* . . .

'Here,' he says, opening a tiny connecting door that I only just notice as he walks to it. 'It seems my father thought of everything.'

Thank God there's a toilet.

'Right! I'll take it!' Aimee says, brightly.

It's only when Patrick and I go back to the house, while Aimee is unpacking her stuff, that I realise something's bothering me and I can't let it go.

'I'm not sure I'm happy she's sleeping out there,' I say.

He looks puzzled for a second. 'What's wrong? Why not? She's perfectly safe. I was only joking about the bears.'

'I know . . .' I feel myself clamming up and am aware he's observing the slight change to me. 'It just feels like she's sleeping in an outhouse or something. Like we've shoved her down the bottom of the garden.'

He is momentarily stunned. 'No . . .' he shakes his head, disappointment filling his eyes. 'Not at all. It's not an outhouse. It's a guest house. But she's welcome to stay in here if you want . . . I just thought this way we'd get a bit of privacy.'

'Ah,' I say. I was right. He *is* pushing her off down the garden.

After a moment I walk over to a sofa chair and sit down.

'You're upset,' he says, following me.

I stare at the knots on the wood to the left of his feet. I am trying to get the better of a sudden surge of emotion that I can't even explain to myself. *Don't make this bigger than what it is!*

'I didn't think it . . .' He upturns his hands in a sort of shrugged apology. 'I've tried to make her vacation fun for her.'

I realise I'm being irrational and unreasonable. 'You have,' I say. 'You totally have, and I appreciate it . . . We both do.'

There is an unsettling moment where he looks at me as though saying, *Well, if you do you've certainly got a funny way of showing it.* And I register it's the first little bit of friction that's come between us.

'I'm sorry,' he says, looking like he needs to say it again. 'I thought she'd think it was an adventure and . . . I just wanted to maybe get a little alone time with you. That's all.'

We say no more about it. He cracks open two beers and I remind myself that Aimee's having a great time and she's happy with the sleeping arrangements. Therefore I should be too.

I try not to dwell on the one thing I know. Mike wouldn't have taken her to cottage country in the middle of nowhere and wanted to be so many feet apart from her while we were sleeping. He wouldn't have rested in his bed.

I am uneasy the first night. But next morning when Aimee tells me how cool it is that she's got her own place, and I witness the genuineness of her pleasure, I start to see that I may have overreacted about the whole thing. From that point forward I put it to the back of my mind and have to admit that those next nights that I'm alone with Patrick in his cabin with the pine walls could easily be the happiest of my life. We don't do much except go out on the lake by day; I swim while Aimee sits and draws more shoes, and only once do we go for a long drive looking for a bear or a wolf – though disappointingly we don't see any. Just plenty of white-tailed deer, which Aimee takes some good pictures of, and a couple of moose.

Patrick tells me a lot more about the book he's writing his outline for – a foreign correspondent's inside view of Iraq. He talks surprisingly little of his new job, nor do I really feel like mentioning it. All I know is that he's due to start it by Christmas. One night when we do actually put the telly on, he shows us the man he will be replacing.

'Cool!' Aimee says, well into the idea of Patrick being famous. 'Won't you get to go abroad, though, and do those news reports from wars and things anymore?' she asks him.

'Sometimes,' he says. 'I'll do live news reports on location when the need arises.' He looks at me and adds, 'Really, it was the right decision to take it.'

When we go to bed, after we make love, I find myself thinking about how he seems to keep dropping in these comments about how it was the right thing to take the job. They always seem to be a little apropos of nothing, which makes me wonder if he's trying to convince himself of it – or me. With the discussion of him starting by Christmas, I tell him that a couple of days ago I had an idea to perhaps throw a New Year's Eve party for my clients. 'Maybe a masked ball . . . I could get every client to invite a couple of guests who are single. Everybody keeps their masks on until midnight, when they take them off and finally see who they've hit it off with.'

If he's wondering why I'm telling him all this, he doesn't show it. 'That's not bad,' he says, looking quite impressed with the idea. I notice, though, that he doesn't say, 'But I was hoping you and I would spend Christmas and New Year's together . . .' which is perhaps what I'd been fishing for.

I flip on to my front, resting my face on my arm, turned away from him so he can't see my disappointment. He kisses my shoulder and writes letters on my bare back – the same words he wrote with the tip of a dried-up leaf while I lay in my bikini on the sand, while Aimee suntanned and read a book beside us. 'I love you,' he wrote. When I smiled at him, he smoothed it away with his hand, as though perhaps he'd never written it in the first place.

I love you, he writes now, only this time he doesn't rub it out. Perhaps he has read my thoughts.

I realise I haven't said it back to him. Now would be the perfect time but I just find myself clamming up. Why did I have to spoil things by letting my mind go to Christmas?

It's our last night before we return to the city; in two days we will be flying home. We are in bed again. I don't want to ruin everything and yet I have such a horrible, restless dissatisfaction running rampant through me. It's as though I can't enjoy the now for always pitching ahead. I can't be where we are for needing to know where we're going. So I cautiously whisper the one question that seems to be so familiar to us. I ask him, 'Have you given any thought to what we're going to do?'

'I have,' he says, after a small sigh. 'And I don't know.'

There's a long silence and I'm busy thinking, *Is that it?* when he turns me on to my back, making me look at his face in the moonlight, and says, 'There is part of me, Celine, that says you should come live here. Aimee could go to school here. You could do the same line of work. Or maybe you'd be happy to not have to work for a while. I'd be earning enough.' His fingers do a rapid pitter-pat on my shoulder. 'Aimee could go back to England as much as she wanted – you both could, anytime, to see your sister and your dad.' His fingers stop moving and hover a couple of inches above my skin and then he takes his hand away altogether. 'But it wouldn't be reasonable to drag Aimee away from her father, would it? And even for my own reasons, I'm not sure I can have you come live here.' He rolls on to his back and stares at the ceiling. His eyes look deeply set and shadowed, as though I'm only just seeing that he's carrying a burden – perhaps one that's been around for quite a long time. 'I did that with Anya, moved her away from her life. Hauled her off into the unknown. Made her put me and my career ahead of everything else.' He turns to me with unfettered honesty written all over his face. 'It wouldn't be that much different, would it? You'd be in the same position as she was in, and I have a feeling it would be doomed. And I can't have that responsibility on me. I just can't.'

I don't know what to take issue with first. I'm gutted by him saying *doomed* followed by *responsibility*. 'I've never felt like somebody's responsibility before,' I say. 'And, in any case, when you're part of a couple you do have an obligation to ensure it works. And you actually want that obligation! That shared purpose is what marriage, or partnership – some might argue, *life* – is!' How has he missed this?

'I know all this,' he says.

But I just can't help thinking, *Do you? Really?* I sit up, wriggling to one side of the bed a little, unconsciously putting an inch or two of distance between us. 'Anyway, I'm not sure Anya is a good comparison to me,' I say. 'I'd have said the difference is you love me and you feel we were meant for each other, whereas you didn't have that feeling with her.' If he was being truthful. I have never doubted him before.

It devastates me that he doesn't instantly agree. 'I'm not sure that is the difference,' he says, after perhaps too much thought. 'I think it's more about putting too much pressure on the situation. On me – to make it all work out.'

Wow.

He watches me as I quickly clamber over the top of him. 'What are you doing?'

I pull on my underwear and a jumper that got thrown on to a chair. 'I need air.'

'I'm just trying to be realistic,' he calls after me, his tone regretful and slightly bemused, and slightly hopeless.

251

I am already outside, my temples pulsing, wishing I could scrub those words out – in fact, all of the last five minutes. Admittedly part of what he has said is right: I couldn't drag Aimee away from Mike – not that I can really believe he has Mike's interests at heart; it's just convenient for him to say that. So why am I wishing I were being offered something I don't even want or see as possible myself?

He doesn't instantly follow, which also speaks volumes to me. I sit on the sundeck and stare at the moon, which appears to be suspended by invisible cords on the top of the water, feeling very alone. More alone than at any time in my life. And I register something. In all my years of marriage, of deciding if it was better or lesser than it seemed, I never actually felt alone. Mike has never made me feel as bad as I feel right now.

I want the impossible, I think. *That's my trouble. I always did. I am my own worst enemy.*

Then he's standing behind me. 'I didn't mean it like that,' he says.

I can't look at him. All I can think is of his girlfriends. This one in the Middle East. That one in California. He's forty-three years old and he's never known true commitment. Why would I think he's capable of it now?

'Look at me,' he says. 'Please, Celine . . .'

I let out a huge involuntary sigh. I look at him.

'I would love to promise you that we can do this, and it'll work out. I've tried to see it from every possible angle . . .' He sits down beside me and gazes at my profile because I've turned away again. I just can't hear any more buts. 'There is not a single doubt in my mind that if we both lived in the same country – in the same place – it would work out. Not a single doubt. But—'

'We don't and we never will,' I finish for him. 'What we had should have been left in Vietnam. I don't even know what that was anymore, but what I do know is that not much has really changed.'

'That's not true,' he says, unconvincingly, sounding slightly disapproving and hurt.

'How is it not true?' I say.

When he doesn't reply, I realise something I wish I'd realised earlier because despite Patrick having come back into my life it remains true. The one who got away is always built up to be the big mischance of life. But the truth is he was probably meant to.

After a while of us sitting beside one another, wordlessly, he stands. 'Will you come back to bed?'

I continue to sit there for a moment or two longer, then I get up. We go back inside. Back to bed. Patrick holds me but it no longer feels the same.

Something is gone from the holiday. An air of transience overlays us. There is an economy to my words, to my affection. I want to be alone. Even Aimee senses it. She draws and colours in quietly, her burgeoning shoe-design collection a replacement for having to make unwanted conversation. I wonder if she'll tire of shoes the second we're on the plane and then she'll want to start painting waves again, with her granddad. By the time we're back in Toronto, and I am packing our bags in Patrick's apartment, a part of me can't wait to get on that plane.

Driving to the airport, it feels like a long time since he came to meet us here two weeks ago, maybe because we've done so much. Aimee stares out of the back window but with less curiosity about Canada than she had when we arrived, her travel bug now satisfied. Patrick and I say very little in the car. In fact, so little that he ends up switching on the radio to fill the silence.

When the girl at the check-in desk asks me my destination, I find myself saying, 'Newcastle,' with a certain fortitude.

'Look, do you want to grab a coffee before you go through security?' he asks. I can tell he's desperate to part on a better note than this.

'No,' I say – though not easily. 'Best not. You know me and goodbyes.'

'Hey,' he kisses my downturned lips as Aimee trots off to the toilet. He lifts up my chin with his index finger so I have no choice but to look in his eyes. His face is drawn, but as handsome as ever, and for a second I could crumple at the realisation that we have come to this. 'I'm not giving up on us, Celine. You might be, but I'm not.'

I want to say, *I'm not either*. To lie as brightly as he is lying. But I can't say anything.

When Aimee comes back from the toilet Patrick reaches a hand to the top of her head. 'It's been a great two weeks,' he says to her.

'Thanks . . .' she smiles. 'I've had a really nice time. It's been a lot of fun.'

'You've been lovely to us,' I tell him, because it's so true. He isn't a husband or a father but he really did give playing family a good stab. 'You couldn't have handled us better,' I smile. 'We won't ever forget Canada.' My eyes are telling him so much more, but if I say any more I'm going to cry.

He looks almost bereft, and kisses me again as I fight back tears. Handing over our passports before we go through the security gate takes me back to years ago, to leaving Vietnam. Only he wasn't there to watch me. He'd already gone. A part of me felt I'd dreamed him, and the reality is I could be still dreaming him. Nothing much has changed.

Before we disappear, I turn and look at him and he holds up his hand in a wave. And I take a mental picture of him, letting my mind slowly process it. Because it's quite possible I won't see Patrick again. I don't know why I have such a strong sense about this, but I do.

FORTY-SIX

I never imagined I'd find myself celebrating my sister leaving. But here I am, on this early-September day, along with twenty-two other close family and friends, at Blackfriar's restaurant in Newcastle, partaking in a medieval banquet of suckling pig and leg of lamb, served to us by monks and buxom wenches. It also happens to be Jacqui's thirty-fifth birthday.

Mike is here with Jennifer. I notice she talks to him a lot. And I notice something else. That his eyes are on me every time I glance his way. Even when I'm trying not to make it obvious that I'm looking.

'How was Toronto?' he asks, at one point. He has to speak across three other people. It's awkward for both of us, and I'm sure for Jennifer.

'Good. Aimee had a really nice time.'

'Yes,' he says. 'I heard all about it.'

I try to imagine what she might have said. If she would have kept her account strictly to the fun things she did – if Mike would have broken his 'I don't want to know anything' policy when it was his daughter he was talking to rather than me.

'She was positively glowing with all the stories!' Jennifer says cheerfully, though I sense something about it is a little forced.

Mike's eyes meet mine again. 'But did you have a good time?' he asks. There is something sad and hard in his expression. I hope Jennifer can't see it. I think he's going to say more but fortunately we're interrupted by Jacqui chinking her spoon off her wineglass. 'A few words, please!' she says, standing and pushing back her chair. The table falls silent.

As she thanks everybody for coming, I notice for perhaps the first time how much weight she's lost since splitting up with Rich. In a clingy dark-brown wool dress to mark the sudden shift into autumn, her chest looks bigger, her waist smaller, her hair somehow shinier and her eyes even more luminous. But sitting here about to listen to her say goodbye to us, I wish so much that she wasn't going that I just want to disappear, hide behind coats in the cupboard and cry.

'I'm standing here and I'm still rocking on my feet,' she says. 'This has been such a whirlwind – from my applying for the job, to the interview, to my hearing I'd got it. Then the trips down to London to find a flat.' She swipes a hand across her brow. 'Whoosh! But I'm excited! This is what I haven't felt in a long time. About anything.' Her gaze swings itself past me, taking everybody in, including a couple of her friends who weren't so supportive about her leaving Rich. 'In getting here I've had to recently make a lot of very tough decisions in my personal life. Ones that some people maybe still don't understand. But believe me, I have lost sleep over it all, as I take my actions very seriously. Much as I'm excited to move to London, and much as I tell myself I'll be back up here every weekend, and nothing's really going to change, I also know that a lot will.' Her gaze slides to me now. 'The one thing I would love to be able to do is put Celine in a bag and bring her with me.' She smiles, and her eyes fill. 'Because ever since I was very young I've had Celine right by my side, supporting me and encouraging me in all that I've ever done. I'm going to have to find somebody else to drop in on at all hours of the night, somebody else to pop out for a pint with on the spur of the moment, somebody else's personal crises to balance out my own, and absolutely no one is going to measure up! When I've needed a friend, there's no one I could imagine offloading to in quite the same way as I have done to Celine. To me, the fact that we don't actually come from the same parents was just an accident of birth.' She wipes a tear. Then she picks up her wineglass and raises it, surveying the table again. 'I just want you to know that you're all welcome in my new flat in Hammersmith. Only not all at the same time, as it's only a little bigger than my car.'

She flops back down in her chair and we all whoop up the applause. Somewhere, in my intent focus on her, I failed to notice that Mike got up and left. Jennifer is sitting there looking at me with faint alarm in her eyes. She pulls a tight, plaintive smile.

Time seems to fly. Aimee and I start planning The Love Market's New Year's Eve party. I thought I'd put her artistic leanings to good use and have got her designing the invitation.

'Doesn't one of your rich clients own a big castle or something?' she says, when I bemoan the fact that so many of the good venues around town are already booked up. If only I'd thought of the party idea sooner.

The penny drops. 'Gosh! Yes! David Hall, the man who doesn't wear underwear, owns the spectacularly fabulous Strickley House!' I had the pleasure to visit it once, and felt like I'd died and been re-born as royalty. After Kim dumped him – apparently she never saw his house because he took her to his flat instead, and I often wonder whether if she had, things might have been different – I set him up with Paula Nicholson, a forty-three-year-old wedding photographer who is the granddaughter of the chauffeur to the Duke of Northumberland. I don't know why, but I thought the connection was neat. Plus, when she's not shooting a wedding, she has a thing for artfully capturing stately homes and castles – and, I'm hoping, for men who don't wear pants! She had an exhibition of her photography a few months ago, in Newcastle. I went to see it, and it was quite fantastic.

'Well, it's a long shot but I suppose I could put in a call to him.'

Aimee scowls. 'How do you know he doesn't he wear underwear?'

FORTY-SEVEN

I have noticed that in the weeks since getting back from Canada our FaceTime calls don't seem quite as regular. In my low moments I think, *So I was right in not truly believing him when he claimed he wasn't giving up on us.* But then I berate myself and wonder if I'm just looking for faults to support my own case. I find myself reviewing every minute of our time together, starting with seeing him again in London, searching for clues that he might not have been as emotionally committed as I'd sensed he was. After turning it all over in my mind I decide that all I've really got to doubt him on is the fact that he's taken a job in Toronto and he didn't mention us being together over Christmas. Suddenly I feel a little better about things.

Until the next time we speak.

Patrick is tired, he tells me on this particular FaceTime call. Because he's just flown back from a whirlwind trip to Barcelona. He was there reporting on Catalan independence.

The words are slow to sink in. Ridiculously, I find myself grappling for something intelligent to say on the topic – something I've picked up from the newspaper – to bluff my way through my shock and disappointment. But we know each other too well for me to do this. So I find that all I can actually say is, 'Oh . . . You were just in Spain?', trying to keep the note of reproach out of my tone.

'Yes,' he says, after a small hesitation. 'Like I said, it was whirlwind. Got in and out in less than forty-eight hours.'

We hold eyes and I suddenly hate this impersonal medium of communication and the fact that he is staring at me so closely and yet I can't really feel any true emotion from him; there is this annoying barrier. What had he said in Paris? He'd have flown me there even if we'd only had two minutes . . .

'Hey,' he says, gently, after a moment or two, when I look away and stare hard across the room, cautioning myself not to get upset. 'You wouldn't have wanted to be there, I can promise you. Aside from the fact that I had literally no time, it wasn't a very nice environment to bring you to with everything that was going on.'

Please say no more, I think, suddenly embarrassed that he's trying to make this about the issue of my safety.

'Look,' I say. 'I've got to pick Aimee up from swimming. I'm already a bit behind . . .'

'Celine . . . ?'

'Really, I do have to go.'

'Wait!' he says, holding up a hand. So I wait. 'I wanted to ask if you and Aimee would want to come here for Christmas . . . I was going to go about it in a better way than this, but anyway . . . there it is.'

I don't know if he's just saying this because he knows I'm pissed off with him. Either way, has he forgotten I have a party planned? How can I be in Toronto when I'll have so much last-minute stuff to do? And even if I could, tickets at that time of the year will be so damned expensive. I can't afford transatlantic dating!

'It's impossible,' I tell him. And I give him all the reasons why. I am suddenly so very defeated by the logistics of a long-distance relationship. Yes, they can work. If they are a means to an end. Not if they are an end in themselves.

'Well, I can't come there, unfortunately,' he says, though it needs no saying. He'll have just started his job. 'I really need to see you again soon,' he adds. 'I miss you. In the summer I had your visit to look forward to but now I don't have that . . .' The fact that it's been almost two months seems to underscore the significance of him not telling me he was going to be in Spain and inviting me along. I hate feeling like our relationship has become a burned-out candle but I can't help myself.

We hold eyes, then I say, 'Like I told you, I really do have to go.'

He looks dejected and I feel a little bad. But I don't want to prolong this.

I am the first to click 'End Call'. There is a ping and then I'm just sitting here staring at a blank screen.

FORTY-EIGHT

Jacqui is back for a visit and wants us to go for dinner but I tell her I'm not feeling up to it. I try to concentrate on work. I've a couple of new client leads – recommendations from an existing client – that I should follow up on but I find myself dragging my heels. I just can't rally myself to be bothered with other people's happy endings. I've never been much of a pessimist or pouter so I hate that I'm being one now, but I just can't snap out of it. Because Christmas is around the corner, I am able to immerse myself in that. There's a certain comfort to the distraction of crowded shops, the carols, the rambunctiousness of office parties spilling out of every pub.

The party preparations fortunately demand a lot of my attention. I spend an inordinate amount of time putting together preliminary plans: talking to caterers, contacting a client who is an event planner for a DJ recommendation, researching costumes. I find a site on the internet that sells exclusive, handmade ostrich-feather masks that Aimee's going to love. Then I suddenly think, *Well, hang on, we can put feather boas in vases instead of flowers.* It'll be fun and far cheaper.

David Hall has agreed to loan me his house. Well, part of it. He said it was the least he could do, given that I've introduced him to someone he's falling for – plus, he said, the house has needed a party for a long time.

I went over there and saw the room that he thinks we should have it in. Now I have the whole place envisioned: a couple of chrome martini bars decked in silver tulle and strung with silver and gold mini-lights, nests of silver Christmas balls on high-top tables, silver candelabra, silver and gold tableware – I must find out where to rent it. And it might be fun to kick things off with a dance lesson! I'll invite an instructor to teach everyone the Viennese waltz. Or should it be the merengue? Perhaps the waltz will be more original. Plus, it encourages intimate contact.

Three weeks to go, and I have seventy confirmed guests, most of whom intend to bring a friend or two. Paula – David Hall's photographer girlfriend – is going to take some snazzy photos, hoping to land us in the local newspaper. My event-planner client referred me to the world's finest hors d'oeuvres caterer who knows how to do things with an asparagus spear that boggle the mind. And Trish, who claims she's an expert in alcohol, has been having tons of fun designing weird and wonderful martini concoctions that I'm going to serve. All I need to find is my dance instructor and I'm set. Aimee claims she doesn't want anything for Christmas, only the right to spend up to £100 on things for her costume.

The article on The Love Market came out in the November issue of *Hers* magazine, angled slightly differently. They ended up sending a photographer here to shoot me, and a lovely picture of Vietnam led the piece. Because of the publicity, I've had eight phone calls from women keen to join, and, interestingly, one from a man: a thirty-nine-year-old consultant heart specialist. He filled out my personality questionnaire and sounds interesting. By his photo he looks quite nice, and I've suggested he comes to the party.

Aimee has a copy of the invitation she designed pinned up on her wall. 'It's good,' I tell her.

'Granddad says my wave looks more like a toenail.'

I tut. 'Your granddad thinks being hard on you will motivate you.' I remember how he used to encourage me to draw. But because I knew he was trying to mould me into an image of himself, I deliberately made myself fail. 'He liked the sand dunes you did.'

'He said they looked like breasts.'

I groan.

She wipes the back of her wrist over her cheek. 'I'm useless. I can't even get a good mark when I copy somebody's exam.'

'You copied somebody's exam?'

'Once.' She flushes. 'But I copied the wrong person. He was even dumber than me.'

'Aimee! Don't ever call yourself dumb! I never got good marks in school and I've done fine! There's more to life than being measured against everybody else. Sometimes you have to just be proud of what you achieve for yourself, and stop comparing yourself to other people, or you'll never be happy. There's always somebody better, cleverer, prettier.'

'You really don't think I'm useless then?'

I smile. 'On a scale of one to ten – ten being the least useless you could ever be – you're a seven.'

She looks horrified.

'You could still try much harder to beat your dad at Wii tennis. You could try putting a load of dark laundry in without washing my white blouse with it. You could get a Saturday job as a farmer . . .'

I see her smile.

'But other than that, I can't really think of anything else that's useless about you.'

Mike comes to pick up her up on the second Saturday in December.

'She's Christmas shopping at the Metro Centre, with Lauren – do you not remember?'

He slaps his palm off his forehead. 'I forgot. Damn.'

'She'll be back in an hour or so, I think. Do you want to just come in and wait for her and have a cuppa? It seems a waste to go all the way home . . .'

His eyes tick around my face. 'I suppose,' he says, after some thought.

I make us tea. It's splashing rain and we sit there listening to the knock-knock of the loose downspout.

'Why don't I just fix it,' he says, somewhat impatiently, taking his mug to the sink.

'Don't. I can get somebody out to look at it.'

'But it's annoying,' he says. He goes to the back door and removes the small key that unlocks the shed where we keep the stepladders.

He's up there a while. I keep looking out to make sure he's all right. Drops of rain cling to the fading rose bushes like hundreds of the world's tiniest fairy lights. It suddenly strikes me that Northumberland is beautiful. The mists. The rain. The vastness beyond my window. I do want to live here. And Patrick was right: come what may, I do have a lot to be thankful for.

Mike is quite soaked when he comes back in. He goes to the sink and washes his dirty hands, then takes off his jacket and puts it over the back of the kitchen chair while I re-boil the kettle.

'Thanks,' he says, taking the mug of tea from me. I have one of those surreal moments where I still feel married to him; I can't believe he ever left.

'Patrick asked me to go to Canada for Christmas,' I find myself telling him, punctuating our silence. 'But I'm not going, obviously.'

'Why not? I'd have thought you'd have jumped at the chance.'

I give him the same reasons I gave Patrick.

He listens, says nothing. I watch him closely, try to read him, but it's difficult. It's as though there is a blanket over his emotions, which has the dual effect of buffering us both from them. 'I have a feeling things aren't going to work out between me and him,' I say. It's the first time I've verbalised it and, oddly, I'm more accepting of the concept than I'd thought.

He looks at the space on the floor between his feet. 'Oh? I had no idea,' he says, somewhat disinterestedly.

I go on watching him, but he doesn't look up. 'What about Jennifer? Are you in love with her?' I say.

'No.' He finally looks up. 'Jennifer is a terrific person. I enjoy spending time with her. In many ways she's everything a man could want and would be lucky to get. But no, I'm not in love with her.' He shrugs.

He casts his gaze out of the window. There is a sad, solitary air about him, a canyon of disconnect between us that I want to reach out and bridge. He looks back at me and makes a slow study of me that seems to have no ending. Then he says, 'You see, the thing is, I suppose there's something I've always known about myself. I only ever wanted one woman. And I married her. And, unfortunately for me, I still love her.'

FORTY-NINE

I open my mouth to speak right as his mobile rings. After a moment he reaches to the chair, for his jacket pocket. He looks at the call display, puts the phone back in the pocket. 'It's Jennifer,' he says, and huffs, ironically. Then he adds, 'I should probably go. You can buzz me when Aimee gets back . . .'

He stands and plucks his jacket from the back of the chair.

'Don't go,' I tell him, quietly. 'We should talk.' But I'm not even sure what I plan on talking about. I want him to leave. I want him to stay.

'About?'

I search his face. 'Us.'

He frowns, half-shrugs. 'Celine, you're with somebody else. Fine, there are glitches – nothing in life is easy; people aren't easy – but I'm sure you'll work it out.'

'Why did you kiss me in the park?'

The air seems to tighten. He sighs, still holding his jacket, making no move to put it on. 'That's a good question. I don't know. I shouldn't have. I couldn't help myself. Nostalgia?'

I get to my feet too. And we stand here, caught in a moment of truth. 'Mike,' I venture. 'Do you think this isn't over for us?'

He casts his gaze out of the window again, just inches past my head, as though the answer is somehow out there, corporeal, yet beyond us. When he finally looks back at me he has that same air of detachment that I noted about him earlier. 'You know, Celine, there was a time when I hoped it might not be. When I emailed him, there was a small part of me thinking that if you got back together with him and it didn't work out, then I might get you back. That you'd have finally seen sense . . .' He shakes his head at himself. 'Mad, eh?'

Then he glances at the ceiling; above us is the bedroom we once shared. 'I don't feel like that now,' he says.

His words take me aback. There are no ifs, ands or buts. Yet not a part of me doubts him. I see it clearly in his face. Mike is no longer in love with me – not really, not as much as he might think. He's still harbouring a fantasy; love is the last habit to die.

'I think it was just something I had to go through. I had to hold out some hope I'd get you back, just to lessen the pain of losing you. But now I know I'd never want to go back. I had doubts in the beginning about your feelings and I chose to ignore them. I convinced myself that what we had was good enough for me for a very long time. But the fact of the matter is, I deserved so much better.'

He continues shaking his head long after he stops speaking, as though he's slightly disgusted at me. 'I don't know what you're really asking me, or really saying, but I hope you're not even thinking that you want to get back together, Celine. We had our chance. Now you have to take a chance on somebody else, and so do I.'

'Are you going to marry her?' I remember what he said long ago, about how we learn things: that just because you're in love doesn't mean you're going to be happy, and just because you're not in love doesn't mean you'll be any worse off.

'I don't see me marrying anyone again, actually,' he says. 'I think being married to you was probably as good as anyone could really expect marriage to be. But if that's as good as it could ever be, well, then it's not worth it.' He watches me passively, while the blood rushes to my head and my heart hammers. 'But the good thing is, moving forward I know it'll never feel as bad as this has been, so there's some comfort in that. Because this has been pretty bad, I have to admit.'

He nods me up and down, as though indicating he's done. He walks to the door and I follow him down the passageway. As he's about to open it he says, 'Don't kid yourself, Celine; you don't want me back either. Not really. And you know you don't. Not deep in your heart. Go with your heart. You're the kind of person who should, maybe more than others. It's the only thing that works for you.'

FIFTY

I am not sure this part is exactly what you'd call going with my heart. But it's definitely going with my head.

On Thursday night I do what I inherently know has to be done. I phone Patrick and when he answers I tell him I can't do this anymore.

'Having you come back into my life made me believe in something again,' I tell him. 'And you know what? We are a lovely dream, and part of me wants to just stay sleeping, but we're no better off now than we were all those years ago, if we're being honest. We're just older.'

After a long pause, where he must be waiting for me to say more, he says a very quiet, 'My God.'

We sit there, processing what I've said, while I process his reaction. After another while he says, 'Are you seriously doing this? I mean . . . I can't believe you'd do this. I thought we were fine.' He sounds utterly aghast. 'What prompted this? Something has . . . Surely not Spain?'

It's the first time I wonder if my interpretation of his actions or his signals has been wrong. He sounds as though this has completely blindsided him. 'No,' I say, less confidently. 'It was before that. Maybe after you told me you were taking the job. I think that was when it started to feel hopeless.'

I can still feel him hedging his way around his shock. 'But . . . but if it hadn't been that job, I'd have probably been going back abroad. To what I've done for twenty years. How is this any different?'

I laugh a little. 'It's not! That's the point. It doesn't make it any better; it just makes it the same. And for me, I know I'm not the kind of person who can keep coming over there to see you, having such a fabulous time, getting more and more attached, and then having to come home and live my life looking forward to the next time, however many weeks or months away that will be. It's no way to live. And maybe I'm saying that because I've been married before, and deep down, that's what I'm used to – someone *there* – and that's what I like.'

'Celine . . .' he says, as though he's flabbergasted.

I jump in quickly. 'I'm not looking for you to say you want to marry me!' I knew this would all come out wrong.

'And why wouldn't I want to say I did?' he says, his turn to blind-side me.

I scramble to sort out what this means, what he's really saying, but there is hope in his voice again.

'What I was going to say was Aimee's nearly a teenager. In a few years she'll be grown up and moved out, and you can go and live and be who you want to be, and do what you please!'

I laugh again. 'A few *years*? Patrick . . . no!'

'Why not? We waited fifteen years to meet again; what's a few more to properly be together? We could make it work! I can't believe you're being so defeatist, that you're just so quick to throw in the towel . . . It doesn't seem like you. I still don't know what's prompted this.'

My heart pounds. I open my mouth to say I'm not any of that, but I remember that I am and for good reason. 'Just . . . no,' I say, though those good reasons are becoming fudged again. It strikes me that this could be another slightly more storybook version of the classic rebound situation. Jacqui sort of said it. I am barely divorced from Mike then I'm hurtling back to my old flame. Maybe I just need time in between.

'I still can't believe it,' he says. 'I honestly thought we were doing all right. I thought we were fine.'

'Well,' I say, 'I have a feeling it probably is fine enough for you. But as for myself, I just know I can't get on with my life, talking to you nearly every day across an ocean, and not being able to really have you in my life, and having this be so open-ended.'

'In my mind it's not open-ended,' he says. 'It never was.'

I feel we're going around in circles. I am so glad we are not on FaceTime, as I couldn't have handled it. And yet more than anything right now I wish I could see his face. For one last time.

'Look,' I say, hearing the emotion in my voice and trying to steady it. 'Let's just agree to recognise what we had for the lovely thing that it was. And leave it at that.'

'I'm not prepared to do that,' he says, quite certainly, with a strident urgency.

But I try not to hear it. It sounds so much like something I've heard too many times before. So I say the hardest words I've ever said.

'Goodbye, Patrick.'

FIFTY-ONE

Jacqui comes back up for Christmas and that's the only thing that stops me from going off the rails. I never thought losing someone could feel like this. Certainly not someone who was never even fully mine.

I have invited my dad and Anthea, and Mike, for Aimee's sake. Jennifer was asked to a cousin's in Dundee, and at the last minute Mike decided he didn't want to go with her. It's the worst Christmas I've ever suffered through, even though I try my best not to show it; I don't want to spoil it for everybody else, and neither do I want the attention. I just want to crawl under a rock. We eat turkey, wearing paper hats that Aimee made, and listen to Bing's 'White Christmas'. Afterwards we watch two films and drink copious amounts of wine, my father squeezed on to the couch between Anthea and Jacqui.

We won't have many more Christmases together like this, I think as they all start preparing to leave. As each year ticks over we become more entrenched in the new steps we've taken. There won't be this comfort in gravitating to what's familiar – each other. Because it won't be so familiar anymore. That's just the way life is.

Throughout the day I try very hard to ignore the fact that Patrick hasn't tried to contact me. Not even today, to wish me Merry Christmas, which would have been a bridge back to something, had he wanted to cross it.

He doesn't want to cross it.

The realisation hammers home. I try not to dwell on it but I'm sure it's there on my face, in my delayed responses, in my absent gazes, in my regretful grouchiness. I'm sure it's there for anyone who cares to see, or even for those only half-looking.

I see off my dad and Anthea at the door. 'You've got a good woman there,' I tell him, when she decides to pop to the toilet.

'What can I say?' he says. 'She's a companion. I light up her life.'

I smile, even though I've found very little to smile about this day.

When I see Mike off, he kisses me once on the cheek. I don't know if word has got back to him that I have ended things with Patrick. But from the way I've caught him slowly studying me a few times, I suspect it might have. As I watch him walk down the garden path in his skinny jeans with his thigh-length sheepskin jacket, I realise something that not so very long ago would have made me come apart at the seams: I will always love Mike. I will love him equally as much as I have always loved him. Because Mike, in many ways, is still my family and he probably always will be.

But he was right. He knew something I didn't know at the time: that I don't want him back. My time with Patrick these months – despite the unconscionable heartbreak of having to let him go – has made me see that with crystal clarity.

I know who the right person for me was. I've known that all along.

Divorce is like hacking down a mature tree; it leaves an unsightly gap and you want something to quickly grow in its place. You find yourself staring at it and remembering not why you cut the thing down in the first place, but only how nice it used to look. But eventually you can look at the space it occupied and a part of you forgets it was ever there.

FIFTY-TWO

David Hall's stately pile opens its doors to, among the more notable: a red devil, Playboy madam, Phantom of the Opera, Cinderella, a black cat, Batgirl, Batman and four court jesters – all of them in masks. Jacqui wears a stunning silver-sequined floor-length gown and is, she tells me when I can't guess, 'a masked Hollywood actress at the Oscars'. She tuts. 'Isn't it bloody obvious?'

'Which one?' I ask her over the top of Barry White singing 'Let the Music Play'.

'Angelina Jolie and Kate Winslet rolled into one,' she grins under disco lights, showing white teeth framed by ample red lipstick.

'When are you coming home?' I ask her.

'Never.'

'Please?'

'Sorry. I'm never coming back up to this dump.'

'Don't call Newcastle a dump! Just because you're a Londoner now!'

She laughs. 'I'm just happy down there now! Except for missing you. It's almost perfect. And perhaps almost is as good as any of us gets in this life.'

'Oh. My. God!' Someone taps me on the shoulder as Jacqui and I are trying to move a giant candelabra that got placed dangerously too close to the edge of the martini bar. When I turn around it's Trish and James. 'Your dress!' she says. James whistles as I do a twirl for them.

'I'm one of the professional dancers on *Strictly Come Dancing*,' I tell them, holding out my arms to show off the dramatically slit bell sleeves of my frock, which I ordered from a website selling second-hand ballroom gowns.

'It's the most stunning thing I've ever seen!' Trish says.

I look down at myself, still amazed that, other than a little let-out around the hips, the dress fits me so well. It's aquamarine, with an asymmetrical neckline and a low waist that leaves my entire back bare. The bodice is what the description called 'cracked ice' lace, and the skirt is a full soft charmeuse satin. It came with a wrap that I knew I'd never wear, so I had a seamstress turn that into a mask. Aimee helped me choose my high silver stilettos – insisting on only one thing: that she could buy a similar pair.

'What are you?' I ask Trish, happy to see her and giving her a hug before I introduce her and James to my sister. She's wearing a white towelling bathrobe, a white towelling hairband pushing her hair back off her face, and a bright-orange silicone eye mask with two holes in it for her to see out of.

'Can't you guess? I'm a spa diva!'

'Oh!' I chuckle along with Jacqui.

'Truth is, we went to the costume-rental shop and they didn't have much left. So we had to use our imaginations, which was quite hard, given that we don't have one between us.'

'And I'm . . . well, guess what I am,' says the extremely handsome but un-costumed James, who has his arm around her like a man who never wants his arm to be anywhere else. I can feel Jacqui doting on them with her eyes.

I look him up and down. 'Well, unless I'm missing something, you're a man in a blue shirt and a pair of jeans with a surgical mask dangling around your neck – which breaks the rules, by the way! It's supposed to be faces covered all night. No masks off until midnight! Then you finally get to see the person you've met.'

'But I've met her already!' he says, squeezing her into him. 'Thanks to you. But then I'd met her before you. So, truthfully, I'm all confused.'

'I am just pleased she isn't a girl with all those issues!' I joke, remembering his comments about the last ten women he dated.

'Oh she is,' he says. 'She's got loads of them.' He smirks at her. 'And I love every last one of them.' He kisses the side of her head.

Trish chuckles like it's the funniest thing anyone has ever said, and she gazes at him, utterly besotted. Sometimes you see two people together who just look so right for one another. And they are it.

'You still haven't told me what you've come as,' I remind him.

'I'm a dentist,' he says. He pulls a toothbrush and a tiny tube of toothpaste from his shirt pocket and waves it at me.

'If you misbehave we'll make you clean the toilets out with that,' I say.

He laughs. 'If I get drunk enough I'll do it without being told.' Then he drags Trish off towards the bar.

'He's quite tasty,' Jacqui says. I think she's talking about James, but then I see that she is indicating across the room. To a tall, masked, blond man in hospital scrubs.

'A doctor and a dentist tonight! That's Dr Michael Hill, a thirty-nine-year-old consultant heart specialist at the Freeman Hospital. He filled out my personality questionnaire. Contacted me after he saw the article in *Hers*. Remember, the article they had to completely restructure because of you?' I tease her.

'He's a doctor and he came dressed as one?' she laughs. 'Oh dear! But he looks very sexy. There's something about him.'

'So you want to meet him, then?'

She grins. 'I don't want to meet someone who reads women's magazines.'

'He doesn't. His secretary showed him the article. Apparently they've all been trying to set him up since he got divorced. And he doesn't want to date nurses.'

'Interesting,' she says. 'How about architects?'

'Oh, come on.' I drag her over there.

'But you can't let me like him!' she says. 'And you can't let him be as good as he looks! Please! Not now that I live in London and I'm just getting my life sorted! I can't fall in love with a man back up in Newcastle!'

'Of course not,' I tell her. 'I'll try to guarantee it.'

The music changes to Earth, Wind and Fire's 'Let's Groove', even though I specifically warned the DJ not to get into cheesy tunes until everyone was wasted. But somehow it has the effect of drawing everyone to the dance floor. After I introduce Jacqui to the doctor, I go and work the room, and I'm happy to see Sandra, my spa owner and my father's muse, chatting away animatedly to my wounded footballer Liam Docherty, and Liam looking happily ridiculous in his red-devil costume. I'm just deciding not to bother interrupting them when she waves me over excitedly. 'Oh, Celine.' She hugs me as Liam asks her what she's drinking and then walks over to the bar. 'I've been meaning to phone you since before Christmas but I was so busy at the spa. I wanted to tell you how the sitting went, with your dad.'

'Oh! I didn't know you'd actually done it. I thought you might have just been putting him off.'

'No!' she says. 'I was very keen. I mean, obviously not at first.' She laughs. With her large boobs spilling over her gown, she looks like one of the most pornographic Snow Whites I've ever seen. 'I did it as a treat to myself for Christmas. Had my staff work a few miracles on me.' She laughs again. 'It was lovely. I never expected I'd feel so comfortable with all my clothes off, but he put me completely at ease.'

'He did?'

'Yes. And his drawing was wonderful. I couldn't believe it was me. So when all this is over and things settle down a bit, I want you to come to the spa for a free massage and see it.'

'It's at the spa?'

She beams. 'I had it framed and hung it in the powder room. If anyone asks me who did it, I'm going to give them his card.'

'I don't think my dad has a card.'

'Apparently he's getting them made.'

'Oh!' I hide my grin in my hand.

'I was fat as a teenager. It took me years to lose the weight. Then I ended up in the spa business, but somehow never lost the self-esteem hang-ups.' She throws up her hands. 'But your dad made me think that maybe I don't have to be so hard on myself all the time.'

Aimee comes and pokes me in the back, right as Liam returns with Sandra's drink. I cuddle my little Tinkerbell in her short green mini-dress, with her white footless tights with holes poked into them, and her silver mask on a stick.

'Mind my wings,' she says.

I look at her feet, in silver sandals a bit like mine. And then . . . 'What are you drinking?'

'A martini, of course,' she says and takes a sip. 'Without alcohol.' She looks across at the cute young barman I've hired for the night, on loan from Karma restaurant, where I go on my Fake Dates and they think I'm a prostitute. 'Mark made it for me.'

Then she flits off like a butterfly across the floor.

I survey the room. A great turnout, and most did bring a couple of guests. David Hall, dressed as Mr Darcy, said that only Kim had guessed who he was. He's a perfectly good sport about having his house taken over by nearly 200 people whom he's never met before. Kim, otherwise known as Elizabeth I, is here with Andrew Flemming, my client in the music business. When I go over and ask her how it's going, her first words are, 'Nice house,' as she looks around.

'It could have been yours,' I say.

'But Knickerless would come with it.' She smiles. 'And no, actually. It's not "going" with Andy. You seem to think I'm here with him, but I'm here by myself. As is he. We just happen to be talking.' She smiles. 'We've been on four very good dates. He's lovely – the first man you've introduced me to who has absolutely nothing wrong with him.'

Nothing hanging out of his nose? No patent lack of shoulders? He didn't pick up his fork before she picked up hers? I'm floored. 'What's wrong then?' I ask.

'There's just no chemistry,' she says.

Finally. A real reason to not see him anymore. And, alas, one I cannot fix.

'This is progress, though, isn't it? In a weird way?' I hug her.

She chuckles. 'I think.'

'Who is this hunk?' Jacqui comes up to me and whispers in my ear. When I look to where she's pointing, a part of me dies. Over by the Christmas tree, a diminutive highwayman is talking to a masked devil in a miniskirt wearing horns.

'Oh my God!' I say.

Jacqui chuckles.

My dad, the diminutive Dick Turpin, has got his beige pants tucked into knee-high boots and is wearing a long, purple velvet cape.

For one moment his eyes meet mine. He grins at me, and I would recognise those teeth anywhere.

I notice, as we all dance and chatter and drink, and swipe hors d'oeuvres from trays the second they come near us, that Jacqui and Michael, the doctor, are getting on very well. They become quite engrossed in conversation, and then, when we have to take our partners for our lesson in the Viennese waltz, they take the floor together, and Jacqui sends me a look that could contain pornographic content. At one point, when we meet in the middle of the floor, she says to me, 'He's fabulous! We've totally hit it off! This is a catastrophe!'

Diminutive Dick Turpin dances his way over to me with his tall young companion. 'She's a horny devil,' my dad says, touching the pointy things on top of her head. 'See . . . horns.'

'Yes, Dad, I think I get it. Where's Anthea?'

'She's not a big New Year's Eve partier,' he says, and sighs like it's a cross he has to bear.

Then he takes my arm and pulls me aside. 'Did you know Mike broke up with Jennifer?'

I frown. 'What? I don't think so. He's gone up there for Hogmanay with some of her family and friends.'

'No,' he says. 'I bumped into him in the village a few hours ago. It's over between them. I think he's going to a work party tonight instead.'

As we approach midnight I'm aware I'm giving too much thought to Mike having broken up with Jennifer. I move with the music in the act of dancing, a colourful moonflower pattern of lights spinning around my feet, and I feel suddenly unspeakably sad. But not for too long. As Slade brings in the New Year with 'Cum On Feel the Noize', everyone takes off their masks, and I hug and kiss my daughter, my sister, my father . . . and I realise something. It is no longer the year I got divorced. We have moved on, technically only by minutes, but it feels like miles.

Aimee puts her arms around me while I'm chatting to Jacqui. 'Can we phone Dad?'

'You do it,' I tell her. 'Wish him Happy New Year from me.'

When Aimee flits off, Jacqui raises the tip of my chin so my eyes meet hers. 'Sad thoughts are not allowed. Not tonight.'

'I know.'

But the sad thought I'm thinking is not about Mike.

That's when I decide to do it. I pick my moment and then I make my escape.

In one of David Hall's many bathrooms, I take my mobile out of my clutch bag. Sitting on the toilet lid, I punch in the numbers. It'll only be 7:30 p.m. in Canada. He could easily be at work.

It rings and rings, as my heart beats at an electrifying pace. Maybe he sees who is calling. Perhaps he's deliberately not going to answer. I sink when I realise I could be right because it clicks over to voicemail.

'Hello,' I say, a moment or two after his recorded voice stops speaking. I force myself to inject a smile into my voice.

'Patrick . . . it's New Year's, and I just wanted to phone you and say . . . I miss you and I have a horrible feeling I've made a big mistake . . .' I leave the words there – happy that I've managed to say them – until I can work my way around other ones. 'Plus I should have told you what I didn't tell you before. I should have said I love you. There were so many opportunities and I never did . . .' I have to take a steadying breath. 'I convinced myself I couldn't say those words when I had such a strong sense that I was going to lose you, but I want to say them now because they've always been true, and you should know that, even though I'm sure it changes very little. Anyway . . . I've probably said enough to an answer machine. I'll end by saying I wish you the happiest of new years, and a very happy future.' I hang up, feeling frustrated that it still doesn't feel like enough. Downstairs, Elvis Costello is singing 'Alison'.

I go on sitting there on the toilet-seat lid. I can't face anybody yet. New Year's Eve is such a strange night of the year for me. I am always hoping that the year ahead will bring me a certain peace with myself, a certain acceptance that my choices have been mine and mine alone, and that they've been good ones. That life is good. Exactly how I'm living it. Because to think any different is at best ungrateful, and at worst tempting providence.

I hope the same hope every year.

After a while, I force the temptation to just go on sitting here and reflecting on a few things out of my mind. The song switches to something more upbeat, a tune I don't recognise. I stand up, straighten out the skirt of my dress again, and go back to my party.

When I enter the room, my sister says, 'Where have you been?' She looks a bit shaken up. 'Go outside.'

'What?'

'Just go!' She pushes me, not so gently, in the direction of the door.

My first thought is that it's my father getting it on in the bushes. I prepare to be extremely embarrassed – and to murder him. But when I step outside into the moonlit darkness I see right away that there is a taxi at the door, not fifty feet ahead of me. A moment or two later, the taxi door opens. Then there is a man getting out of the taxi. And I know this man. I know him so well that it makes my world become a surreal sort of still.

'Patrick?'

My mouth has gone dry. My heart is a strange clash of disbelief and delirium.

He sets his suitcase down on the path. Then his eyes find mine and we are held there while a part of me tries to make this real. The taxi pulls away, scrunching gravel, and still we go on looking at one another, neither one of us speaking. And I am swept back to that pivotal time I first saw him. In the café, in Hanoi, in the middle of a typhoon. The stranger I thought was indifferent to me. Before I had loved and lost him. When my heart was still a blank slate.

'Good heavens,' I say. Nothing else will come.

And now we are standing here, just Patrick and me, in the gravelled grounds of a starlit stately home, in the first minutes of 2018, a year unencumbered so far with plans and promises and hopes for the impossible. He holds up a hand with his mobile phone in it, breaking the spell we're both under. 'Tell me that part again . . . about how you've been meaning to tell me you love me.'

I must be beaming the biggest smile because his face lights up with pleasure. 'But . . . how are you here?' I can't work my way around the logistics.

'I didn't take the job,' he says.

'You didn't?'

He walks towards me, slowly, looking briefly at the ground, like a man building up to say something big to a woman. 'I didn't want it badly enough.' He reaches for my hands, runs his thumbs across my knuckles, clasps them down by our sides. 'Or what I should say is, I wanted something else so much more.'

As I try to read his face, he studies me with that same vigorous intensity I've seen in him so many times.

'But how did you know . . .?'

'Where the party was? Aimee emailed me some photos of the holiday, and she tacked on an invitation. You've got a clever daughter . . .' He reaches into the pocket of his jacket. 'The only mask I could manage was this one, I'm afraid.' He pulls out a British Airways sleep mask.

I stare at it and chuckle, pressing my fingers to my mouth. Was he really going to wear it? 'You're a little late. We ditched those at midnight.'

'I'd planned on being earlier. Airline's fault. They lost one of my suitcases. You look beautiful, by the way.' He looks me over with a sort of awe.

Pieces of a puzzle are floating before me, only I can't grab on to them. From inside the house, Seal is singing 'Kiss from a Rose'.

'What you said on the phone when you told me it was over . . . about what you wanted . . . I want to be your *someone there*.' He looks moved and humbled by his own words, a shade of him I haven't really seen before, though I like it. 'When I heard you say that, I knew I wanted that more than anything – though I've probably always known it.' His eyes scour my face again.

'Patrick, I . . .'

He places a finger over my lips. 'Whatever impression you've had, whatever fears you have about how sincere I am, I want you to know that I was in love with you from the very minute we met, and you're the only woman I have truly loved. And there is nothing I won't do if it means not losing you. I wasn't quite sure how to express how serious I am when I say that. And then I realised there is a way.'

For some reason my eyes go to the suitcases.

'That's a lot of packing for a short holiday,' I tell him, counting three.

'Because I'm not here on holiday,' he smiles. 'I've taken the lease on a flat in London. It's for a year. Renewable, of course.' He drops an enthusiastic kiss on my slightly open, surprised mouth. 'I'm going to be based here. I can cover Europe and Brexit for the network and work on my book and see you at any and every opportunity, as often as we can make possible, if you will let me . . .' He looks delighted with the fact that I'm obviously so stunned. 'Please don't think I did it assuming any-thing. If you tell me we don't deserve to have every shot at making this work, then I'll accept that.' His serious face breaks into a slightly cheeky smile. 'But no matter what you say, I'm not going back to Canada.'

I let out a small laugh, tempted to trust him completely yet reckon-ing there must be a catch. 'I can't believe it,' I say, slowly shaking my head and trying to take in everything that he's said. 'You're moving to London? Seriously? You've rented a flat? Already? Sort of . . . just like that?'

He grasps me by the shoulders, such ardour pouring from his eyes that it makes it impossible for me to doubt him. 'I told you before: a long time ago I let you go because I couldn't really think of a way of keeping us together. I'm not repeating history. The only question that remains is: I know it's not perfect, but can you live with this for now?'

I scour his apprehensive expression, the furrow that has just arrived between his brows, as his question holds us captive there. He seems genuinely worried that I'm going to say no.

'I can absolutely live with this for now,' I say.

ACKNOWLEDGEMENTS

I grew up watching films like *Brief Encounter*, *Casablanca* and *Gone With the Wind*. My heroines were Elizabeth Taylor, Doris Day, Bette Davis. I would have much rather gone on a date with William Holden than with Tom Cruise. I was a romantic, a dreamer. I really did believe that life and love would play out exactly as they did in the movies. So it's probably no surprise that at some point I was going to write a love story – albeit one that's grounded in a little more reality. *The Last Time We Met* was a joy to write, and I owe huge thanks to my publisher, Lake Union, for bringing this and my other novels to you, my wonderful readers. In particular, my editor Victoria Pepe – I thank her profusely for the thought and insight she brings to elevate my stories and make them the best they can possibly be. Huge thanks are also due to Sammia Hamer, and to Bekah Graham and the entire marketing, sales and promotions team. I am so lucky to work with you all. To Lorella Belli, thank you so much for being the agent any writer would want in her corner, and for believing in my writing from day one. I also thank my mother, who passed on the writing gene, and who will happily sit there all day brainstorming book titles; and my husband, who has supported me unflaggingly from the moment I told him I wanted to write books – and mine was not a swift and easy route to publication.

I would also like to thank all my readers who have bought my novels, recommended them, left lovely reviews . . . I love hearing from you, so do find me on Facebook or Twitter. Sign up for my newsletter at carol@carolmasonbooks.com – I will send you a note when I have a new book coming out. And, lastly, thanks to my fourteen-year-old dog, Sadie, and my three-legged cat, Tria, for being two other heartbeats in my often too-silent writing room.

https://www.facebook.com/CarolMasonAuthor/

https://www.twitter.com/CarolMasonBooks

https://www.instagram.com/CarolMasonAuthor/

FROM *AFTER YOU LEFT* BY

CAROL MASON

2013

The alarm goes off, and, for a moment or two, in my semi-awake state, I think I am still in Hawaii. I slide a hand across the mattress and make contact with his mid-back. I can hear his mammoth breathing, never quite a fully-fledged snore. With the gentle clawing of my fingers on his bare skin, he rolls over now. He looks across at me, sleepily, and we smile.

But the rainbow-coloured bubble of my happiness doesn't hold. Instead of Justin's warm, waking body, I am patting cold sheets. Then comes the blunt, quick scutter of disbelief. I am endlessly astonished how I can be hit so unexpectedly by something I already know.

I've made a terrible mistake. I can't go on, for everyone's sake. I'm sorry.

Events of four days ago have cruelly lain in wait on this side of my consciousness, keen to be relived – as if I haven't played them over enough already. But each time I do, it's neither more, nor less, real.

I woke up in Kauai, like I've just woken up now. Justin wasn't there. I imagined he'd gone for a swim, like he'd done the previous three mornings. I got up, drew back the white voile curtain to let the sun in.

I stood there in its path, gazing out across a blazing turquoise ocean to where the black army of early morning surfers was riding the waves.

I couldn't see him. Of course, I wasn't even remotely perturbed. I just liked spotting his head. *My husband.* The noble-shaped skull and thick, dark hair. His arms windmilling as he cut a course at right angles to the tide. It's my favourite thing to do: watch him when he's unaware, imagining I'm looking at a stranger.

I let the curtain fall away, and went to the minibar to take out the cream. I was just about to insert a coffee pod into the Nespresso machine when I saw the tented piece of paper beside the two cups and saucers. On the front, *Alice*, in his writing.

I remember the hesitant reach of my hand. The words on the page that didn't make sense. Then the open wardrobe door. Half a dozen or so empty coat hangers. The bare luggage rack where his suitcase had previously sat open.

The Hawaiian cop was a blank-eyed bulldozer of a woman. Her hair was shaved off, leaving only a clump of spiky fringe like a goatee at the wrong end of the face. I wanted to describe her to Justin when he came back, and tell him how intimidating she was, but then I had to fathom it all over again: Justin wasn't coming back. The hotel manager had been the one to call the police; he was nice enough to let us use his office. I'd been wandering around, disorientated, in my bathrobe, telling people that my husband had disappeared. A couple of hotel staff had helped me search the beach. They were very kind, but I could tell right away that the policewoman wasn't going to be.

Leaning forward, she dropped her enormous breasts on top of the desk. 'Sweet cheeks, this is not a suicide note, if that's what you're thinking. Someone who is about to kill himself doesn't disappear in the middle of his honeymoon with a laptop and a suitcase full of his clothes.'

I hadn't said a thing about suicide. The word landed and revolved in my head.

I can't go on . . . ? She was giving me that look that said, *I'm only tolerating you because you're English, blonde and possibly a lunatic.*

Then she read the note out loud again, as if I could have possibly forgotten it. She clapped it down in front of us, looked at me quite gravely and said, 'Honey, you've been dumped.'

ABOUT THE AUTHOR

Carol Mason was born and grew up in the north-east of England. As a teenager she was crowned Britain's National Smile Princess and subsequently became a model, diplomat-in-training, hotel receptionist and advertising copywriter. She currently lives in British Columbia, Canada, with her Canadian husband. To learn more about Carol and her novels, visit www.carolmasonbooks.com.